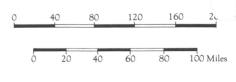

THE ONLY MAN EATER IS THE MOTEL.

INCLUDING

A SUMMARY HISTORY

OF

ZANZIBAR

AND

AN ACCOUNT OF

THE SLAUGHTER

AT

TSAVO

TOGETHER

WITH A SKETCH

OF LIFE IN

NAIROBI

AND AT

LAKE VICTORIA

A BRIEF AND

WORRIED VISIT

TO THE

UGANDAN

BORDER

AND A SURVEY

OF ANGLING

IN THE

ABERDARES

MAN EATERS MOTEL

AND OTHER STOPS ON
THE RAILWAY TO NOWHERE

AN
EAST AFRICAN
TRAVELLER'S
NIGHTBOOK

DENIS BOYLES

WITH NUMEROUS
PHOTOGRAPHS BY
ALAN ROSE

TICKNOR & FIELDS
NEW YORK
1991

For information about permission to reproduce selections
from this book, write to Permissions, Ticknor & Fields,
Houghton Mifflin Company, 2 Park Street, Boston,
Massachusetts 02108.

Library of Congress Cataloging-in-Publication Data
Boyles, Denis.
Man Eaters Motel and other stops on the railway to nowhere :
an East African traveller's nightbook, including a summary
history of Zanzibar and an account of the slaughter at Tsavo :
together with a sketch of life in Nairobi and at Lake Victoria,
a brief and worried visit to the Ugandan border, and a survey
of angling in the Aberdares / by Denis Boyles ;
with numerous photographs by Alan Rose.
p.   cm.
Includes index.
ISBN 0-395-58082-X
1. Kenya — Description and travel — 1981–   2. Zanzibar —
Description and travel.   3. Railroads — Kenya.   4. Boyles, Denis —
Journeys — Africa, East.   I. Rose, Alan.   II. Title.
DT433.527.B68   1991   91-8106
916.7604'4—dc20   CIP

Printed in the United States of America

Book design by Robert Overholtzer

DOH 10 9 8 7 6 5 4 3 2 1

Portions of this book have appeared, in different form,
in GEO, Esquire, Men's Life, Rod & Reel, and
World Monitor: The Christian Science Monitor Monthly.

THIS BOOK IS DEDICATED TO

GEORGE LEINWALL

A GREAT EXPLORER

Acknowledgments

This book mirrors my life so far, in that what started as a highly personal obsession has quickly turned into a mad, desperate scramble for money.

As a consequence, few people could share my thrilling sense of urgency during the course of writing this book. Some did, however, and they helped more than they know. I must, of course, first thank Bob Dattila, my agent, and John Herman, the editor who acquired this book, the first for his ruthless bargaining style and the second for finally acquiescing to the first, then rescuing it from a hideous fate at the hands of unbelievers.

My wife, April Reinking Boyles, deciphered, uncovered, discovered, and otherwise salvaged various parts of this book, and if I hadn't had her help, this whole project would have been a big mess. Caroline Sutton read an earlier version of the manuscript, and I am grateful for her very helpful suggestions.

Many other friends, acquaintances, and colleagues were universally encouraging and supportive, notably Tony Archer, Norman Bleichman, James Butler, Timothy Corfield, Anthony Dyer, Monica Gesue, G. Barry Golson, Terry and Suzan Hall, Claude, Marikje, and Ruben Hamilius, Jan Hemsing, Uta Henschel, Christine Hultgreen, Georg Kajanus, Maggie Kassner, Tim Warren and Tom Kavanagh of *The Sun* in Baltimore,

Richard Kimenyi, Arthur Kretchmer, Karen Kriberney, Guy Martin, Norbert and Christiane Missault-De Soete and their family, Peter Moore, P. J. O'Rourke, Ellen Popiel, Nick Raab, Alan Rose, Fred Schruers, David Sheff, Alain and Annick Soubry, Allen Spaulding, Gregg Stebben, Harry Stein, Bob and Patricia Waldman, Alan Wellikoff, and Spence Waugh.

I also owe a debt of thanks to Robert Burke and to the staffs of both the Enoch Pratt Free Library, Baltimore, and the British Library, London, for valuable assistance.

Although I mention other sources elsewhere, I want to especially thank the late Charles Miller, whose book, oddly entitled *The Lunatic Express,* has given me great pleasure and assistance over the years, providing not only a well-organized and entertaining overview of East African colonial history, but also a model of what a book of popular history ought to be. At the moment, Mr. Miller's book is out of print, except for a paperback edition published in Kenya by Westlands for the tourist trade. Then, Mr. Miller and I both owe thanks to M. F. Hill, whose two-volume history of East African railroading, *The Permanent Way,* really is the definitive work.

Finally, I owe two friends — David Hirshey and Gene Stone — thanks not only for their encouragement with this project, but also belated thanks for their collegial assistance with my previous book on Africa, *African Lives.*

And as always, I thank my father, mother, brother, and sister for their loyalty and love, and my daughter, Hattie, for her constant good cheer.

Of course, none of those above have anything to do with any errors in this book, each of which I will have carelessly crafted myself, and many of those I have listed will disagree with my conclusions about African politics and history.

Everett, Pennsylvania   D.B.
September 1990

Contents

INTRODUCTION
xiii

Part One
ZANZIBAR
I

Part Two
MOMBASA—TSAVO—NAIROBI
49

Part Three
NAIROBI AND EVERYPLACE ELSE
143

Part Four
THE END OF THE LINE
193

Appendix I
A LION PRIMER
215

Appendix II
WITH RYALL AT KIMA STATION
227

INDEX
243

INTRODUCTION

Good neighborhoods, like bored wives and tuna, go bad if ignored too long. Take, for example, Zanzibar, one of the last
places on Earth, and not just alphabetically speaking. Little
more than a century ago, the fabulously rich Sultan of Zanzibar was titular head of a long, skinny empire that stretched
along the east coast of Africa from the Horn to the middle of
Mozambique. Slaves, ivory, and everything else of value in Africa came to market in Zanzibar; missionaries working door-
to-door, so to speak, among the front porches of the Great
Unclad made Zanzibar their headquarters, just as explorers
would subsequently make the island their jumping-off point.
In fact, a hundred years or so ago, Zanzibar was all *anyone*
knew about East Africa because everyplace else in East Africa
was someplace else — but nobody was sure where, since most
of East Africa was unmapped.

Now most large cities in Europe and America have a bar
named Zanzibar, so the place is not quite forgotten. But it's
certainly been eclipsed by the rush of books, articles, and
films about East Africa, and especially about Kenya. There's
some irony here if one is inclined toward that sort of thing:
Kenya started its modern political life as a large, underpopu-

lated, disease-ridden, extremely inconvenient piece of tribal-war-torn real estate that stood between the two points of interest in that part of Africa, namely the Zanzibari coastal ports — especially Mombasa — and Lake Victoria and the source of the Nile. Now Kenya is the paved road of Africa, a thriving tourist attraction and a vibrant demonstration of what good business sense and a working telephone system can do for a young, modern African state with ambition. The Sultan of Zanzibar, meanwhile, is hiding somewhere in London.

To appreciate fully Kenya's enormous success, it must be seen in the odd manner in which it was achieved. Quite simply, it was this: To bridge the gap that unhappily existed between the coast and the lakes in Africa, the English built a railroad there. One thing led to another, and soon enough people had gotten off the train early — first for agriculture, then for hunting, and finally for package tours — to make the railway's final destination, a sleepy town on the shores of Lake Victoria, somewhat incidental. Kenya was invented in the space of a lifetime along the tracks of a railway going nowhere.

This is not a reference book, nor is it a definitive guide to anything other than a few of the author's passing interests. Indeed, this book has a very modest scope, as a highly idiosyncratic travel portrait and historical sketchbook of what was once one of Zanzibar's more forgettable hinterlands. It uses the railway from Mombasa to Kisumu as a device for threading together a few good stories and a lot of personal observations. Some of these observations will no doubt offend, since, for many, Africa is not just a place, it's a moral proposition — or, worse, a place that generates a great deal of poetic, excessively romantic, occasionally patronizing, frequently zealous introspection and is therefore exempt from ironic commentary.

Maybe this book will be used by visitors to Kenya and

Zanzibar as a sort of secondary guidebook.[1] Or — who knows? — maybe some unsociable soul will pick it up as something to read through the night on the long journey by rail inland from the coast. Lots of people write books about Africa,[2] after all, and Kenya, the easiest place in sub-Saharan Africa to visit, is especially well documented.

All that said, I do hope that if you've chosen your traveling library with special attention to companionability this book will amuse you. And, of course, even if you never go to Kenya and climb aboard its peculiar railway, I hope you'll enjoy this ride.

---

[1] For a good guidebook to Kenya, budget travelers and late-blooming hippies might try *Africa on a Shoestring* by Geoff Crowther, a source of much useful detail. But for most people, the best by far is John Heminway's *African Journeys: A Personal Guidebook,* a book I must recommend to anyone interested in a Kenyan holiday.

[2] Allow me here to pay special tribute to Michael Weber, a remarkable writer. An avid adventurer and traveler, Weber once crossed the Sahara from East to West (or maybe the other way round), traveling in the back of trucks, entertaining children in small villages by performing juggling tricks and other feats of legerdemain, sometimes sleeping rough, and sometimes traveling on foot. The journey took months, and he accomplished it at some measurable risk to his life. But his great literary skills notwithstanding, the reason Michael Weber is a remarkable writer is that he never wrote a book about this prodigious accomplishment, thus becoming the only writer — most obviously including this one — who has spent any significant time in Africa without bringing home a first draft as a souvenir.

PART
ONE

- - - - - - -

ZANZIBAR

I SAT IN A SWELTERING TAXICAB PARKED NEXT TO A goat and dried the sweat off my glasses. Outside, the driver, Mohammed, froze into a pose, as if I were photographing him, grimly displaying yet another coconut, the sixth of the day; behind him, a dense, green coconut grove gave way to a beautiful, white, sandy beach where young boys armed with poles and round, metal discs were fishing for a terrifically belligerent local version of barracuda, a foul-tempered fish with razor-sharp teeth in a mouth the size of a coffee can. Just over Mohammed's shoulder I saw a boy hook a fish; his friends shouted, and suddenly the fish leapt from the surf, its huge jaws open wide, aiming for the thin chest of his antagonist. The kid moved deftly to one side, conked the fish on the noggin as it passed, then bent over and picked it out of the water. Even as the tears of sweat filled my eyes, I could see it was a beautiful sight: serious Mohammed; the coconut; the dark boys on the white, sandy beach; green trees above, blue beyond. I wondered how a place that looked so much like paradise could be so much hotter than hell.

▼▲▼▲▼

I had ridden from one end of the island to another in Mohammed's 1959 Bedford taxi looking for a little overgrown history, something that would make clear to me why, for many
hundreds of years, Zanzibar was to Africa what London,
Paris, and Rome were to Europe. In other words, I was a tourist. I wanted to know what it was about this hot, soggy sea-
bound speck that had once compelled the imagination of gen-
erations of schoolboys, driven the Germans and the English
to the brink of war, and merited one of the earliest American adventures in Third World diplomacy. I figured that if I
stumbled around the island long enough, I'd see it the way the
Europeans saw it little more than a century ago — as the
dimly lit edge of a place of great darkness and myth.

Throughout the latter half of the nineteenth century, Zanzibar was one of the most important places on Earth. But in
1901, when the British completed the Uganda Railway, a
hobby-gauge railroad from Mombasa, a sleepy beach town
just across the water and once a part of the Sultan of Zanzibar's coastline empire, to Lake Victoria, the curtain went
up on modern East African history. Eventually, Zanzibar became just another exotic African place-name. Today, if you
talk to people about Zanzibar, they'll nod knowingly, but
sooner or later most people will ask where the place is.

Zanzibar didn't die instantly, of course. Long after the construction of the Uganda Railway, the sultans still ruled in Zanzibar and on nearby Pemba Island and the booming clove
market still made a healthy export crop. But the island became
somehow incidental to the reason the British were drawn to
East Africa in the first place: their wish to guarantee unfet-
tered access to India. The British put together a whole empire
by settling and colonizing peculiar places that seemed to have
no value greater than their strategic importance for secure
commerce with the crown's most important colony. In the

case of East Africa, London wanted the coast kept safe for the Cape-to-Bombay run, but even that was secondary to their desire to keep the headwaters of the Nile secure in case some foreign rival tried to put Egypt out of business, thereby threatening the Suez Canal, Britain's crucial shortcut to India.

The railroad through what is now Kenya prepared the way for the development, colonization, and subsequent politicization of Kenya and Uganda, and, indirectly, Tanganyika. Perhaps the railroad also had met its tactical purpose, since no one had stolen the water from the Nile. But the real effect of the rail line was to open the inland territories to Europeans who came first as adventurous farmers, then as ambitious hunters, and finally as tourists to clog Nairobi's streets and jam into the overcrowded game parks.

The interest in East Africa, the construction of the railway as a part of some grand global security scheme, and the consequent development of the territory through which the railway passed have occasioned a colorful history that has been so thoroughly romanticized that it now seems like a sequence of fables, a collection of anthro-fiction, a mythology involving a long, pre-colonial golden age in which gentle, pastoral tribesmen watched their flocks as mystics studied the heavens and visionaries built mysterious cities. According to this romance, the golden age was rudely interrupted first by roving gangs of white chaps who overpowered local chiefs, then kidnapped millions of natives and took them to Louisiana and elsewhere. Finally, rapacious colonizers delivered the death blow to life in Eden. A few white folk manage to creep into this epic and, thanks to Hollywood, emerge as heroes: people like Karen Blixen, the precious, affected, patronizing, self-absorbed Dane who was more concerned about her aristocratic title than almost anything else in her life, portrayed by Meryl Streep in film, the only version of her life that matters, or perhaps

Henry Morton Stanley, the murderous explorer, canonized in the movies by Spencer Tracy. These lives, so richly embroidered, have no meaning, since, in terms of real history, these lives have no context.

Still, even in reality, the story of modern African history is appealing enough — especially to the American sensibility, since the episodes, characters, and situations often have much of the substance of frontier conquest, with the added patina of (usually) British imperial grandeur. To me, an intriguing portion of East African history was manifested in the strange rail line that ended at Lake Victoria, the way some people see a portion of American history in, say, old Route 66. The more I read about the railway, the more I felt convinced that not only was the Mombasa-to-Kisumu line a fine feat of Victorian engineering, it was also a handy device upon which a fellow might hang a tale or two of Saturday-matinee African adventure.

But I also knew that from a more modern point of view, whatever had happened in East Africa had had its origin in Zanzibar. I had done my homework, I had a little list, and Mohammed and I had checked everything on it. My mission for that day with Mohammed, for example, was to find the site of an abandoned seaside resort. To be specific, it was someone's failed get-rich-quick scheme — but it was also some magazine editor's notion of what might make a good story and hence a little get-rich-quick scheme of my own. Alas, it was a chore that Mohammed had dragged out mercilessly with stops for tropical fruit every ten minutes. I felt like I was sweating Hawaiian Punch. "A papaya!" he would shout, and we'd stop, he'd grab the papaya, display it, then put it in the front seat next to him and describe how it would taste when he got home, patting it affectionately as he spoke. Now it was nearly dusk, and it was clear that I was never going to find the place. I thought of making a dash into Zanzibar Town to the airline office, but it was too late. Another lost day in Zanzibar.

But at least I had closed the gap on history, since I had found myself doing what virtually every other visitor to Zanzibar had done in the last hundred years: I was swooning in the big heat, looking at fruit, and dreaming of easy money and far-away places.

I fueled Mohammed with another handful of abstract Tanzanian currency and pressed on again through the hot haze. Alongside the crater-filled road — what would be Zanzibar's national highway if Zanzibar were still a nation and had a highway — slow-moving locals waved languid greetings. Papaya, coconut, banana, and citrus trees blocked the view of the small, tidy settlements filled with children napping under the giant palm fronds in the steamy air. Food was everywhere you looked — on the ground, in the trees, growing from vines, in the hands of the children; I marveled at the children's cool, clear faces. From time to time, Mohammed, filled with the zeal he saved for the island's occasional tourists, stopped and got out to show me an especially compelling piece of fruit. When he did, I'd lean out the window into the wet heat, grimace, and nod my approval as he split a pineapple or plucked some cloves or scraped some cinnamon or pointed out a patch of nutmeg or black pepper, while hot, spice-filled air would fill the taxi. And suddenly I'd grow hungry. No wonder. Zanzibar smelled like a baked ham.

But I didn't. I was soaked with perspiration, and Mohammed — sensing my discomfort and not wanting his meter to stop ticking — suggested buoying my wilted spirits by returning to the slave cave, the underground passageway that led to the sea through which slaves were once brought from the heart of Africa to be sold in Zanzibar's market by Mohammed's ancestors. It was the coolest place on the island and one of the more intriguing tourist stops, but once was enough. "No, let's go back to town. No more today."

Mohammed looked down at his feet. He was disappointed

and trying to come up with a redeeming idea, something that would prolong his fruitful quest. It isn't often you can watch a man's thought processes: Mohammed squinted in concern and gestured quietly to himself; he looked at the darkening sky, nodded a few times, then looked at his feet again. He was a former schoolteacher, barely fifty and barely five feet tall, and his sweat-soaked shirt barely covered his belly. He stammered a half-dozen more suggestions, came up with a few excuses, and finally surrendered to a hopeful question. "We'll go again tomorrow?"

I felt bad for him. By his own account, Mohammed was descended from a race of fabulously wealthy Arabs, masters of the thriving East African slave and ivory trades. But where once Zanzibar had been home to merchant princes, today it is the home of twenty-five or so taxi drivers, all of whom keep their ear to the ground and pray for tourists. I was the end of the rainbow for Mohammed — a journalist on an expense account covering the island by car and too lazy to drive. Over the course of a few days bouncing around in his taxi looking for one point of interest after another, he had come to regard me as a personal resource, the guy who would be able to eliminate the budgetary deficit he'd built up over a lifetime teaching school for twenty dollars a month. But there are only 640 square miles of Zanzibar, and I felt like I'd caromed through each one. We'd seen ancient Persian baths and cooperative farms and museums filled with stuffed birds and deformed calves; we'd passed through tropical forests, dodged the island's peculiar colobus monkeys, and wound our way through endless groves of coconut palms. I had caught a glimpse of the remains of an old, seven-mile-long railway, built by an ambitious Yankee just after the turn of the century. Once, driving along the road that paralleled the transparent blue sea, we'd clocked twenty-seven kilometers of perfect, absolutely deserted white, sandy beach. I had even hired a fishing boat one afternoon and gone out first to visit Grave Island and then on to neighboring Prison Island. Zanzibar is an incredible place, the sort of eccentric African destination I love, but I was anxious to get to Mombasa on the Kenya coast, where vast beach resorts house teeming throngs of yellow-haired, sun-reddened Scandos in air-conditioned splendor. "No. Tomorrow I'm leaving."

He positively wailed, a long, low keen that was followed by a series of grunts. "It's impossible," he finally said. "You know nothing here."

I agreed. It was time to go.

"You can't go." He said it flatly and not as a matter of opinion. "When will another tourist like you come again?"

▼▲▼▲▼

He needn't worry. A year or so from now, the Aga Khan, the spiritual leader of the island's Ismaili Muslims, will open a luxury 200-room Serena hotel — not unlike the opulent spa he opened at Sardinia's Costa Smeralda — on the island's northwest coast, the first of many such developments, and, alas, for the first time in a quarter century, Zanzibar will not only have tourist attractions, it will also have tourists.

This incipient transformation of one of Africa's most exotic and unusual places has transfixed both Zanzibaris and foreign visitors alike. Only a year or so ago, every taxi driver's dream was a full tank of gas. Now every taxi driver dreams of buying a minibus, and every minibus owner dreams of buying a fleet of rental cars. In the dark, dense medina streets of Zanzibar Town, shops that have been closed for decades are reopening, new mosques are being constructed, and the phenomenally beautiful houses — many built with improvisational eccentricity around the antique, ornately carved teak

THESE ANTIQUE, ORNATELY CARVED TEAK DOORWAYS HAVE COME TO
SYMBOLIZE ARABIC ARCHITECTURE.

doorways that have come to symbolize Arabic architecture at its unpredictable best — are being bought up by foreigners, their investments finally gaining the apparent protection of the government.

For the last twenty-five years, tourism in Zanzibar has been heavily discouraged — and it's just as well, since Zanzibar is the sort of place that twenty-five years ago would have become a mecca for hippies, if hippies had been allowed to make the pilgrimage, which, mercifully, they weren't: Zanzibar with a few Mr. Zig-Zag posters, a bucket of poster paint, and a black light or two could have become a psychedelic paradise, maybe Africa's Goa. Instead, Zanzibar was forced into a marriage with Tanganyika and transformed by a band of local thugs, all puppets of Tanganyikan mainlanders, into a sort of offshore Uganda.

Now the mainland government is letting go of its disastrous and lethal experiment in reclusive socialism, triggering a hopeful spurt in the economy, and suddenly tourism is on everyone's mind. The few visitors who show up are recruited as consultants by Zanzibaris anxious to acquire some cash that has meaning. Mohammed had asked me if I thought he should throw in a luncheon stop as part of his planned "spice tour"; it was a curious question, since there's only one restaurant on the island that might be acceptable to tourists from Parma or Paris on a package tour. But Mohammed was living in the future.

As Zanzibar slowly comes to life after a quarter century in a political and economic coma, its history falls into perspective, coloring the scenery, creating a mask behind which most Zanzibaris hide. After all, once upon a time Zanzibar was the richest place in Africa. But because it is in Africa, most of its wealth was acquired in hideous ways, including the selling of slaves — although ivory was a more valuable export at most

times during the island's history. Beyond Zanzibar's commercial appeal, a measure of its reputation was also built on
the unbelievable stench emanating from its harbor; visitors
claimed they could smell Zanzibar before they could see it;
"Stinkibar," David Livingstone called the place.

▼▲▼▲▼

For years, Zanzibar was a sort of down-market Hong Kong
for Africa, a bustling port governed by local agents of a dynasty of freewheeling Omani sultans.[1] In 1828, Sayyid Said —

[1] For much of the historical information in this chapter, I have relied on standard
texts — notably *A History of the Arab State of Zanzibar*, by Norman R. Bennett
(London: 1978); Sir Richard Burton's indispensable *Zanzibar; City, Island and
Coast*, Vols. *1 and 2* (London: 1872); a useful study by Frederick Cooper, *From
Slaves to Squatters: Plantation Labor and Agriculture in Zanzibar and Coastal
Kenya* (New Haven: 1980); *East Africa and Its Invaders*, by Sir Reginald Coup-
land (London: 1938); Basil Davidson's *The African Slave Trade* (a revised
and expanded version of *Black Mother*; Boston: 1980); Sir John Milner Gray's
History of Zanzibar from the Middle Ages to 1856 (London: 1962); David
Livingstone's *Journeys and Researches in South Africa* (London: 1851) and his
Last Journals (two volumes, edited by Horace Waller; London: 1874); *Zanzibar
in Contemporary Times*, by R. N. Lyne (London: 1905); *The Swahili Coast*, by
C. S. Nicholls (London: 1971), an excellent source of trade information; *Isles of
Cloves*, by F. D. Ommaney (London: 1955); *Zanzibar: The Island Metropolis of
East Africa*, by F. B. Pearce (London: 1920); and a most valuable and entertain-
ing volume by Esmond Bradley Martin, *Zanzibar: Tradition and Revolution*
(London: 1978), a book I recommend to anyone wanting a quick, lively, and per-
ceptive survey of Zanzibar's history. During the last decade, little useful informa-
tion about Zanzibar has appeared — a situation that should change as the place
becomes more familiar to tourists and vacation planners. *The New York Times*
Travel Section has already headlined Zanzibar ("Zanzibar's Exotic Medley," by
Barbara Diamonstein; 30 April 1989), so it appears likely that a lot of adventurous Manhattanites are in the island's future. Among recent books, Nigel
Pavitt's *Kenya: The First Explorers* (London and New York: 1989) has some interesting asides about Zanzibar in the nineteenth century, while Thomas J.
Herlehey and Roger F. Morton's "A Coastal Ex-Slave Community in the Regional
and Colonial Economy of Kenya: The WaMisheni of Rabai, 1880–1963" in *The
End of Slavery in Africa*, edited by Suzanne Miers and Richard Roberts (Madison:
1988), contains much helpful information on the establishment of coastal communities of ex-slaves. Every now and then, some astute editor can be convinced
to run a short travel piece on Zanzibar, as Anita Leclerc at *Esquire* was not so
long ago. The result was Paul Schneider's very amusing dispatch, "How Far to
Zanzibar?," in the January 1988 issue.

who had become the reigning Omani sultan[2] by killing his
cousin, the previous sultan, in 1806 — visited Zanzibar and
Pemba while on a tour of the lower East African stretch of his
sultanate, a Twiggy-thin territory that extended from the
Horn to northern Mozambique. He apparently liked what
he saw, for he returned again briefly in late 1831, declared
Zanzibar his home, went back to Muscat for his things, and
returned to Zanzibar again in 1833 for a longer stay. For
much of the next twenty-three years, until his death in 1856,
Zanzibar was the Sultan's home, a change of circumstance
that almost immediately made itself felt on the island's economy, already a healthy one, at least by contemporary African
standards. In the ten-year period between 1833 and 1843, the
value of the island's exports — mostly ivory[3] — grew fivefold
to more than $750,000 and a small diplomatic community had
settled into Zanzibar.[4] By the time Sayyid Said died, Zanzibar
was the most important commercial center in East Africa,
with exports of ivory, cloves, cowrie shells, and copra worth
more than $1.25 million. A year later, after the departure from
Zanzibar of Sir Richard Burton and John Hanning Speke's famous 1857 expedition to discover the source of the Nile, the
island became famous among explorers and geographers as
the starting point for most important East and Central African expeditions, including missionary Johann Krapf's travels
beginning in 1844, David Livingstone's final departure for Af-

[2] Sayyid Said's official title was Sultan of Muscat.
[3] After 1843, cloves began to rise steadily as Zanzibar's most valuable asset.
[4] The American consulate was established first in 1837, followed by the British in
1841, and the French three years later. American interest in Zanzibar focused
mostly on the acquisition of ivory. In fact, a small Connecticut city, called
Ivoryton, was at the other end of this economic chain. In Ivoryton, and in other
towns, manufacturers turned out billiard balls, knife handles, bookmarks, combs,
collapsible toothpicks, collar buttons, and piano keys made from Zanzibari
ivory. For an interesting account of the Zanzibar–New England ivory trade, see
Richard Conniff's piece, "When the Music in Our Parlors Brought Death to
Darkest Africa," in the July 1987 issue of *Audubon*.

THE SULTAN'S HOME

rica in 1866, and Henry Morton Stanley's absurd publicity stunt in 1871 to "find" Livingstone (who, after all, was not lost at all, but only somewhat lackadaisical about keeping in touch) for James Gordon Bennett's New York *Herald*. Most expeditions were manned by porters from Zanzibar, who quickly formed informal guilds, each of which owed allegiance to different unsavory leaders. The best-known of these brigands, the infamous Tippoo Tib, was an Arab slaver and trader whose caravans crisscrossed much of Central Africa and who formed badly executed working agreements with the likes of Stanley. Tippoo Tib's house is still standing in Zanzibar Town; behind its heavily carved teak door live many families, all informal tenants, and, from what I could determine by asking around, all were unaware of the significance of their dwelling but grateful for the apparent absence of rent. "How can we thank him?" one friendly, slightly confused man asked me.

In Europe, Zanzibar was probably best known for its busy slave market. There is no way to get a real fix on exactly how many slaves were brought out of East Africa by Arab and African slave traders to be sold on the block in the middle of Zanzibar Town, but Esmond Martin reports that he and T. C. I. Ryan, a University of Nairobi economist, calculated that between 1770 and 1896, 1.3 million slaves reached markets both on the coast and in Zanzibar, of which approximately one-third were sent to the Arabian peninsula or to India. By Nigel Pavitt's account, in *Kenya: The First Explorers*, an average of 15,000 slaves were sold every year in Zanzibar. Basil Davidson cites an unnamed "British observer" who claimed that by 1839 "between 40,000 and 45,000 slaves were being sold there [in Zanzibar] every year," although this figure for that date is probably very high; by Ryan and Martin's calculation, the slave market peaked between 1870 and 1876, when they reckoned some 30,000 slaves were brought to the block in Zanzibar each year.

But these are crazy numbers. One slave or 10 million slaves, no matter the number, the wretched crime is there. And it's still there today. The Anti-Slavery Society, the London-based organization that has fought slavery for more than 150 years, has documented the persistence of chattel slavery in parts of sub-Saharan Africa (although not to the tremendous levels it has reached in Asia), most recently in the Sudan. According to a statement issued by the society to the United Nations Economic and Social Council in August 1987, "Reports reaching the Anti-Slavery Society in recent weeks indicate that the civil war in the Sudan is producing the predictable results and especially the re-emergence of chattel slavery. Regrettably, the Sudanese government appears to be taking an extremely passive role in this matter, though it might be an exaggeration to say that the government is actively encouraging slavery." It should also be said that, owing to a persistent and particularly brutal civil war, there is no actual government in much of the Sudan. (The Sudanese civil war pits the Arabic, Islamic north against the Nilotic, Christian, and animist Southerners; it is a war that may abate from time to time, but probably will not end until the country, arbitrarily united in the first place, is successfully divided.)

The idea that slavery exists in Africa in the late twentieth century seems a peculiarly repugnant betrayal of history.[5]

[5] It also must seem unlikely, even to those who should know better. Amnesty International USA, for example, claimed in several of its ubiquitous solicitation letters that slavery "is all but extinguished throughout the world," a claim it continued to assert even after informed of its error. Such assertions in the sort of mass mailings that wealthy groups like Amnesty International USA produce in order to churn cash can only harm the efforts of the small, financially hard-pressed Anti-Slavery Society, which must feel that a large part of its work is in making people aware that slavery is indeed an ongoing concern.

Yet, the Society's reports, such as the ones I'm quoting here, might just as well have been made by an early precolonial observer, so vividly do they portray a situation that most of us thought had long vanished.

Our information [the 1987 report continues] is that it is the Dinka people who are the principal victims of this recrudescence of slavery in a region which was once, of course, notorious for the practice.[6] The Dinkas are especially vulnerable since they live in the border zone between the two sides in the present conflict.

The Sudanese government has been arming militias drawn from Arab communities and it is these armed militia who are largely responsible for much of the new wave of enslavement, especially of the Dinkas, which is at present causing us such concern. The main concentration of Dinkas is in Equatoria province. In the late 1950s and 1960s a policy of Islamisation and Arabisation was enforced upon the population of the province which, until then, had been mainly Christian or animist and whose élite spoke English. The local chiefs were forcibly converted to Islam under threat of losing their lands and their authority. This attempt at forcible conversion has left a legacy of suspicion and mistrust between the Arabic peoples

---

[6] In 1874, the Egyptian Khedive, Ismail, appointed Colonel Charles George "Chinese" Gordon governor of the southernmost Sudanese province of Equatoria, replacing Sir Samuel Baker, an explorer and adventurer who had encouraged the territory's annexation by Egypt in the first place. Equatoria was — and perhaps still is — ravaged by slavers, mostly Arab tribesmen. Gordon, one of England's most famous Victorian soldiers, who earned his nickname for his brilliant suppression of the Taiping Rebellion and who, for my money, is the last modern hero, suppressed slavery in the southern Sudan, but just long enough to realize that Egyptian corruption would only cause it to flourish again. He resigned in 1876, but, partly to mollify European critics, Ismail convinced him to return as governor-general of the entire Sudan. Gordon took up the antislavery cause again after his reappointment, but left the country once again when Britons of the official temperament — always Gordon's enemies — gained the ascendancy in Cairo. Gordon was finally killed by Islamic fundamentalists in 1885 in Khartoum, abandoned by Gladstone and his government, which had sent him to the Sudan for the third time. The most recent biography of Gordon, entitled *Gordon of Khartoum*, is by John Waller (New York: 1988).

such as the Rizeigat and the Misseirya and the Dinkas; the Dinkas and the Rizeigat live in adjacent territories where the Bahr-al-Kiir river is their effective "frontier". To the north of this river is the province of Darfur whose principal town, Dhain, is the headquarters of the Eastern District Council. Dhain is in Rizeigat territory and its mixed population of about 60,000 includes some 17,000 Dinka adults and an indeterminate number of Dinka children. On 27 and 28 March 1987 possibly as many as 3,000, but certainly more than 1,000 Dinka men, women and children were killed in a violent attack by mainly Rizeigat gangs which included women and boys and well as men. During this massacre the Rizeigat also took slaves.

This is not the first time that the Dinka have been attacked by the Rizeigat; in 1976 a notorious clash took place and it was then that open slavery in the Sudan can be said to have been reborn. On that occasion 1,000 Dinkas, mostly women and children, were taken. A government enquiry was instituted headed by Judge Martin Magier Gai. Only 300 of the missing Dinka were found and the official report was suppressed. As a result the judge resigned and joined the opposition in the south of the country.

The existing atmosphere of inter-community suspicion and the renewal of the old tradition of slavery has been further poisoned by the arming of the Arab militias who are thus given ascendancy over the Dinka. Unfortunately it seems that even the Sudanese army itself is not innocent. When units are posted to distant parts of the country, the officers and senior ranks acquire their "servants" who are frequently sold in other parts of the country when that particular unit moves on. In the northern village of Meiram, south of Muglad, we have reports of an auction of captured children which took place early this year; a boy could be bought for about S£700 [approximately $235 at the official rate; half that on the black market] and a girl for around S£900. In February 1987, for example, Regimental Sergeant-Major Ahmed Omer of the Haganah unit of the Sudanese Army was transferred north from the El Obeid region in south Kordofan. He was found to be the owner of three child slaves: two boys aged about eight and a baby girl of two. The boys are now in the care of the local Dinka welfare committee, but the whereabouts of the sergeant-major and the little girl are unknown. All three children came from the To-posa community of Kapoeta, hundreds of miles to the south in Equatoria province.

For some 30 years now there have been rumors of a clandes-tine slave market in Omdurman and of a renewal of the traffic in slaves across the Red Sea. Now we hear of the Marahaleen, as the militias are called, using their strength and privilege to terrorise the Dinkas. The Marahaleen are accused of com-mitting grave abuses of human rights including the rape of women and young girls as well as their enslavement. The girls are taken far away in the traditional manner: roped to one an-other by the neck. As far as the army is concerned the name of Major-General Burma Nasir was frequently mentioned during 1985 and 1986 with destruction of Dinka villages and the enslavement of the inhabitants. Major-General Nasir is a Bagara Arab.

The following year, The Anti-Slavery Society expanded its investigation and found that the situation in the Sudan had grown far worse and that more and more slaves were being taken by armed militias of Arab tribesmen. (The Society has also been active investigating and monitoring other reports of slavery in one form or another in Mauritania — where the government only abolished slavery in 1980 — as well as in Mozambique, Kenya, South Africa, and other African coun-tries, in addition to an even larger number of reported cases in India, South America, and Southeast Asia.)[7]

In Zanzibar, the selling of slaves was a popular spectacle. Thomas Smee, an 1811 visitor to the island, recorded his view

---

[7]The Society, founded in 1839, is supported by donations which should be sent to the Director, The Anti-Slavery Society for the Protection of Human Rights, 180 Brixton Road, London SW9 6AT.

Slavery is an old story in Africa and frequently a confusing one. On the back of

of the slave market with the callousness of a theater critic:
"The show commences about four o'clock in the afternoon,"
Smee wrote, after the slaves had been "set off to the best advantage by having their skins cleaned and burnished with
cocoa-nut oil, their faces painted with red and white stripes,
which is here esteemed elegance, and the hands, noses and
feet ornamented with a profusion of bracelets of gold and
silver." Slaves of both sexes were lined up with the youngest
and smallest in front and the larger, older slaves in the rear.
Leading this bizarre column was the slave owner and his body-

---

one recently published account (Davidson, *The African Slave Trade*), for instance, the hyperbolic copy reads thus: "Between the fifteenth and nineteenth
centuries perhaps fifty million men, women, and children were captured, bought,
or kidnapped from Africa by European slave traders to labor in the mines and on
the plantations of the western hemisphere." (A perhaps less heavily invested
book, Miers and Roberts, eds., *The End of Slavery in Africa*, covers more completely the social history of the pre- and early colonial period of African history.
The Miers and Roberts book, of course, leaves virtually untouched a central
problem, namely that slavery hasn't yet reached an end in Africa.)

Reliable figures are difficult to come by, but, if a consensus of other students of
slavery is correct, it seems more likely that 10 to 12 million slaves were taken
from Africa to work on plantations in the Western Hemisphere — especially in
the West Indies and in Brazil, where labor to harvest sugarcane was desperately
needed to meet the growing demand for the commodity. European and American
markets during the sixteenth, seventeenth, and part of the eighteenth centuries
certainly intensified the demand for slaves, but Europeans did not wander the
African bush kidnapping them — there were too many local chiefs and other African and Arab traders willing to do that sorry work.

Slavery is an ancient, complex social and moral phenomenon that has become
a political and rhetorical phenomenon, and the grotesque charade is played by
both sides. In forms both blatant and subtle, slavery — like its sister crime, pros-
titution — is a part of the history of nearly every society. At some time, virtually
every social group has been enslaved by someone else. I say that not to diminish
the hideousness of the African slave trade. But it's important to overcome the notion that slavery is an institution of European design that flourished briefly, then
died once Europeans (and Americans) were no longer interested in owning slaves.
That perspective has only produced a great deal of obnoxious posturing and
added to the harmful rhetoric that has helped masquerade the atrocities that continue to be committed in Africa and elsewhere today — for the most part without
European or American connivance. Do we commit a suspect act by pointing out
that slavery continues to this day in Africa? No. The bottom line is this: We must
be as concerned about the future of slavery as we obviously are about its history,
and if as much outrage were vented on the crimes of the present as is spilled on
the crimes of the past, perhaps African, Asian, and Latin American men, women,
and children would not still be enslaved today.

guards "armed with swords and spears." The column followed the bodyguard in a procession as the owner proclaimed, in a loud chant, the qualities of his slaves until somebody expressed an interest in buying one of them. At that point, "the line immediately stops, and a process of examination ensues, which for minuteness is unequalled in any cattle market in Europe." After checking the general health and constitution of a slave, the prospective buyer "next proceeds to examine the person; the mouth and teeth are first inspected, and afterwards every part of the body in succession, not even excepting the breasts, etc. of the girls, many of whom I have seen handled in the most indecent manner in the public market by their purchasers." According to Smee, the young female slaves would most likely have already been raped by the dealer selling them. Finally, the examined slaves are made to walk or run to make certain their feet are in good condition, and "if the price be agreed to, they are stripped of their finery and delivered over to their future master,"[8] who may well have been a Zanzibari plantation owner. By 1890, when the British Protectorate of Zanzibar (not including many of the mainland territories, most of which were administered by the Imperial British East Africa Company) was finally declared and British colonial law was imposed, the population of Zanzibar was about 150,000 and the majority of the residents were domestic slaves owned by Arabs, Africans, and Indians.[9]

When the English decided to pursue an imperial policy in East and Central Africa in the latter half of the nineteenth century,

[8] Smee's account appears in Martin, *Zanzibar: Tradition and Revolution,* and in a very slightly different form in Pavitt's *Kenya: The First Explorers.*
[9] M. F. Hill, *The Permanent Way: The Story of the Kenya and Uganda Railway,* Vol. 1 (two volumes, Nairobi: 1949, reprinted 1976). Hill's book is the semi-official account of the Uganda Railway's construction, and for a long time, it was difficult to obtain. A valuable thing has been done by Westland Sundries (Nairobi)

as we've already seen, they were primarily interested in safe-
guarding their commercial routes to and from India. As a result, they had long ago laid claim to the Cape, and, once the
Suez Canal had been completed, they had secured their position in Egypt. They were still interested in two areas where
they saw potential threats to their Indian preoccupation: the
eastern coast of Africa and equatorial lakes in Central Africa.
Regarding the equatorial lakes, the British reasoned thus:
Whoever controls the equatorial lakes controls the headwaters of the Nile; whoever controls the Nile controls Egypt;
whoever controls Egypt controls Suez; and whoever controls
Suez controls access to India, especially if there were no English ports on the eastern African coast offering protection for
ships travelling around the Cape. So the territory that is now
Uganda and the island of Zanzibar became geographic oddi-
ties of crucial importance to England. The Sultan of Zanzibar's coastal empire suited the needs of British strategists,
since, following a pattern typical of their colonial expansion,
they sought to rule through an already functioning local
political institution, namely, the Sultanate. Rivaled first by
the Germans, who, until the English gave them the island of
Heligoland in 1890 in exchange for most of their East African
ambitions, also laid claim to the sultan's possessions, then, in
Madagascar, by the French, the British consul at Zanzibar finally came to be the head of a colonial government that ruled
all of East Africa save only Tanganyika, a territory retained by
the Germans until the First World War, and Mozambique,
painfully occupied by the Portuguese. In some places, like
Zanzibar, where the British agent "advised" the Sultan, "indi-
rect" British rule was more or less direct; in most of the Sultanate's mainland territories rule was through the Imperial Brit-

in promoting its reissue. Hill's study is exhaustive and completely necessary to
anyone wishing to know more than what is here about the Uganda Railway.

ish East Africa Company, the IBEA, on behalf of the Sultan of Zanzibar.

Forging a credible political unit out of the IBEA's often imaginary territorial sphere was obviously a stopgap measure. After endless parliamentary debates and expensive African surveying expeditions, on June 15, 1895, the government announced that a protectorate over East Africa would replace the territories administered by the IBEA. On July 1, Sir Lloyd Mathews, the Sultan's wazir, conducted a brief ceremony in Mombasa renouncing the Sultan's inland claims. The formal language of imperialism is interesting enough to include here. "I have come here today," the wazir intoned, "by order of our Lord, Seyyid Hamid-bin-Thwain, to inform you that the Company [the IBEA] has retired from the administration of this territory, and that the great English Government will succeed it, and Mr. Hardinge, the Consul-General at Zanzibar, will be at the head of the new administration, and will issue all orders in the terrirory under the sovereignty of His Highness. And all affairs connected with the faith of Islam will be conducted to the honour and benefit of religion, and all ancient customs will be allowed to continue, and his wish is that everything should be done in accordance with justice and law." In exchange for his coastal possessions, the Sultan would receive a £11,000 rent per annum. The East Africa Protectorate was officially declared by the Foreign Office on August 31, 1896. The Protectorate of Uganda, replacing the IBEA's most ambitious project, had been declared earlier, in June 1894.

It didn't take long for the English to realize that governing and administering the huge expanse of territories that would later be known as Kenya and Uganda from a small island off the coast of Tanganyika wasn't going to work, so, despite great parliamentary opposition, the government decided to build a railroad from Mombasa, on the Indian Ocean, to Lake Victoria.

So final was the eclipse of Zanzibar after the turn of the century that only rarely does something of interest on the place show up in newspaper indices — a modest spark of unrest, an incendiary coup, then nothing. (Nowadays, no news agency keeps a stringer in Zanzibar.) Once the railway was finished, ivory and other natural resources were brought to markets on the coast by rail, slavery was effectively eliminated, and with a railway in operation between the sea and the inland lakes, the need for Zanzibari porters was drastically reduced.

So Zanzibar slipped out of the African spotlight. For Europeans, Zanzibar was always at the end of a long, unpleasant commute — a steamer down from Suez or up from the Cape. The action in East Africa shifted first to Mombasa, and then, after the turn of the century, to the new capitals of Dar es Salaam and Nairobi. The suppression of slavery had badly disrupted the island's plantation economy, and the annexation by Britain of the Sultan's mainland empire had greatly reduced Zanzibar's status as an offshore market port. In the end, Zanzibar was left to peddle its cloves and find a future as best it could.

In 1914, at the beginning of World War I, H.M.S. *Pegasus* was sunk by the German ship *Königsberg* in Zanzibar harbor;[10] the British dead were buried on Grave Island alongside scores of Britons who died fighting the Arab slavers in the

---

[10]The *Königsberg,* in turn, was sunk by the Royal Navy off the coast of southern Tanganyika in 1915. Many of her guns were stripped off her by the German general Paul von Lettow-Vorbeck, who carted them along through the Tanganyikan countryside on his endless East African campaign against the British. One of the *Königsberg*'s guns ended up at Fort Jesus in Mombasa — as did one of the guns from the *Pegasus.*

nineteenth century. The cemetery is overgrown now, as much forgotten as the role the English played in stopping slavery in this part of Africa. Between the wars, irritable, formally dressed British administrators gossiped and quarreled at the English Club and drank and dined at a number of movie-set restaurants, the most popular of which was the Africa Bar just opposite the main post office. The Japanese occupation of Southeast Asia during the Second World War was an economic tonic to Zanzibar, and the value of the island's exports more than tripled between 1938 and 1945, only to stagnate again in the 1950s. Nevertheless, the Zanzibaris were better off than their neighbors in Kenya and Tanganyika: "No one in Zanzibar went hungry," Esmond Martin notes. Indeed, starvation would be hard to achieve in a place where food literally falls down upon your head.

As the mainland moved toward independence after the Second World War, Zanzibar seemed likely to make the transition painlessly. The Sultan was still on his throne as a constitutional monarch and the head of a dominant minority community of 50,000 Arabs. There were about three times more Afro-Shirazis, most of whom were descendants of immigrants from the mainland and from the Shiraz region of Persia, who, after a thousand years of close living, had become Zanzibar's largest single ethnic group. There were also some 20,000 Indians and Pakistanis; 55,000 Africans, many of whom were relative newcomers, brought to do agricultural work after the end of slavery; 5,000 descendants of immigrants from the Comoro Islands; 500 whites; and 300 Goanese. In 1957, the British began encouraging self-rule by holding elections which were marked by an extreme nationalism that had the effect of only partially and temporarily ameliorating racial differences. For years, the British, acting on the supposition that Zanzibar was an Arab state, had been appointing Arabs to the consultative council, often at the expense of the Afro-Shirazis, the Indians, and the Africans, among others, and four years before the election, the British had tried to ensure the bureaucracy's neutrality by forbidding civil servants to play an active part in politics, effectively excluding many educated Africans from participating in the electoral process, including those who, for the most part, had sided with the Arabs. In 1957 the Afro-Shirazi Union won the elections; for the ASU, under the leadership of a militant African ex-seaman named Abeid Karume, and with the direct assistance of Tanganyika's Julius Nyerere, had successfully united both the African and Afro-Shirazi factions.

In January 1961, new elections to a larger legislative assembly were conducted. The Zanzibar Nationalist Party, originally the party that represented the Arabs' political interests, expanded away from its narrow Arab constituency to include Pembans and conservative Africans who rightly thought the Afro-Shirazi faction was being manipulated by mainlanders. The ZNP won nine seats. The right-wing Zanzibar and Pemba People's Party won three seats, all from Pemba. The Afro-Shirazi Party won ten.

Predictably, a coalition proved unworkable and new elections were conducted the following June; Karume's ASP again won ten seats, but this time the ZNP also won ten and the ZPPP won three, so a coalition between the Zanzibar Nationalists and the Zanzibar and Pemba People's Party forced the ASP into parliamentary opposition. Following a pattern that has worked well elsewhere in Africa's brief flirtation with participatory democracy, the ASP responded by encouraging racism and agitating violence that by mid-July had resulted in perhaps as many as one hundred deaths and hundreds of casualties, almost all of them Arabs.

At the same time, Julius Nyerere, whose leadership of an independent Tanganyika was by that time assured, began pushing for a union between the mainland and Zanzibar.[11] On Zanzibar, the ASP refused to work with the assembly, and so the British, anxious to conclude the independence process, again called elections, in July 1963. This time, the ASP took thirteen seats; the ZNP took twelve, and the ZPPP took six, once again forcing the ASP into opposition. Independence was declared on December 10, 1963, so the July 1963 election was the last free election held in Zanzibar's history. On January 12, 1964, a Ugandan national named John Okello promoted himself to field marshal and led a lightning coup. One of his first moves was to advise the Sultan to kill his wives and children and commit suicide.[12] Almost instantly, Okello formed a provisional government with Abeid Karume and the ASP. By the end of the year, all other parties had been banned and many of their leaders had been imprisoned by Nyerere on the mainland; Okello was back in Uganda; Swahili had replaced English as the official language; all the rickshaws in Zanzibar were burned; all land and most businesses were nationalized; as many as 5,000 Arabs had been killed; almost all the whites were gone, along with a large number of skilled Asians; Chinese, Russian, and East German workers were imported to replace the whites and Asians; "indoctrination centers" were set up throughout the island and political correctness was taught in the schools; and Zanzibar, with its £25,000,000 in hard currency, was part of a United Republic of Tanzania, with Julius Nyerere, that zany socialist

---

[11] Nyerere, one of postindependent Africa's most ambitious imperialists, also wanted to include Kenya in a union that he would dominate, but Nairobi did not welcome the idea and it was promptly scuttled. Ironically, the East African Union that did emerge after independence was broken up by Nyerere, who had grown frustrated at his inability to control the much more successful Kenyans.

[12] Sultan Jamshid ibn Abdullah and his family escaped in the night for England. On his arrival in Southampton, the Sultan made quite a splash, generating a great amount of publicity. Things are different these days; there's a listing in the telephone book for Sultan of Zanzibar, but the Pakistani who now has the number knows nothing about the Sultan — or about Zanzibar, for that matter.

prankster, at the head. Karume was given the post of First
Vice President with almost absolute power over the fate of
Zanzibar.

The inevitable decline was even more precipitous than an-
ticipated. By 1972, the economy was in ruins, food was ra-
tioned, and most Zanzibaris were living on bananas and co-
conuts. The shops were empty and the only growth sector of
the economy was in the domestic intelligence industry, for
Karume ran a brutal police state, not just listening in on telephone conversations, reading mail, and following people
around, but driving people out of their homes and telling
them where to live, how to dress, how long their hair should
be, and, by banning makeup, how they should look. He enforced his whimsical decrees with long sentences at hard
labor. At the same time, he encouraged nepotism and corruption, began the forced exile of all non-Africans, and, by
engaging in systematic beating and sexual abuse, coerced the
daughters of some Persian families to marry members of his
Revolutionary Council. Nyerere, busy with his own goofy
brand of social engineering, successfully ignored even the
worst of Karume's excesses. Finally, in April 1972, Karume
was shot dead by plotters. In his eight years, he had killed
thousands of his people and exiled tens of thousands more.
Arabs were blamed for the assassination, and Karume was
elevated to martyr status.

Under Karume, Zanzibar had become a bloody fiefdom, a
once sovereign state that even now is effectively occupied by a
foreign power. The police and soldiers are all imported from
the mainland, and the island's sole source of electricity comes
from a long extension cord plugged into a socket someplace
in Dar es Salaam, the capital of what is now Tanzania. Since
Nyerere stepped into the background, a Zanzibari has been

the figurehead president of Tanzania, but the islanders aren't fooled: In Zanzibar, people gesture obscenely behind the backs of mainlanders. Indeed, if Tanzanians were white-skinned, the Zanzibaris' situation would generate in America the hot wrath of bumper-sticker rhetoric instead of the head scratching of old-fashioned geography. The Zanzibaris have made occasional, halfhearted attempts at rebellions of one kind or another, but Zanzibar is a small, unarmed island, and Africa is a large, well-armed continent. Zanzibaris seem content to fight for their freedom with irony.

Tanzania, of course, is just another entry on the long list of African nations crippled by megalomania and bad government, and recently Zanzibaris have been quick to distance themselves from the mess on the mainland. "Last year, we were only thirty kilometers from the mainland," one merchant told me. "This year, we are fifty." Soon, the mainland won't be visible from Zanzibar, and the sense that something is going to happen soon is a kind of social carbonation that has already buoyed the spirits of the islanders. "We are only waiting for Nyerere to go," a Zanzibari told me. "Then we will move forward. We will be a free port again, I think." Foreign investors have been told of the new legislation protecting their capital — "Winds of Change in Stinkybar," headlined the *Financial Times* — and even the local functionaries from the mainland government who run the tourism ministry can see something's up. "We will have many new hotels," an official told me. He rattled off the names of a half-dozen projected development schemes. "We expect foreign investment to create new projects." He held up a UN document that he said suggested tourism was a crucial part of any economic reconstruction in Zanzibar. "This is our Bible."

"Good," I said, and asked about the impact mass tourism will have on a place like Zanzibar. The official looked at his assistant, a bright local lad who had invited me in for the interview. The assistant looked at me, then back at his boss. We all looked at each other.

The official finally cleared his throat and asked, "What do you mean?"

I explained that I simply wanted to know what kind of cultural and environmental changes they saw coming in on the wave of tourism. I described the people I had met alongside the road, offering me food and hospitality. "What will happen to those people?" I asked.

Instead of answering, the official made a crack about my shirt — wet with perspiration — and my sunburned scalp, asked me how long I had been in Zanzibar, then told me what I already knew — that I wasn't an expert — and suggested that I didn't know what I was talking about. He picked up the UN document again and repeated, "This is our Bible. And our people are well trained to preserve their culture." He opened his Bible at random pages; charts and graphs whizzed by; he did everything but thump the thing.

As I stood to leave, the assistant, anxious that we all part pals, started making small talk but ended by suddenly blurting, "Mass tourism will ruin the culture."

His boss looked up, startled.

"We don't want to make Zanzibar a second Mombasa," the assistant continued. "We want . . ." But his boss shut him up, and I was out the door.

▼▲▼▲▼

From time to time, I imagine life on Earth to be a doppel-gängers' convention, where a bunch of people hang around looking like somebody else. You must have seen it yourself — there goes Jimmie Stewart, here comes Mamie Van Doren, that sort of thing.

I ran into Tippi Hedren's double in Zanzibar. I was alone in the Dolphin restaurant, struggling through another piece of curried fish, when a cool, composed Tippi-type walked in, sat down, looked at the brief menu scrawled across the wall — grilled this and curried that — looked at me and said in French, "I just can't do it again," and left before I even had a chance to say howdy.

Wherever you are, lady, I know what you mean — if you were talking about the food, that is. I know part of the charm of travel in exotic places is eating the exotic food. But here's the truth: In many parts of Africa, the food may be exotic because it's African, but even if you're the type of tourist who goes temporarily native, it really isn't very good. I mean, do you think a typical African worker would rather eat manioc root and bad rice out of a tin plate or a steak and an all-you-can-stand salad bar?

Before you answer, here's an illustrative scenario: Let's say you're in Zanzibar, you work up a real sweat touring the countryside, then you come back to town hungry and find that your hotel has flat run out of brown curried solids. You know that there are other restaurants in town, and that if you were in, say, New York, a Zanzibari restaurant would be a popular choice, crowded with half the student body of the New School, all happily eating curried fish and reading garbled professional outrage in the *Voice*. But you're stranded in Zanzibar, and your notions of exotic food have become extremely situational. So. What do you do?

Until recently, this would be a trick question, and the answer would be, "Nothing." Because, until quite recently, you could wander through Zanzibar's dark, thick warren of markets and alleyways, crowded with ornate but neglected Arabic architecture — huge ramshackle, once whitewashed buildings inside which passages and rooms wind in a cool maze — only to find that there wasn't an ethnic restaurant on the whole

ORNATE BUT NEGLECTED

island, that, gastronomically speaking, the place was like
an Indianapolis suburb with nothing but franchised burger
joints. While today the tourist population in Zanzibar rarely
exceeds two digits, by the early nineties, Zanzibar will be
a major tourist destination and its white, sandy beaches will
be decorated with thousands of grunting, sunburned Germans, plumping like steamed bratwursts in the equatorial
sun. But that's then. Now, if you asked somebody in Zanzibar
where he wanted to eat, his reply would probably be, "On an
airplane."

No sense blaming the Zanzibaris. They want a life, too,
just like the one they used to have when the island was an
oasis of wealth on a continent well acquainted with poverty.
Maybe someday, they say, they will reopen some of their swell
hotels and restaurants, just like back in the good old days
when the currency was a little less theoretical.

There are places to eat, of course. There's the place where
the Frenchwoman materialized; it's called the Dolphin, it's
near the old post office, and it's not bad. There's the dining
room of the New Africa Hotel — once Zanzibar's English
Club — which is atmospheric, but the terrace bar overlooking
the sea is the attraction, not the kitchen. And there's the Spice
Inn, which sometimes serves food to nonresidents, but where
the sullenness of the staff eventually becomes tedious. The Ya
Bwawani, Zanzibar's principal hotel, a government-run enterprise, has a real restaurant, but the meals are decidedly in-
stitutional, the sort of stuff Third World postal workers might
feed each other. Finally, there's Local Food in Zanzibar, a
dark and eternally empty café; the owner's looking to draw
tourists, but when I suggested to him that he'd be better off
hanging out a sign that said something simpler, like Mustafa's
Eats, he only smiled shyly. All these places are extremely in-
expensive, and they all serve large helpings of rice along with

LOCAL FOOD IN ZANZIBAR, A DARK AND ETERNALLY EMPTY CAFÉ

some local protein source, and tropical fruit, which grows with enthusiasm just outside the kitchen door.

Fortunately for recent travelers to the island, a thin, sandy-haired, raggedly debonair Kenyan chemist and a burly, hearty French butcher from Mulhouse were both stranded in Zanzibar when their plans for a holiday resort crumbled under the weight of bureaucratic meddling. The two became so desperate for money that they opened a restaurant, the Fisherman, in an empty building near the old yacht club.[13] That was in the spring of 1988. Now the Zanzibari epicurean spectrum has been widened to accommodate some fine seafood dishes and a wildly spiced avocado vinaigrette.

"It is real progress, the restaurant," a man from the Tourism Ministry told me.

"It's a nightmare," René Hairsine, the white Kenyan chemist, told me.

To Hairsine, it must have seemed like a good idea at the time. Put yourself in his shoes: A young and ambitious man with several thousand pounds to spare, Hairsine gets a call from a rich stranger one afternoon, and the next thing you know, presto! he's suddenly in Zanzibar as a partner in a scheme to build a big luxury beach resort. He'll give up chemistry, he'll buy a motorcycle, he'll eat fruit all day and carouse all night and he'll be rich, a restaurant prince in Zanzibar.

A year passes. Then, oh-oh. Something goes wrong. The beach resort becomes a muddy building site overgrown by jungle. The motorcycle breaks down. Hairsine finds himself living off the land and shedding weight like a rabid Oprah. He's broke, held prisoner by his poverty, and, in one golden, sun-drenched afternoon, his paradise goes to hell. While the rich stranger explains what happened to his money, a man

---

[13]I was told as this goes to press that the restaurant is now located on Prison Island.

ANCIENT FREIGHTERS, REEKING AND RUSTY, LITTER THE HARBOR AT
ZANZIBAR.

from immigration interrupts to tell him he should give up hope of ever working in Zanzibar. Hairsine rubs his eyes. Everywhere he looks there are ruins: buildings collapsing into narrow alleyways and grim bazaars; dark shops half filled with things no one can afford; red-roasted tourists wandering the streets in a sunstroked daze, all of them stranded by an airline with an Einsteinian concept of time or by the vagaries of a Hovercraft that only occasionally provides escape to the mainland; a bad-ass bunch of foreign policemen all over the place; and power-jealous authorities who observe him with a kind of scientific curiosity. Egad, he says, this isn't Pleasure Island. This is Zanzibar.

While he probably wouldn't choose to view himself as a pioneer, Hairsine was among the first to recognize the potential for tourism in Zanzibar. With Mohammed, I had gone to the site of the Aga Khan's proposed resort, where the clear, deep blue water washed up on a blindingly white beach. I sat in the shade of the coconut palms and imagined the Aga Khan sitting there with me, looking at it all, and saying, "Looks good to me. Pave it."

For the white population of Zanzibar, tourists will be welcomed not only for their hard currency, but also for the conversation they might make. After all, the permanent standing of the chemist and the butcher meant that the island's resident white community had swollen to double digits: Hairsine and his partner, Daniel Tschambser, joined a couple of low-level diplomats and a Danish family named Mortensen — an ambitious father and daughter who, under the trade name Zanea Tours, are trying to get the tourist ball rolling.

Finn K. Mortensen is worth looking up, if you ever get to Zanzibar. He's one of those permanently smiling, itinerant chaps who, in the course of a career as a UN technical specialist, seems to have taken Africa in alphabetical order —

happy with his lot until he reached the end: Zaire was so-so, but Zambia was terrible. But Zanzibar, he says, is the best of a lot that for him began with Algeria back in the 1950s.

The morning I met him, he was instructing the Zanzibari mechanics on how to repair the Hotel Ya Bwawani's never working air conditioner, dropping off some Texas safari brokers at the airport, then going to find a crane to help maneuver a new generator into place on Prison Island. I had dinner with him — he knew everyone, it seemed, and the men at the tourist ministry had rolled their eyes impressively when I mentioned his name — but I couldn't keep track of what he was up to: The adventures of the Danish Family Mortensen were varied, indeed. His daughter gave me a homemade brochure with a piece of clove stuck to it, and it still gives a certain unexpected fragrance to my filing cabinet. All I could get from Finn was a repeated claim that Zanzibar was the greatest place on Earth, but somehow his enthusiasm wasn't terribly contagious. As I listened to him, I energetically assaulted a delegation from the insect kingdom determined to share my brown, vaguely squamous meal. "Air conditioning makes them stay away," Finn said as I dripped and swatted and flicked and fanned my way through dinner. "Inside my home it is like Denmark. My wife makes Danish sandwiches and we drink Danish beer." I tried to imagine what it must be like to go from Zanzibar to Denmark in one step, but I failed.

Unfortunately, most of the dozen or so whites in Zanzibar have little good to say about each other, so Hairsine's restaurant clientele tends to the tourist crowd — if crowd is the right word for the few foreigners who occasionally turn up on the island. Hairsine lives upstairs; at night, he is the maître d' and Tschambser, who is up early to buy fish and produce from the locals, is the chef.

If opening the restaurant was a desperate ploy by the two

men to pick up some cash, its immediate success has both frightened and amazed its owners. The restaurant had been open only two weeks the first time I tried to eat at the Fisherman, and I foolishly hadn't booked a table. The place was full. "It's been quite a surprise, really," the Kenyan said, adding that he expected the restaurant's good fortune would invite trouble from his nemeses, the local bureaucrats.

After a series of brief encounters, I suggested to Hairsine that we meet for a more formal interview. We discussed meeting in the restaurant, but he said he was tired of the place, and so we ended up at the yacht club drinking the usual beer and watching the lateen-sailed dhows in the harbor.

We chatted briefly about the calm beauty of the place, about its special sense of exotic remoteness. I asked him if he would do it all over again, and he looked at me with that special disgust we reserve for unexpected fools. "Not on your life," he said.

Zanzibar resembles Venice only in that it is best approached from the sea. The white, gleaming facade of the House of Wonders, the rough stolidity of the old Arab fortress greet a visitor returning from Prison Island, Zanzibar's Lido, where a large ruin — the prison itself, built by a slave trader to house recalcitrant slaves — backs against a newly reopened guest house, originally built by the English but now operated by the government for the benefit of tourists. In fact, the island does attract a few visitors who must pay two dollars, hard currency only, for the privilege of landing there. You'll see the tourists as you arrive: Sullen white kids flop around on the tiny beach, a strand the size of a Renault. The prison is a colorful pile of rubble that was taken out of the hands of the slave trader and made into a jail after the English arrived. Nobody was ever locked up in the place, though. A short dis-

tance from the prison is an old quarantine center where in-
fected immigrants to East Africa were housed; it, too, has
long been abandoned. Tortoises, discarded gifts to a long-
dead Sultan, roam the island past broken bed frames and in
and out of the prison, their shells punctured by tourists who
want to see what happens when you poke a hole in a tor-
toise's shell. Visitors can spend the night in the guest house or
in old hospital rooms and spend the day wandering along the
banks of a water-filled quarry or sitting on rocks looking toward the mainland.

▼▲▼▲▼

If Air Tanzania's fantasy became a reality, it was to be my last
day on the island, so I wandered around town, down the clut-
tered, confusing labyrinth of corridors that sometimes opened
out onto a familiar market but sometimes curled around into
an elaborate dead end. Merchants sold shoes, ice-cold Fantas,
old tables, and coffeepots and pipe tobacco in dim, closet-
sized shops bedecked in signs and advertisements from the colonial era. Twice I passed the Anglican cathedral, built more
than a century ago with grand overstatement by the British on
the site of the slave market, then I stumbled across the Goanese Catholic cathedral, painted pastel pinks and blues inside,
with little plastic pennants (souvenirs of Easter) everywhere. I
stopped for a drink at the New Africa Hotel, browsed among
the books in the abandoned library of the English Club — *Fly
Fishing in the Four Corners of the Empire* — and wandered
through the billiard room, the table covered and apparently
unused for twenty-five years. Near the Soviet consulate, I
passed a granite marker displaying the distance in miles from
Zanzibar Town to points closer to the center of civilization:
"BVBVBV 6¾," it read, the U's etched in a classic style, like
V's, the better to enrich the Zanzibaris' cultural background.

Then, at the top, in letters no larger than the rest: "LONDON 8064." Once, a tiny train ran from Zanzibar Town out to BVBVBV, but no more; only the cuttings and bridges remain. Finally, I found myself in a neighborhood of cemeteries, where the abandoned Goanese graveyard, situated across the street from the abandoned Zoroastrian temple, suffers in comparison to the German cemetery next door ("Hier Ruht Hans Georg von Nostitz Kapitan zur see und Kommandant S.M.S. Stosch Geb. 17. Janr. 1810 Gest 5. Aug. 1885. Geweidment von den kameraden"), where all the grave markers were knocked over during a war, but where the lawn is neatly trimmed.

To a stranger, walking Zanzibar is like strolling through the fun house; you are eternally lost. But everywhere you go, you either see the same twenty or so tourists that come over on day visits with the MV *Virgin Butterfly,* the unlikely hydrofoil that links Zanzibar with Dar es Salaam and the neighboring island of Pemba, or you see the half dozen visitors transported by air from Dar and Mombasa, then held prisoner by fluctuating flight schedules. It was as if we were all at the same group sensitivity seminar: We knew each other intimately, and we never spoke.

One unmarried couple in particular interested me. He was forty, French, bespectacled, trim, and prosperous; she was maybe thirty, Belgian, and cute in that Jean Seberg kind of way. She wore T-shirts and shorts everywhere and she always walked as if she were wearing high heels so that even a casual stroll across a hotel lobby looked to me like what anthropologists I think call presenting behavior. When they arrived, they were happy and singing silent, telepathic love songs to each other. But after a hot, sticky day dodging Arabs on bicycles and swatting mosquitoes, their ardor had cooled visibly. After several days, they barely spoke — though he guarded her at-

A NEIGHBORHOOD OF CEMETERIES: THE ABANDONED GOANESE GRAVE-YARD, ACROSS THE STREET FROM THE ABANDONED ZOROASTRIAN TEMPLE, SUFFERS IN COMPARISON WITH THE GERMAN CEMETERY NEXT DOOR, WHERE ALL THE GRAVE MARKERS WERE KNOCKED OVER DURING A WAR.

tentions vigorously — and merely made the rounds of the same old tourist spots over and over again, starting each morning at the airline office hoping for a flight. Every now and then, she would stare at me without expression but also frankly and without embarrassment; once her companion caught her looking, took her by the shoulders, turned her toward me and held her there, a mortifying thing for all three of us, although we all immediately acted as if nothing had happened. It was clear that she *hated* Zanzibar. On my way back from the German cemetery, they passed me heading for the harbor, and, as he stepped ahead of her, she half turned and very carefully smiled at me. So naturally I followed them, lurking behind corners like a sweaty character actor in a cheap film.

Down at the docks, the hydrofoil from the mainland had discharged another batch of day-trippers. Mostly young backpackers, they had wandered in a daze off the vessel and into what must have seemed like a Hollywood set: Ancient freighters, reeking and rusty, took on bulk loads of cloves and spices; soldiers tried to control noisy crowds of Zanzibaris and mainlanders anxious to board the hydrofoil or one of the freighters for the return ride to Dar es Salaam; dhows and derelict East European cargo ships littered the harbor, and everywhere stevedores screamed into the salty, putrid air.

I followed them through the crowds and past the customs office, but my attention was diverted by a sikh I had met the day before, and I lost them. I looked everywhere, even along the endless rows of stalls selling pungent fish. I knew the *Virgin Butterfly* was sold out, so it was my last stop.

The hydrofoil was ready to go and all the passengers were on board. I asked the ticket officer on the dock if he had seen my pair, and I described them brilliantly. Sure enough, the Frenchman had managed to get the Belgian woman on board. "She insisted," he told me. "So the man, he talked to the captain and she is on board."

But where was her companion? I squinted at the hydrofoil's windows, then hoped I hadn't been caught. The man shrugged. "I don't know."

I found him back at the Ya Bwawani. Most of the hotel's rooms look out on a swamp newly improved by a rice paddy, beyond which rise huge, hideous, dull gray, uninhabitable East German-built blocks called the Michenzani Flats, one of Karume's not-so-good ideas. Karume demolished a large neighborhood of typical Zanzibari huts and had the mammoth complex built exactly to his specs. Unfortunately, the East Germans couldn't figure out a way to get water to the top floors, so the whole hellish complex has become a sort of vertical village, with the inhabitants carting trash cans filled with water up and down concrete steps. There are other, smaller hotels in Zanzibar Town, but while they may be more atmospheric, they were no better than the Ya Bwawani. The hotel had also been designed by Karume when he was in his architectural frame of mind, and built, of course, by East German craftsmen. But Karume had forgotten to install air conditioning, so window units were put in hastily after construction was complete. They quickly broke down and were removed; consequently, the rooms, which had been sealed to accommodate the new air conditioners, filled with fungus and the tiles peeled up off the concrete floors. Karume also forgot to include a kitchen or a dining room in his plans, so they were added on later. The replacement central air conditioning unit — another fine East German job — had expired on installation and had become one of Finn Mortensen's ongoing interests; I saw the Dane negotiating with a workman one morning as he was on his way out to inspect his kelp beds, a new project. Mortensen had hired a Korean kelpmeister to come to Zanzibar and grow seaweed — "the food of the future," he told me — but the chap was threatening to leave if he couldn't find some way to escape the heat. The Ya Bwawani is run, after all, by the same people who run the Tanzanian banks and the Tanzanian air line, and the management prefers toxic gas to nets for the constant mosquito problem, so the atmosphere in the hallways and in the rooms is tangibly chemical. In fact, the only way to avoid malaria, which is widespread in Zanzibar, is to sleep with a huge fan blasting across you to make it impossible for the mosquitoes to land.

I found the Frenchman sitting in the bar drinking a beer in front of a fan. He looked somehow relieved, a little happier, maybe. I nodded, he nodded. Because of the weird social dynamic that existed on the island, this was the first time we had acknowledged each other, aside from his angry display of jealousy. "How do you like Zanzibar?" I asked.

"It's hot," he said, "but very beautiful." I nodded. He asked if I had been to the swimming beaches. "You should go to the beach at Bwejuu," he said. "It's a beautiful beach, nobody there. It's like a paradise."

I nodded, he nodded. We both looked at the bar.

Two hours later we were drunk. We had sat together silently drinking, taking some small comfort in each other's presence as we watched the hotel's guests make their evening sorties: a walk through the bar to confirm their fear of boredom, dinner, then another walk-through, a quick drink, then out. Some kid, a tourist on a motorcycle, came in with his girlfriend. They had a few drinks, then they necked at the bar. We watched them. I guess the Frenchman and I exchanged maybe ten words all night, then, apparently tired of watching the two drunk kids, he retired. I stayed on to see if the kid would cop a feel at the bar, but no dice.

Fifteen hours later, the Frenchman and I, along with virtually everyone I knew on Zanzibar, were on a plane to Mombasa, and an hour after that, I was bribing my way through a health check: It was quick; the health officer said my yellow fever vaccine was expired, I said it wasn't, we went to his office next to the passport counter. I didn't sit down, I just said, "Look, gotta run, here's ten bucks, see ya." We shook hands and that was that.

On my way out, the health officer's accomplice was leading the Frenchman in. He looked at me imploringly, but I looked over his shoulder and spotted his Belgian girlfriend waiting for him just outside passport control. I kept walking. As I left the passport check, she approached me, preceded by her chest and followed respectfully by her bottom, walking that wild high-heeled walk. No. It wasn't a walk. It was a parade. I smiled, she didn't. She said, "What happened to him?"

Amazing how much we shared of each other's lives. Such familiarity: "What happened to him?" What happened to him? It was so sad . . . The world's easiest straight line: "What happened to him?" You mean, what happened to *him*? Well, let me tell you. The guy walked into a bar with a duck on his head and the bartender said . . .

"A yellow fever check," I said stiffly, in the bizarre manner I have of speaking English to people whose mother tongue is something else. I enunciate very clearly and I myself affect the accent of somebody who speaks English quite well as a second language. In Germany, for example, I speak English the way Germans spoke English in old movies. "It will cost him approximately one hundred francs. It is no problem. In five minutes he will be free."

"Thank you," she said, already forgetting me. I noticed by the way she immediately looked past me, searching for her friend, the guy with her ticket back to Belgium, that absence had made her heart grow fonder and her skin redder. A morning spent around the pool of an expensive Mombasa surf resort, I wagered. Probably in a very tiny bathing suit. Bored.

Waiting for something to happen. Staring with unabashed abandon at her admirers, maybe. Later, clad in some thin and gauzy frock, she probably strolled casually over to the open-air bar as the sun set over Africa. She probably laughed easily and occasionally shook her hair out of her eyes as she endured a series of frivolous conversations that never quite got to the point. And, when she finally stood to leave, the brilliant moonlight reflected off the calm waters of the Indian Ocean and silhouetted her perfect legs, as if her dress were a mere nod to convention. Yeah. That's probably the way it was.

"You're welcome," I said, overstaying my welcome. "Uh. Don't worry."

"Thank you," she said again. A nanosecond passed. Then she *smiled*. I had it made in the shade, she was mine, anything could happen.

So I jumped in a cab and in twenty minutes I was at the train station, just a half hour ahead of the scheduled departure of the last train for Nairobi. I found my carriage, tossed my bag inside, then went back out to light a pipe.

They were there: Out on the platform, the Belgian girl was almost pulling him along; the Frenchman had all the bags. She saw me and, somewhat startled, gave a little wave that said small world. But the Frenchman, he hated me again. For him, the world was much, much smaller.

PART TWO

MOMBASA—TSAVO— NAIROBI

ONCE, I FLEW IN AN OLD CARGO AIRCRAFT OVER THE civil war in Angola. Below me, lush, green fields covered the earth and the rivers ran clear and clean. The only signs of war came at the abrupt end of roads, the bridgeless punctuation at each canyon and rift.

Next to me, a graying pilot, still too hung over to fly, but too valuable, apparently, to leave behind, sat on a crate and looked out the small window in the freight door. "That's the thing about life on Earth," he said. "The higher you get, the better it all looks."

Imagine, then, the lofty eye of our distant God. Easy for Him to look down at all He made and pronounce it good: The higher you get, the better it all looks. But on this planet, crime is in the details, in the long look, up close — and even then, what you see isn't necessarily what you get. If it were, we would find truth in television and there'd be no divorce.

Most visitors to Mombasa, for example, are holidaymakers and sunbathers bent on gaining an intimate knowledge of only the first few hundred meters of Africa. To them, Mombasa might resemble a Condé Nast picture of paradise, with little thatched pavilions on a platinum blonde strand and a sky of process blue. Lots of people go to Mombasa and recall little about the continent outside the Mediterranean-style beach resorts and perhaps the sprawling, labyrinthine Old Town that washes up against the buttresses of ancient Fort Jesus, a gigantic, crenellated, hyperbolic statement of resolve uttered by stubborn Portuguese in the fifteenth century.

After Zanzibar, Mombasa's Arab Quarter is somewhat tame, but there's more money in Mombasa than there is in Zanzibar, so there's a lot more business and traffic and the oldest part of the city, stretching away from the harbor, is crowded and busy: tinsmiths and tailors, greengrocers and butchers hawk their merchandise at full volume. Carts and taxis struggle through the narrow streets amid the roving gangs of tourists who dutifully follow a local guide from one point to another, usually ending up at Mombasa's own slave cave — through which slaves were brought to dhows for the trip to Zanzibar's slave cave, thence to market in Zanzibar Town — or back to Fort Jesus, below which local fishermen work the harbor's waters. On the northern shore, some visitors look for what remains of Frere Town, the settlement named after Sir Henry Bartle Frere, a former high commissioner for South Africa, and built by the Church Missionary Society for ex- and runaway slaves and where the small but influential tribe of "Bombay Africans," as the descendants of Indian workers and local natives were known, strutted like English gentry a century ago and lorded it over the rest of the Frere Towners. On the ground, in the streets and dark passageways, Mombasa is a wet Araby, a stifling hot and humid relic surrounded by beaches packed with European tourists.

During my last visit to Mombasa, six months or so earlier, I had decided to make a series of quick stops at the beach resorts along the coast, each resembling the next — each with its own disco, its own highly sentimentalized tropical bar, its

FORT JESUS

own shop selling upmarket souvenirs, its own authoritarian entertainment scheme — and all resembling the cheerfully dull beach resorts of southern Spain or Italy or the Caribbean or the Texas Gulf Coast or Acapulco.

I had stopped first in the middle of town at the Castle Inn, a rummy but atmospheric rendezvous for tourists who wish to sit in the hot sun, drink cold beer, and eat sandwiches made from pastel-tinted meat so old that each bite seems invested with a certain dangerous thrill. My object had been to meet a friend who would lend me a car.

My original plan was to visit the bars of the seaside lodges, then either to return to Mombasa in time to catch a charter flight back to Nairobi or to stay the night at the Diani Reef hotel, a stewardess-infested, air-conditioned, well-appointed dive with a well-stocked bar — in short, a model of the sort of seafood-buffet and swimming-pool accommodation I unfailingly enjoy — some forty-odd kilometers south of Mombasa.

By very late lunchtime, I had reached my destination. Rather than check in, I had gone straight to the bar, where, in an effort to order a drink, I met an English chap whom I will call Jack Marsh. The previous night, while in a state of accelerated saturation, Mr. Marsh and a friend had hitched a ride — "for a lark" — with a caravan of minibuses carrying a German tour group from Malindi, a resort-clogged town farther up the coast, where he said he feared he had left his fiancée. His friend had apparently found solace with one of the German tourists, but Mr. Marsh, after a night of chronic misdemeanor, was anxious to get back to his future and begged me for a lift at least as far as Mombasa.

With Mr. Marsh behind the wheel, we set off back along the A14, Kenya's well-traveled coast road. I tried to make small talk with the Englishman, but all he wanted to talk about was his fiancée. We quickly settled into a fuel-inefficient cycle: He would volunteer that his fiancée would be furious

with him, and as he spun out his complex speculations, the
car would slow gradually. When the slow pace of the car
reached a sufficiently dangerous level and trucks and other
cars were swerving wildly to get around us, I would agree
with him that, in fact, "furious" was too mild a term. This
would agitate him, he'd stew in silence, and he'd accelerate
rapidly.

We were heading north, so Africa was to our left, with the
Indian Ocean, and, eventually, Borneo, to our right. At one
point, we passed a turnoff to the Shimba Hills Reserve, where
a dazzling assortment of bird life can be found in the reserve's
coastal jungle forest. But Mr. Marsh was driving with his
heart, not his head, so he dismissed the notion of a detour.
"We went to Amboseli when we first arrived," he said, "but
we didn't care much for Africa."

"But you're *in* Africa," I pointed out.

"No, but I mean . . ." He hesitated. "You know what
I mean."

▼▲▼▲▼

If you're like most tourists in Mombasa, there's an 80 percent
chance you're German, that you stayed six nights and seven
days at one of the beach hotels where you ate a lot of crusta-
ceans and fruit, that you spent one night in Mombasa town
getting drunk on a little prepackaged debauchery, and five
more at a hotel bar or next to a pool drinking stuff out of
coconut shells with little umbrellas stuck in the ice. If you're
like most tourists visiting not just Mombasa, but Kenya, you
never went more than a mile or so into Africa, unless you
signed up for a flight to Amboseli or some other handy game
park for an overnight in the bush. If you're in Mombasa,
you're where most tourists to sub-Saharan Africa come; of
the 700,000 or so foreigners who will visit Kenya next year,
most will stay in Mombasa and won't be bothered with the

imminent departure of the overnight train. They'll skip Nairobi and Kisumu, thanks.

But let's assume you've decided to make the trek from Mombasa to Nairobi and points beyond by train — a bargain at the rough equivalent of $29.95 first-class all the way to Kisumu — and that this little book is your companion. You would have read the bit about Zanzibar and the brief squib about Mombasa in the three hours or so that elapsed between your departure from Mombasa and before the second seating for dinner — the preferred seating, since the dining car staff won't have to hustle you out to accommodate more diners.

You would have booked your seat far in advance to make sure you don't have to ride third-class, no fun but educational in that carry-on-livestock-in-a-box kind of way, and you would have showed up at the station for the second and last departure of the day, the train of choice. You would have arranged for the delivery of your bedding, and you'd be whiling away the minutes reading something like this and looking out the window as the train leaves Mombasa, crosses the causeway to the mainland — Mombasa, remember, is an island — and begins its slow, all-night ascent to Nairobi, where the glories of the African plains will pass just outside your window, but in utter darkness. Dinner is served late, and by the time second seating is called, you'll be hungry and maybe a little restless.

No fear: En route entertainment is as close as the dining car, for feeding time is show time on Kenya Railways. Each train is equipped with one or two restaurant cars and each car accommodates fifty passengers or so at each of two sittings. The meal is served in three courses, starting with the extraordinary Serving of the Soup, in which gallant waiters, clad in white duck, sockless, with unlaced canvas sneaks, ladle consommé from a tureen as the dining car lurches from side to side. It's left to the diners to spill the soup, which they do, and generally to their own amusement.

THE RESTAURANT CARS ARE ELEGANT AND OF INTRIGUING VINTAGE.

Besides, the passengers — Europeans in tight knit shirts, Americans in Banana Republic's tourist-photographer vests — are universally underdressed for the setting. Many of the restaurant cars are elegant and of intriguing vintage — one dates from the twenties and is richly paneled; another is a late-thirties Deco delight. The appointments are genteel-shabby, with frayed but spotless white tablecloths and an assortment of silver. In the course of its history, the railway has been called virtually every name in a railroader's book; teapots, saucers, and forks all bear different markings; some are from the Kenya-Uganda Railroad, some are from a brief bureaucratic experiment called East Africa Railways and Harbour, a spin-off name from an earlier incarnation as the East African Railway; the oldest stuff is the best: it bears a simple "U.R." The seat of choice for this entertainment is the chair at the table for two in the front corner, facing the car. Diners at the first seating are rushed out unceremoniously to make room for more passengers; diners at the second seating are rushed out so everyone can go to bed, but some lingering is allowed.

After dinner, you entertain yourself. You're missing a lot of terrific scenery outside, of course, but you're not missing much on the train. Up front, an engine driver and his assistant sit silently on little black vinyl-covered stools and stare out into the black desert blankness through which much of the trip is made. If you were to ride in the locomotive cab, you'd find yourself leaning against a hot metal panel behind which the diesel engine roars and your only distraction would be watching an occasional antelope bolt into the light, then away again. The train moves very slowly, often cruising at twenty mph or so for hours, the night time tedium interrupted only at the stations where a station attendant passes the key to the next track segment on to the engine driver and at the same time picks up the key to the last segment in an elaborate exchange of wooden hoops in which the keys are lodged; the line is single-track almost all the way, so it pays to know who has the right-of-way. After about three hours, about the time you reach Tsavo, maybe, you'd start to wish you were stretched out on one of the comfortable berths, stiff white sheets pulled up around your neck, reading a good story through the night, after the moon sets on Kenya and before the sun rises just south of Nairobi.

The railway reached Voi — mile one hundred — in December 1897; if you took the last train from Mombasa, you probably reached it shortly after midnight. Voi is an important station, the market center for this part of the Kenyan plateau, so the train will stop for a while: mail on, mail off, that sort of thing.

AN ELABORATE EXCHANGE OF WOODEN HOOPS

A spur runs due west out of Voi to the Tanzanian border. It was built during World War I by the British to help fight the Germans, who, under General Paul von Lettow-Vorbeck, ran the Brits ragged as they pursued him through Tanganyika, Mozambique, Zambia, and back again.[1] A major battle in that East African campaign was fought near Taveta. While the station porters take care of the post, the engine driver and the stationmaster, standing just outside the cab, will quietly exchange gossip, then the train will slowly roll on. Thirty miles farther along the way, watch the window. Eventually, you'll see the highway, and, if you're lucky, you may be able to make out the Man Eaters.

Man Eaters Motel is only a few hundred meters from the bridge at Tsavo. Once, man-eating lions roamed this stretch of the Taru desert. Now the few lions left are busy with buffalo and the like, and the only man-eater is the motel, except there's no motel there, just some gas pumps and the dining room and a small kiosk selling chocolates and soda to the passing road trade. The motel is the last stage in what seems to be the three-phase development of Tsavo. The gas pumps and the dining room were built several years ago, but the motel construction is running way, way, *way* behind schedule.

Done by daylight, the train ride from the south is a high ride through hell. No passenger service is operated during the daylight hours,[2] so the freight trains own the line while the

---

[1] General Paul von Lettow-Vorbeck's insistent campaign in East Africa is on every military historian's ten-best list. Charles Miller tells the full story in *The Battle for the Bundu* (New York: 1974), but William Boyd's novel, *An Ice Cream War* (London and New York: 1982), based on the von Lettow-Vorbeck campaign, is brilliant fiction, one of my favorite books, in which this extraordinary story is wonderfully researched and told with affection and rich imagination.

[2] Limited daylight passenger service was introduced in 1989 by Kenya Railways, but it was discontinued after too few tourists took advantage of it to offset the loss of revenue from locals, who refused to use it. A Kenya Railways official told me that people don't want to arrive in Nairobi at night. "It's too dangerous," he said, "and besides they like to sleep on the train."

sun's up. Often the trains seem like the only things able to stir during the incredibly hot day. You can stand by the track and watch a freight train come and go, appearing uncertainly on the floating horizon, then disappearing into the Taru, which stretches away into a scrub-filled zone of tedium that vanishes without a point, without really seeming to end. With a little marketing, you could fill this desert with young professionals seeking a perfect two-hour tan, but a full day will give you a sweet melanoma glow and a week or so of arm dangling out of a covered jeep will give you an elbow full of little, blistering sun sores.

The last time I was on a train going upcountry toward Tsavo, it was a daylight run on a long freight. I rode in the caboose, no doubt to the muted consternation of the occasional travelers who also sought a lift and who climbed on and off the train at each tidy, flower-bedecked station. The stations along the main line all compete for a prize — usually a plaque — given to the best-kept station. As a result, the tiny station buildings on the Kenya Railways line are among the best-maintained colonial structures I've ever encountered anywhere in Africa. In Khartoum, the library of what was once called Gordon College might be quite unshelved, and in Kinshasa, the Belgian legacy might be covered with tin roofing and militant vegetation, but the railroad stations in Kenya — aside from those in Nairobi, Nakuru, Mombasa, and the other major stations — are well-scrubbed, quaint bungalows set in small, obsessively manicured gardens and almost without exception they are the centerpieces of the dusty villages the railroad's presence helps preserve. Inside each neatly swept building are the machines of an earlier technology: Painted iron, well-oiled wood, and polished brass fill the offices of the stationmasters and the ticket sellers. These modest gems are for the most part unseen, except by the locals and the engine

THE TINY STATION BUILDINGS ARE AMONG THE BEST-MAINTAINED CO-
LONIAL STRUCTURES, WELL-SCRUBBED BUNGALOWS SET IN SMALL,
OBSESSIVELY MANICURED GARDENS.

drivers on the railway, since, as you well know by now, interested visitors pass each way along the line only in the night.

I arrived at Tsavo sometime after lunch. The assistant stationmaster, Cowence Agweddo, slightly irritated at my sudden appearance, quickly donned his white heavy cotton uniform coat and retired to his office, one of two small rooms in
the station building, to give my travel permit a slow once-
over. A station porter shadowed me while I waited on the station porch, where a flowering vine climbed the walls and the
roof supports. A neat garden swept along the track. Opposite
the station, some outbuildings had been occupied by an extended family of baboons. The assistant stationmaster finally
emerged with my letters of introduction.

A cluster of modest buildings occupied a slight rise between
the station and the highway, but they appeared to be empty.
On the far side of the track was a valley, at the bottom of

A SORT OF WELCOME TO TSAVO. BOTTOM: TOMBSTONE-SIZED ANTHILL

which was the ruins of a small stone building. Some distant hills interrupted the flat desert plateau. "I'm looking for the town," I said.

He pointed in the direction of the Man Eaters and shrugged.

No, I said, I mean the village. "Isn't there a village around here someplace?" I had in mind something quite *civic*, sort of a Welcome-to-Tsavo-Lions-Club-meets-first-and-third-Thursdays kind of thing. "Why," I asked him, "would there be a station here without a village?"

"There is nothing here," Mr. Agweddo said.

"No, I mean, is there a monument here, or a marker?"

"There is nothing," he repeated.

"A shop, maybe, or something else?"

"There is nothing."

"No animals, even? Do you ever see lions here?" I looked around.

"Yes, we used to see lions here in the day. Now sometimes at night, the lions come." He pointed, but I wasn't sure what he was pointing at. Not at a lion, I hoped.

"But no man-eaters, eh, ha-ha?"

"No. Now there is nothing."

By gad, he was right. By day at any rate, there is nothing at Tsavo save a few tombstone-sized anthills and the distant Man Eaters. You'd think there'd be a little more to the place. After all, Tsavo gave its name to two of the largest game parks in Kenya and the Tsavo River flows through here. Once, there was even a small tannery in operation at Tsavo; the remains are visible from the railway line. On the old maps of East Africa, Tsavo is one of the few place-names that would be familiar to a modern visitor, and on the old globe in your library, the chances are Tsavo is a place you could still spot quite easily. Partly that's because of the unfortunate occurrence at Tsavo in the late 1890s, in which a slow slaughter — a topic to which we will presently turn — held up construction of the

Uganda Railway for nearly a year, making Tsavo a railroad town of significant size for quite some time. Partly it's because the river crossing at Tsavo is one of the rare points of cartographic interest in the Taru desert. And while Tsavo is still on the map, these days there's not a lot to keep a tourist in the neighborhood. A government-scheme village — whitewashed huts with standard native thatched roofs — is situated some distance from the road near the railroad bridge, and a mile or so south is the station. If you want a tin of milk or a bag of beans, you've got to go twenty-odd miles down the road to Voi. But if you want a Coke or a chicken curry, Tsavo's your town, the Man Eaters your place.

The Man Eaters is distinctly modern. You can see it from a distance perched on its pedestal, like Monsanto's home of the future, all modular and overfenestrated, a giant white TV set floating above the hot desert. To get to the restaurant, you climb the stairs over the breezeway, past the candy-and-soda kiosk and the toilets, to the dining room. An empty barroom — no bottles, no glasses, empty barstools — occupies one half; the other half is filled with black Naugahyde chairs and modern dining tables. On the wall, you can see maneaters in big blowups of old pictures, but there are no other decorations, inside or out. Under the dining room, a stretch of old, abandoned line leads a few yards through the breezeway to an unfinished swimming pool out back, and tucked neatly out of sight just behind the rack of *Drum* magazines are a few shacks that I guess serve as the employees' quarters.

Considering the rough countryside surrounding it, you might want to do what I did and sit in the Man Eaters forever, looking out at the bright light of African drought as it breaks against scrub and stone. Trucks stop and trucks go and automobiles carrying white people and Asians — but usually not black Africans — pull in for a fill-up and a local Nehi. Once, during my prolonged residency there, a lunar Land-Rover carrying adventurous English tourists from someplace in the rainy highlands to the sea pulled off the narrow highway and into the semicircular drive. The vehicle was a military specimen, with giant tires and a canvas top that had been rolled back to allow the sun to bake the contents: big, confusing cloth bags; some airplane seats; of course a guitar. The thin, uniformed attendant watched warily, but he quickly sensed this was no gas customer; he stretched out again on his beach chair. The driver — beard, aviator Ray Bans, deep bronze — chose to ignore the carpark and its scrawny garden fringe. Instead, he parked out in front, parallel to the gas pumps. A young woman, maybe twenty-five, was the last passenger out. She was badly in need of laundering and pressing, but she had the sort of freckled visage that engenders a parent's blindness, and she had the clear, unblinking eyes of a visionary vegetarian. "We started at Trafalgar Square," she told me. "Then we went through Europe, then Morocco" and so on and so forth, mile after mile, in earnest monotone until she got here, to the Man Eaters. What she saw on the way: animals, some "really heavy" — cosmically, not meteorologically — rainstorms, the desert, the jungle, small villages, colorful people. Four months on the road, and home in another month, right after Zimbabwe.

The rumpled pilgrims — seven in all — went upstairs and pulled a couple of tables together while Samuel, the day-shift waiter, watched them disdainfully. Samuel, a rotund and usually cheerful member of the dominant Kikuyu tribe, had been at the Man Eaters for only a month, but he was plainly fed up with tourists. He had started off the day in fine form, spinning and flicking his white towel and later dancing down the stairs, like a waiter in an old musical. But the day had turned sour, and by the time the English trekkers arrived, he was still cheesed off from the last bunch — an American trio, two women and a man — who insisted they had been overcharged for something. The dispute had raged between Samuel and one of the women (the thinnest one, her hair pulled back severely, her face permanently pissed) for nearly thirty minutes, even though the amount in question was only a few shillings, maybe a quarter or so in American money. "I know what I know," the woman would say whenever it appeared Samuel had her cornered. The rhetorical ploy bought her time, since it obviously made sense to Samuel. Every time she'd say it, he'd look at me, then at the ceiling. I'd shrug. Then, finally, Richard, the stern cook, had to be brought out of the kitchen and into the fray.

The whole thing was ludicrous, and she was wrong all the way. Her white liberal inclination prevented her from verbalizing the ultimate logical fallacy, but you could see she was close to the edge. Besides, it was apparent that she was letting off a lot more steam than a lunch check might generate.

As she talked her way into the social cellar of ridicule, the man slipped off down the stairs and the other woman backed over toward my table, her arms full of bags and T-shirts and her mind full of jealousy, although not entirely her own. Where now there were three, once, when they had set off from New York, there had been four — footloose Manhattanites off on an East African adventure thing. But there had been some predictable confusion among the tents, and the man hiding downstairs had ended up with the woman gossiping upstairs with me, whose own companion (a fiancé, actually) had been on the bitter end of the flip-flop and had lit out for Paris or maybe London or "home for all I know," while the angry woman — once paired with the guy downstairs but now sleeping solo — was now left alone with her outrage, riding in the backseat of a rented Isuzu Trooper II, making acerbic comments "and just spoiling *everybody's* good time." I got all this while Samuel got his.

YOUNG WOMEN WORKING IN THE SODA KIOSK

Out on the highway, a caravan of tourist coaches crossed the Tsavo River and accelerated past the Man Eaters. "They never stop here," Samuel said later, referring to the packed tour buses disappearing down the road. "I am a very lucky man."

Anyway, luckier than the Asian entrepreneur who bought the Man Eaters from its original owner, a former minister in the government of President Daniel arap Moi. "He [the previous owner] was helped by the government," one employee told me somewhat stylistically, "but it didn't help him." The idea behind the Man Eaters was to skim the tourist trade as it rattled down the road and through the desert. Trouble is, there's already a tourist trap or two on highway A109, the road between Nairobi and the coast — notably at Voi, where the two principal game lodges attached to giant Tsavo East

National Park are situated close to the town — and the drive isn't long enough (you can rush and make it in six hours or dawdle and do it in a day) to warrant a lot of overnighters. So, especially during the off season, it seems unlikely that you could fill the Man Eaters with tourists, even if there were a motel room or two to be rented, which of course there isn't.

"Maybe it is the name," ventured one of the young women working in the soda kiosk. She was the Man Eaters' most senior employee; by the time I got there, she'd been on the job for ten, going on eleven months — long enough to recognize a no-future situation, and consequently she was nearing the end of her career in Tsavo. "Too many people do not want to eat at a place with a name like Man Eaters."

I asked her if she knew why the motel was called such a thing, if she knew the story of Tsavo. She wasn't sure, but, even after I told her, it didn't matter. "It is a frightening name." She paused, then said it softly to herself. "Man Eaters."

Her colleague, a younger, more gregarious woman, was busy reading James Fox's book *White Mischief: The Murder of Lord Erroll*. She had only been at the Man Eaters for two months, but she agreed. "It is too hard to stay here." Both women came from distant parts of the country and were far from the families to whom they were sending most of their pay, and they were bored beyond belief. "There is no telephone here, there are no shops here," said the young reader. "There is nothing here. The owner has promised us that something will happen soon, but it never does." She shrugged, then gestured absently. "Besides, even if they build the motel, nobody will want to stay here." She looked out across the desert. Vacancy was apparently a pervasive condition, in and out, of the Man Eaters Motel.

You may, if you wish, put this book away for a bit and stretch. You might even want to sleep. They say sleeping on a train is something on the prenatal side of things. I say it takes some getting used to.

Still, there's something indisputably comfortable about the train's rhythmic sound and movement, the berth, the clean, white bedding, boiled clean, bleached, and lightly starched. Many people have told me they have spent their most restful nights sleeping in a moving train, and I believe them. But it has not happened to me. Still, you can take full advantage of the situation without the business of sleep coming in. If you are an insomniac, as I am, there is no place quite so charming to spend a sleepless night as on a train in Africa.

Long train rides require a bit of reconciliation. The time and distance equation is weighted heavily on the side of time. Time is what preoccupies you, not distance. You will travel X hours, that's all.

If you are sleepless and in such circumstances, you may want a little something to help pass the night. Here, to keep you occupied, is a story about lions, very hungry lions, lions who ate many men less than a century ago just outside your carriage window.[3]

▼▲▼▲▼

Midday in Tsavo: High dust and the white circle of heat.

What's left here is perhaps only the remnants of the big Western, a matinee cliché in which we see the distant, colorless desert hills, and *way* down there, some lonely pilgrim alone in a valley, maybe next to a river, but in any case, down in the valley. He's doing something, some sort of work — panning for gold, or looking for strays, or surveying for a railroad. It's hot, damn hot; the horizon has that sort of nature-on-acid look about it, and you know that our man must be sweating like a pig. Sure enough, he grabs his old bandana,

[3] But as a fallback — in case you want to catch a few winks, after all — a shorter tale, called "With Ryall at Kima," appears in an appendix to this odd book.

takes off his hat, and mops his brow. He glances up at the sky, hoping for a cloud, looking for rain. But all he sees is the relentless sun and the patient carrion birds circling lazily above him. He starts to put his hat back on, but something catches his eye, something high on a ridge top. He can't believe it: Indians! he thinks to himself. Indians! surrounded by the trackless desert, surrounded by billowing volcanic waste. And when the camera pulls back we see them, too: 10,000 Indians. But not *those* kind — not the kind Columbus found; no, the kind he was looking for. Just 10,000 maniacs for money, brought from Bombay to build a railway from the sea across a desert toward a lake someplace in the middle of Africa.

By December 1896, a full year after the construction of the railway began, a man could leave Mombasa after a late and leisurely breakfast, walk the entire length of the Uganda railroad, and arrive at the end of the line well before supper. Although the government had not imposed a strict construction schedule on the railway's builders, there were reasonable expectations to be met and the general consensus was that the project should be finished by mid-1900 at the latest. After the first year, the Uganda Railway, however, still had 558 of its 581 miles to go. George Whitehouse, the thirty-one-year-old chief engineer, had had an easier time building railroads in South America, England, Mexico, India, and South Africa.

But Whitehouse had some pretty good excuses. First of all, he had to work through a troublesome maze of colonial bureaucrats not only in Mombasa but also in Zanzibar, where wilted officials still administered the newly proclaimed East Africa Protectorate. Communications were often frustratingly slow; Whitehouse's outward messages would sometimes go

unanswered, while he would be in regular receipt of memo-
randa urging him to proceed ever more quickly with the
project. Second, the civil service in London proved to be an
enormous, unforeseen problem: The government's railway
commissioners had seriously overlooked the complications
inherent in starting a railroad from an island, which is what
Mombasa is. The necessity to build a 1,700-foot bridge across
Makupa Creek — the small rivulet that separates Mombasa
from the mainland — was not terribly difficult, but because of
the lack of appropriate building materials, it took eight precious months to accomplish the task. Beyond that, the construction of the railroad required lots of men and machines.
So, during 1896, several thousand Indian laborers arrived,
along with hundreds of assorted Indian masons, carpenters,
smiths, clerks, surveyors, and draftsmen. In addition to im-
porting iron houses and tents to shelter his workers and to provide office space for his staff, Whitehouse also had to find water
for the men and for the locomotives that would carry the
men, their equipment, and their supplies into the interior. He
estimated that the construction crews and the steam-powered
machinery, including locomotives, would drink about 10,000
gallons of water a day and that the water would have to be
carried up the line as far as one hundred miles into the Taru.
Mombasa could barely meet the water demands of its own residents, let alone the demands of the railway and its workers, so
basins were built to catch the seasonal rains and the construction of a rudimentary desalinization plant was initiated.

Mombasa was one of the more interesting African ports
during the last half of the last century. The Old Town that's
there now was the only town that was there then. Judging
from contemporary photos, nothing seems to have changed
much, except the streets looked even more crowded then than
now. Men who apparently prided themselves on the ostenta-

tion of their dress pulled peculiar two-passenger trolley cars up and down the narrow, hot, fetid passageways, but since the trolleys were on rails, which meant they couldn't maneuver easily around the giant caravans of camels or the slow-moving Arabs and their donkey trains, Mombasa was in a continual state of gridlock.

Although the British ruled in Mombasa, in the late 1890s it was still a decidedly Arabic place — as it still is — and a minaret rose over the milling Somalis, Indians, Swahili-speaking tribesmen, Portuguese traders, and Omanis who jammed the cramped streets and filled the dark and labyrinthine bazaars. On either side rose the intricate, carved-coral residences of wealthy Arabs, Indians, and other Asians alongside municipal and government buildings and sundry warehouses. The warm air was almost always foul and damp, and during December, tepid monsoon rains fed by the waters of the Indian Ocean washed across the noisy, colorful port city.

One of the biggest problems facing Whitehouse was the fact that the Old Harbour at Mombasa, which for centuries had been fine for Arabs in small dhows, was simply inadequate for landing and distributing the material and supplies Whitehouse needed. The railway construction would require nearly a quarter-million ten-yard rail lengths — each weighing fifty pounds per yard, along with 1.2 million sleepers, most of which would have to be made of steel to render them inedible to ants — and nearly 6 million pieces of sundry hardware. As much as 100,000 pounds of forty- and sixty-foot steel girders would be needed for viaducts and causeways. The railway would also need at least thirty locomotives each weighing thirty tons or so and a large consignment of rolling stock, including tenders, vans, wagons, and passenger coaches. So to make it possible to unload the stuff he needed to build a railroad, Whitehouse had to first build a modern port, with docks, wharves, warehouses, and a wooden jetty with a steam hoist for offloading the rolling stock, which he did, at Kilindini.

And, finally, Whitehouse was saddled with workers who had been recruited by officials in India. They were mostly unskilled, but they all bore contracts that required a minimum wage of fifteen rupees (about five dollars) each month, regardless of the amount of work any one worker did. The laborers were thus relieved of the troublesome burden of initiative.

At the same time, surveying parties were working in advance of the railhead, mapping the terrain that had been sketchily surveyed several years earlier. Because of the thickness of the undergrowth and the need for earthworks, an 1897 report claimed that it was impossible to move the line forward any faster than a quarter mile per day — a speed that would mean the railroad to Lake Victoria would take more than seven years to build — but only if the laborers and staff could survive the illnesses to which they increasingly fell victim. "During the months of November and December 1896 and January and February 1897 the health of the staff and the laborers was very bad," a parliamentary report stated. "The effect of turning up the soil, which in tropical countries almost invariably results in great increase in malaria, has in the present case been aggravated by unusual and unseasonably heavy rains. . . . Ulcers have been very prevalent among the Indian laborers, and over 50 per cent of them have been down with malarious fever. The whole European staff has from time to time suffered severely from the latter." In 1896, one hundred workers died, a miraculously small number considering there were only five doctors on the staff.

Plagues in India curtailed labor recruitment, and it was quickly determined that native African labor would never do to make up the loss. Recruits from the local tribes, unfamiliar with European tools, had to have lengthy, detailed instruction in how to hold and use even shovels and picks, objects previously unknown to almost all of them.

To compound the problems caused by the labor shortage, Whitehouse was shortchanged the locomotives and other pieces of equipment he required. And the draft animals were dropping dead by the thousand, victims of the local tsetse flies or the desert heat.

So building a railway through Africa during the last years

of the last century was a tough job. Whitehouse and the other European staff members were regular visitors to the hospital, and the spirit of the enterprise, so jolly and hale at the beginning of 1896, was grimly pessimistic by the end of the year. The Europeans were demoralized; the Indian laborers were edgy and reluctant to work. All of them, Europeans and Indians alike, felt that whatever the reward of building a railroad to Uganda, it wasn't worth the trouble. They just weren't happy in their work.

And that was *before* lions started eating them up.

▼▲▼▲▼

A man of few words, I thought to myself as I thumbed through one of Ronald Preston's diaries. Here's the entire entry for January 1, 1897: "My birthday. Received orders for Mombassa [*sic*]." That was a Friday. On Saturday: "Passed by medical officer. Played match against Hindu eleven & won."

Ronald O. Preston, thirty-two years old yesterday, at home at 33 Dickenson Road, Bangalore. Kissing his wife Florence good-bye, going off to work every day, patching up the infrastructure of the Indian portion of the Empire, stopping by the medical officer for an okay, followed by a little afternoon cricket. Cricket? Not a bowler, from the looks of him. In a photo taken a month after his birthday, Ronald and Florence Preston are in a tent someplace in the middle of the Kenyan desert. Mr. Preston, now in charge of the railhead, a man who lives always at the end of the line, holds a rifle on his lap; there are zebra skins and hunting trophies at his feet. He's a dark-haired man, built low and close to the ground, with a thick mustache; he sits on a stool looking directly at the camera, his mouth forming a half smile, his eyes serious and dark but not unfriendly. To his right sits Mrs. Preston, a sturdy-looking woman with black hair and broad features, wearing a dark boater, a shirtwaist with a man's necktie and a walking skirt, probably a black one. George Whitehouse — who, as chief engineer was Preston's boss — was an unmarried man, so while Mrs. Preston looks very, very plain, she was, I'll bet, the best-looking European woman in Kenya in 1897. She's gazing placidly, almost vacantly off-camera, as if the photographer and his work were but another once tiresome tribulation to which, after a decade of Indian sweats and now African trials, she has somehow grown indifferent.

Preston's diary has changed, too. While it's no less taciturn, now there is more to write about. There are no more idle afternoon matches against Hindi elevenses. Instead, it's a daily bout of Man *versus* Nature, as Preston inventories his kills, including, on more than one occasion, a lion or two.[4]

By the end of February 1897, Preston was supervising the railhead construction, leading his army of laborers through the Taru toward the plateau on the far side of the Tsavo. The pace of construction had quickened, too, not only because of Preston's expertise, but also because of the military demands placed on the new railway. The French finally had moved in on the upper Nile, establishing an enclave at Fashoda in defiance of British claims. London had dispatched military expeditions toward the area, one of which was to march northward from Kenya after hitching a ride on as much of the

---

[4] Preston's diaries — or what remains of them — are in the possession of his son, Vic, a reformed motorcycle racer — an Isle of Man trophy decorates a shelf in his office — who runs a Shell garage in Nairobi and who seems almost completely without interest in the exploits of his father, who must have been quite old when Vic was born to Ronald's second wife. Vic, Jr., is a world-class rally car driver. Ronald's grandson nearly won the East Africa Safari rally in 1988, covering the whole country in a matter of days. Vic, Sr., discarded most of Preston's diaries, along with any old photos and prints he might have come across. "I suppose I should have kept them," he told me. Ronald Preston excerpted large pieces of his diary and published them as a book, *The Genesis of Kenya Colony* (1946). I've used both the diaries and the book.

Uganda Railway as existed at the time — by the end of the year, a bit more than a one-hundred-mile stretch through the desert. But the expedition was delayed by the mutiny of Sudanese troops in British service in Uganda, a fiercely fought rebellion that disrupted much of the business in the equatorial region until early in 1898. The necessity of rail transportation caused Preston and Whitehouse to lay temporary tracks through much of the Dika Plains past Voi in the western reaches of the desert.

By January 1898, Preston had finally brought the railhead as far as the oasis at the Tsavo River, where the water always ran. Today, there are palm trees lining the banks of the river at Tsavo and the ten-yard strip of undergrowth on either side of the Tsavo is lush and green, in startling contrast to the surrounding dusty, thorn-rich Taru. Everything is identifiable in the old photographs: same rock outcroppings, same sudden thicket of undergrowth. Animal tracks are everywhere here, and on a sign near the highway, a baboon sits nursing her baby, ignoring the passing trucks and the picture-taking visitors.

The Indian laborers took one look at the Tsavo crossing and jumped in the water. While the rest of the railhead consolidated at Tsavo, the crews took advantage of the refreshing, fast-moving river and the administrative holiday that bridge building necessitated. By day, they lounged on the riverbank, but at night in their camps, they told each other stories retailed to them by the local Wakamba tribesmen, stories about the ghosts of Tsavo — a word that means "slaughter" in the local language — and the evil spirits that lurked there. In his diary, Preston dismissed the effect the stories had on the laborers, noting that they could desert whenever they pleased, "if they were foolish enough to run away from their livelihoods." The idea of deserting took on a punning dimension in the Taru. Where, he wondered, could they go? These were In-

A BABOON NURSES HER BABY NEAR THE HIGHWAY

dian workers, a long way from home. He made plans to throw a temporary bridge across the Tsavo and put the troublesome Taru behind him.

▼▲▼▲▼

Once, there was a certain Indian coolie who came to a hasty conclusion just a few months before the nineteenth century did the same. Along with a great number of other Indians, he was helping to build the Uganda Railway, the tenuous metal ribbon that the Victorians hoped would tie Mombasa to Lake Victoria forever.

Our coolie is nameless to us, maybe untouchable to his co-workers. But suffice it to say that he lived a life of profound obscurity until he was one day touched lightly by God, made sort of memorable, and chosen to become dinner for a man-eater.

If you have a taste for a little rough action, this is where you want to get with the story. This is the part where the hapless coolie is strolling along the jungle path, a cheerful folk melody on his lips, when, suddenly, a lion grabs him by the head and squeezes until the poor man's face looks like a science project, until the top of his head becomes meat, until his teeth — that magic smile that once charmed the girls of Poona or Mangalore frozen forever — go flying away from the whole horrible scene.

To his hard-luck Indians, it seemed a desertion had taken place. One of the laborers was reported missing and Preston was compelled to lead a search party to try to find the missing man. The Indian's clothing was found on the riverbank, and it was assumed that he had drowned and his body was swept away. But Preston soon came across the two ends of the truth: "The skull and feet were untouched," he wrote in his diary, "but all the flesh had been torn away from the body." Preston guessed a man-eater had been at work, so he grabbed a rifle and took a party of men out to beat the bush between the camp and the river. No luck.

Three nights later, at two o'clock: a muffled scream, followed by shouts and yelling. Preston quickly dressed, took his Winchester, and rushed out to the camp. It was, he wrote, "a regular pandemonium. Some of the men were yelling at the top of their voice, while others beat drums, the din being greatly increased by the banging of empty kerosene oil tins." Another laborer had vanished, his body not found until dawn. "The remains . . . were much the same as those of [the previous victim] except that in this case even the flesh from the face had been torn off, leaving the teeth exposed which gave the skull an uncanny grinning expression."

The Indians, quite naturally, immediately cooled on the work at hand, but Preston addressed them all, telling them that the sooner they finished the temporary bridge, the sooner they'd be out of terror's way. "The men evidently saw the wisdom of this," he wrote, "and worked like Trojans." Preston's railhead quickly moved away from Tsavo. Nothing was left behind, save the temporary bridge and the river and perhaps the lions. Preston's gang of 10,000 disappeared over another nearby ridge top and into the safety of the dry heat and the thorn and the empty Yatta Plateau.

▼▲▼▲▼

Just before noon on March 1, 1898, Lieutenant John H. Patterson, thirty-one, of the British army in India, a cocksure *pukka sahib* and crack tiger hunter, a builder of Indian railway bridges, sailed into "the narrow and somewhat dangerous harbour of Mombasa, on the east coast of Africa." These days, as we have seen, Mombasa is an altogether hot and dank place, more hazardous perhaps to your checkbook than to your body or soul. But to Patterson, "everything looked fresh and green, and an oriental glamour of enchantment seemed to hang over the island," while the "old town was bathed in brilliant sunshine and reflected itself lazily on the motionless sea." Right. Too much time on a boat, I say.

In his book *The Man-eaters of Tsavo*,[5] Patterson outlines his adventure in breathless, but stiffly Victorian prose. If he spoke as he wrote, he would always be clearing his throat; if his book were to be read aloud, Nigel Bruce would have to read it. With a hearty harrumph, one imagines him dominating a table conversation from the third chair — "Funny you should mention that thing about hedgehogs, because you know, when I was sent out to East Africa, we had this dreadful problem with lions . . ." — while everyone else munched salad in order to drown out that damned lion story again. One thing's for sure, Patterson wrote as he looked. He was a dapper, neat little fellow, perhaps a little too heavily starched for comfort. The Imperial War Museum in London has a picture of Patterson taken shortly after the publication of his book in '07. He's very natty, and in the photograph he's standing ramrod straight, all decked out with a Sam Browne and jodhpurs, and he looks a lot like the way Alec Guinness looked in *Bridge on the River Kwai*. In his book, which is lavishly illustrated in black-and-white photos that are exceptionally hard to make out, he looks more typically Brit-in-the-bush: clad in his jungle best, with the oversized solar topees so popular in those days, generally posed in camp, sometimes next to the body of a dead animal. In fact, the book's frontispiece is a picture of a big stack of heads cut off of dead lions that Patterson had shot while he was in the neighborhood.

[5] London: 1907; reissued in 1979 in England and in this country as part of The Peter Capstick Library series of reprints.

Patterson's reputation preceded him up the line to Tsavo, where he had been sent to build a permanent bridge to replace Preston's temporary one, so by the time he arrived in mid-March he was reckoned by the laborers to be one of the best big-game hunters in the world — not an accurate reflection of his talents, but one which he nonetheless did nothing to discourage, except perhaps by his actions during the first week or so at Tsavo.

For Patterson had not been in camp more than a few nights when he first heard that the two man-eaters that had caused Preston's men such alarm were back for seconds. When a couple of laborers disappeared in the night, Patterson put the blame elsewhere, suspecting that "the unfortunate men had been the victims of foul play at the hands of some of their comrades . . . I thought it quite likely that some scoundrels from the gangs had murdered them for the sake of their money."

Rumors of the reappearance of the lions nevertheless circulated freely in the camp, augmented by gossip spreading back down the line from the railhead. The laborers grew more and more agitated, and a common belief soon spread among the men that the culprits "were not real animals at all, but devils in lions' shape," Patterson wrote. "Many a time the coolies solemnly assured me that it was absolutely useless to attempt to shoot them. They [the laborers] were quite convinced that the angry spirits of two departed native chiefs had taken this form in order to protest against a railway being made through their country . . ."

The coolies' gossip didn't deter Patterson, however. He remained quite unflappable, concentrating instead on the construction of the bridge, which was, after the Makupa Bridge, the biggest project on the line, and, unfortunately for Patterson, one that commanded the attention of his anxious superiors.

But the disappearance in early April 1898 of one of the

jemadars, "a fine powerful Sikh" named Ungan Singh, caused Patterson to investigate the situation a little more closely. He was soon convinced by the tracks near the site that the man had been taken away by a lion. Not only that, but this time there was a witness, one of Ungan Singh's tentmates. "He graphically described how, at about midnight, the lion suddenly put his head in at the open tent door and seized Ungan Singh — who happened to be nearest the opening — by the throat," Patterson wrote. "The unfortunate fellow cried out '*Choro!*' ("Let go!"), and threw his arms up around the lion's neck. The next moment he was gone, and his panic-stricken companions lay helpless, forced to listen to the terrible struggle which took place outside. Poor Ungan Singh must have died hard; but what chance had he? As a coolie gravely remarked, 'Was he not fighting with a lion?'"

Along with a certain Captain Haslem, Patterson set out on a stalk of the animal. "We found it an easy matter to follow the route taken by the lion, as he appeared to have stopped several times before beginning his meal. Pools of blood marked these halting-places, where he doubtless indulged in the man-eaters' habit of licking the skin off so as to get at the fresh blood. (I have been led to believe that this is their custom from the appearance of two half-eaten bodies which I subsequently rescued: the skin was gone in places, and the flesh looked dry, as if it had been sucked.) On reaching the spot where the body had been devoured, a dreadful spectacle presented itself. The ground all round was covered with blood and morsels of flesh and bones, but the unfortunate jemadar's head had been left intact, save for the holes made by the lion's tusks on seizing him, and lay a short distance away from the other remains, the eyes staring wide open with a startled, horrified look in them." Patterson and his men piled stones on the remains of the body, "the head, with its fixed, terrified stare seeming to watch us all the time, for it we did not bury, but took back to camp for identification before the medical officer." It was, wrote Patterson, "the most gruesome sight I had ever seen."

His first experience with man-eaters galvanized his resolve most wonderfully: "I vowed there and then that I would spare no pains to rid the neighborhood of the brutes."

▼▲▼▲▼

Anthony Dyer is the man Patterson needed at Tsavo, I thought to myself. Along with veterans like Robin Hurt, Anthony Seth-Smith, and Tony Archer, Dyer is among the last of the great white hunters — the sort of men represented to a generation of moviegoers by Stewart Granger. I'd been stalking him for two days.

The first lead was from Timothy Corfield, the author of the map I had spread across my accelerator leg. An arc of road, a petrol station, "thick bush," it said, and "rolling hills." Corfield, one of the guides for Ker and Downey's Safaris, had pondered Patterson's dilemma with me and had come up with nothing new.

"You really ought to speak to Tony Dyer about this sort of thing," he told me one night in Nairobi after I'd come back from Tsavo. "Here, let me draw you a map."

I'd already tried the radiotelephone number for Dyer, but the operator had just laughed at me when I complained I couldn't get through. "Nobody can get through, ha." Ha. So there I was in *agri*-central looking for an appropriate left turn. The map said, "gate." ("I can't remember, exactly," Corfield had said, "but I don't think you can go too far wrong." Wrong.)

The region surrounding Timau looks like the promised land to me, the plateau and the Ndare Forest, out past Nyeri, past Nanyuki. You'll know it when you see it — although don't bother looking now; you won't see it from the train.

Timau is far north of Nairobi, in a part of the Kenyan high-lands where the farms are huge and profitable, where the green fields look like oversized Irish imports, where a red Alfa carrying an angry albino and his friend comes running up your ass. The jerk leans on the horn — a very white farm boy out on a toot — then passes crazily over the horizon. Follow the highway along the ridge, past Timau, down a muddy track, through miles of guesswork, following a hand-drawn map, and hope to get a little free advice. In 1902, Joseph Chamberlain, the British colonial secretary, offered Dr. Theo-dor Herzl, founder of the Zionist movement, what Herzl characterized as an "antechamber to the Holy Land" in the form of 3.2 million East African acres scarcely a hundred miles to the west of Timau, where I sat, lost. The idea was that victims of pogroms in Russia and elsewhere could find a safe haven in the wilds of East Africa until a Jewish homeland was established. A delegation of Jews came out, looked the place over, and said no, thanks.

The rumor is that local settlers frightened them off with stories of lions and by sending a delegation of Masai in full lion-headed war dress to greet them.[6]

The road that can take you to hell is the same road that leads first to paradise. If you pass paradise and go too far, as I did more than once before and nearly did again looking for Dyer's gate, you'll find yourself in the volcanic wasteland of the Northern Frontier District, where Somali rustlers cross the border and slaughter whole villages, where Ugandan ban-dits roam the roads, and where you check in with the military

[6]The Herzl plan was only one of several mooted by the British government as a means of finding settlers for the area. Most other schemes centered on the estab-lishment of "colonies" for Indian settlers, but one plan, advanced by the Foreign Office, involved giving land to unhappy Finns. The Commissioner, however, noted that he was "somewhat doubtful whether Finns would find life in East Af-rica congenial," and the matter was dropped.

when you enter and check out with the military if you leave.

Looking for Dyer's, I had driven into Isiolo, a dusty town that serves as a kind of Styx for Kenya's ruined north, and I turned back to get lost in more pleasant surroundings. At the end of a day, I found myself running back to the Suzuki four-wheeler, pursued by a weird-looking bull terrier, after giving up on the only house I saw, while some black guy on the far side of a protective fence laughed at me. I tried another turning, then another, mud up to the lug nuts, streams in full flood, and finally some gardener was pointing toward the kitchen door of a large, comfortable-looking ranch house. Inside, sitting around a huge stone fireplace, were the Dyer family members, youth division, who patiently listened to my apologies for intruding, explained that their father hadn't lived in that house for "what is it, now? Nine years?" then gave me another map ("rock with white letters," "second round hill") and a cheery good-bye.

When they make the Tony Dyer movie, they won't have to look far for a location. Here's the front yard of the last president of the East Africa Professional Hunters' Association: a Piper, a Beechcraft, and an old Helio parked in a hangar next to a grass landing strip. Horses in the stable, flowers galore. Stone walls, English-country style. A huge, rambling old house built by a Dutchman at the start of the century, a colt frolicking in the garden like a hornless unicorn, a rampaging river feeding a waterwheel — the power plant that makes the lights work — and a view of the distant valleys and hills, the world as it once was.

On the verandah, over tea, Dyer set Patterson and me straight. "You don't kill a man-eater that way," Dyer tells me. "You have to limit the options. I mean, Patterson's camps were spread out over an eight-mile length by that time. How can one man patrol an eight-mile front? *You must make the lion come to you.*"

To Dyer, Patterson was just a man doing a job: "People in those days shot huge numbers of lion and what [Patterson] did wasn't exceptional. The fact that he *documented* it was interesting, because nobody else bothered to document [similar events]. And of course the fact that they [the lions] were man-eaters makes it more interesting to the public. But people were shooting lions all the time. Lion was the common enemy; there were many more of them around. In fact, they still are a sort of common enemy."

We talked briefly about the problem faced by Major Ray S. Mayers, who lives on a ranch near Voi, and who had been having a great deal of trouble with lions. Major Mayers, who had accompanied the Prince of Wales on part of his hunting expedition in East Africa in 1928, had told me that there seemed to be as many lions bothering his livestock now as there were sixty years ago. I assumed he was exaggerating, but Dyer thought he was probably right.

"In those days there were large numbers of lions, and there are still many about. I've just been working on an autobiographical memoir — unpublished — which describes lion hunting in that country [the Voi district] . . . so lions were very common, and man-eaters were very common.

"Man-eaters come about in many different ways," he continued. "For instance, epidemic diseases among humans, when a lot of people die, the lions get quite used to picking up corpses, and they develop a liking for them. Man is very tasty and easy to eat."

That created a sort of lull in the conversation.

"People who have eaten man describe it as rather like pork," Dyer noted.

Tony Archer pointed out to me that lions don't know what to make of men. Imagine you are a lion watching a man in a field. The man is slow, with no natural defenses, and he smells rank. He is incapable of disguising himself. His movements are utterly incomprehensible, unpredictably stumbling or waving his forelegs in the air. If you were a lion, you'd say to yourself, "That's very odd food." Even if you could get past the smell of a human, you might wonder how to kill him. Finally, you would retreat from the unfamiliar and look for something else.

Archer, another former professional hunter, told me of being sent into a game reserve that had been closed since World War I and coming upon lions that he thought hadn't seen a human being before. "They were utterly fearless of you, but they don't hurt you. They just don't understand you . . ."

Tony Seth-Smith, a former professional hunter and now a director of Ker and Downey Safaris, told me of the time he took a young newlywed couple — I think he said they were Italian, but I can't recall, exactly — up north on safari. They camped in an open field, with the couple on one side of a thick shrub and Seth-Smith on the other. During the night, Seth-Smith heard an odd noise, followed by lots of commotion. "Newlyweds," he thought, and went back to sleep.

A moment later, he was awakened by shouts. "Help! Bee! Bee!" is the way Seth-Smith described the man's call. So Seth-Smith rolled over, grabbed a can of insect spray, jumped up, and came running round the shrub. Armed with bug juice, Seth-Smith faced two lions. "I guess he had been shouting, 'Beast!' but I hadn't understood him properly."

Taking advantage of the distraction, the couple scrambled for safety in Seth-Smith's nearby Land-Rover. Seth-Smith, meanwhile, started backing away slowly, and when one of the lions began to menace him, he'd give it a shot of insect spray. Eventually, the lions, disgusted, wandered away.

Lions, like men, prefer to eat herbivores — antelope, buffalo, and the like. But indolence is central to a lion's existence, as important as mating and eating, so prides of lions tend to specialize when it comes to finding prey. A pride of zebra-eaters, for example, is not always likely to hunt gazelles because gazelles are more unfamiliar; zebra-eating lions know how to kill zebras with great efficiency, while gazelles represent nothing but trouble. A pride of gazelle-eating lions, conversely, will seek to avoid killing zebras because killing zebras is too much work. Lions do not seek to expand their knowledge by searching out new experiences. Each pride knows what works best with the least amount of exertion. "This is why so many people that get mauled by lions in fact don't die," Archer told me. "The lion will chew you all over the place and scratch you all over the place, but he just doesn't know how to finish you off. Whereas, the lion knows how to kill a zebra, how to break its neck quickly."

Those lions that do have knowledge of how to finish off humans almost always kill men by grabbing them by the head. Once they have rendered a man immobile, usually by breaking the man's neck, they lick the skin off, then devour the torso and legs, often scattering the entrails, then they eat the arms. They almost never eat the head or the feet.

A last note: Despite Dyer's assertion, naturalists quarrel about whether or not we taste good to lions.[7]

▼▲▼▲▼

Within hours of finding the jemadar's remains, Patterson had lodged himself in a tree near the place where Ungan Singh had met his end, hoping the lion would return, but by the time he'd made himself secure, he realized that the tree was full of laborers seeking the safety of his company. Patterson organized the arboreal village he'd created, then checked his weapons—a .303 and a 12-bore shotgun — and settled in for

[7] For more lion lore, see "A Lion Primer" in Appendix I of this book.

the duration. Soon, he wrote, "my hopes of bagging one of the brutes were raised by the sound of their ominous roaring coming closer and closer." Lions always stalk their prey in complete silence, however, and it wasn't long before the roars gave way to a terrifying silence. "All at once, we heard a great uproar and frenzied cries coming from another camp about half a mile away; we knew then that the lions had seized a victim there, and that we should see or hear nothing further of them that night." The lions had chosen to revisit one of the widely scattered railhead camps and had killed another coolie there.

So Patterson spent the next night in a tree near the latest victim's tent, the usual component of coolies out on the limb with him, but this time with a goat tied to the trunk of the tree, a sort of rudimentary bait-and-switch tactic. "A steady drizzle commenced shortly after I had settled down to my night of watching, and I was soon thoroughly chilled and wet. I stuck to my uncomfortable post, however, hoping to get a shot, but I well remember the feeling of impotent disappointment I experienced when about midnight I heard screams and cries and a heartrending shriek, which told me that the maneaters had again eluded me and had claimed another victim elsewhere."

These were the opening skirmishes in Patterson's war against the lions, a conflict he made very much his own — at least, according to his account. He really should have asked for more assistance. After all, the various railway camps stretched from east of the Tsavo to the most advanced railhead camps, some seven miles or so west of the crossing, and the lions seemed to have learned early to be choosy shoppers, visiting a different area for each kill. Patterson found the thick, thorny scrub made an ideal environment for the lions; by day or by night, they had the advantage over any hunter stalking them. And they seemed impossible to track, losing their pursuers when the track crossed over rocky ground, a route the lions seemed to favor on their way to and from their secret lair.

But if Patterson was having trouble figuring out the lions, the lions were having their own difficulty figuring out the rules of man-hunting. Once, they attacked a foolhardy Indian trader, a merchant of pots and tins who was riding on his donkey alone late one night. The lion jumped on him, knocking him to the ground and injuring the donkey. But the lion also fouled his paw in the rope joining the tins together and scared himself so much that he ran off. The Indian trader spent the rest of the night up a tree. On another occasion, a Greek businessman, one Themistocles Pappadimitrini, was sleeping in his tent, when a lion burst in, grabbed the mattress on which the Greek was sleeping, and dragged it out into the darkness, leaving Pappadimitrini in an advanced state of insomnia. And another time, a lion broke into a tent occupied by no less than fourteen sleeping laborers. Instead of going for the meat course, the lion grabbed a huge bag of rice and took it away.

Both sides were only sharpening their talents, however. Patterson's battle against the man-eaters still had almost a year to run.

▼▲▼▲▼

By the time he had been at Tsavo a month, Patterson — whose small tent was pitched in an open clearing and was a more-or-less regular venue for passing man-eaters — was tired of passing his alarming nights alone, so he began casting about for a roommate and some new digs.

Fortunately, the new chief medical officer, a Dr. Brock, had just been shipped up from the coast, and the two men decided to make a new hut, an open-sided affair to allow for evening breezes. Surrounding the hut was a circular *boma* — a fence made of tangled thorn branches — enclosing a yard about seventy yards in diameter, in which the personal servants of the two men also lived in makeshift quarters. Each night, the servants would build a bright fire and Brock and Patterson would sit out in the night air, rifles at hand, looking out into the darkness.

Patterson's domestic architecture was widely imitated, and soon every workman's tent was surrounded by its own *boma*. Not that it mattered much; when the lions were hungry, they simply crashed through the bramble and ate their man, or they jumped over the branches, grabbed a victim, and carried him off. This went on with striking regularity.

The laborers seemed somewhat comforted by their own vast numbers. Preston's railhead camp was still nearby, and according to Patterson, "Each man felt . . . that as the man-eaters had such a large number of victims to choose from, the chances of their selecting him in particular were very small."

But when the large camp, with its 1,500 workers, was relocated, morale dropped in Patterson's bailiwick: "As all the remaining workmen were naturally camped together, the attentions of the lions became more apparent and made a deeper impression," if you'll pardon his play on words. "A regular panic consequently ensued." A full work stoppage was only avoided when Patterson allowed his 470 men time off to improve their already massive *bomas*.

Soon, the camp came to look — and sound — like a settlement of teenage party animals: "Fires were kept burning all night, and it was also the duty of the night-watchman to keep clattering half a dozen empty oil tins suspended from a convenient tree. These he manipulated by means of a long rope, while sitting in safety within his tent; and the frightful noise thus produced was kept up at frequent intervals during the night in hopes of terrifying away the man-eaters." While this must have sounded like a very good idea, it didn't impress the lions much. "In spite of these precautions," wrote Patterson, "the lions would not be denied and men continued to disappear."

When Preston's railhead camp moved, he left its hospital behind. The well-protected facility stood in a clearing away from the other camps and about three quarters of a mile from Patterson and Brock's place. A few days after the railhead camp moved, the lions decided to visit the hospital, with predictable results. The hospital assistant, hearing a noise, opened the door of his tent and was disappointed to see a man-eater standing there. The lion jumped at him, but the assistant fell back into a box of junk and the racket put the lion off. The animal went off to another part of the enclosure and hit the jackpot when he found a tent with eight sick laborers sleeping in it. There were three casualties by the time the lion left: two coolies injured, one eaten.

Patterson ordered the hospital to be moved, then went to the newly vacated site and, once more employing his simian gambit, climbed a tree and waited. "In the middle of my lonely vigil," he wrote, "I had the mortification of hearing shrieks and cries coming from the direction of the new hospital." This time, the lions carted away the hospital's water boy; Patterson sent the man's ring and teeth to his widow in India. The next day, April 23, 1898, the hospital was moved again and an even bigger *boma* was constructed.

We know from his own account and from other witnesses that after the hospital attacks, Patterson's nerves were shaken and he began to doubt his ability to end the rampage. After the last attack, he spent most of the day alone in his camp, perhaps praying that the lions, as they would from time to time, might seek their victims in one of the Wakamba villages that surrounded the railway camps but were outside his protection. Finally, as the darkness began to settle in, Brock came to Patterson to urge him to continue. Patterson must have broken, and at first, the argument nearly came to blows, with the young doctor insisting that Patterson had a duty to continue fighting the man-eaters no matter how vain the attempt. The older man at first attempted to dismiss the doctor from his camp, then perhaps began laughing nervously at his own foibles. He had a reputation, after all, as an experienced big-game hunter, and he should have been able to put an end to the lions within a fortnight of their first appearance. But he hadn't, and he must have had a difficult time facing his own failure on a daily basis. After a sullen dinner together, Brock must have finally encouraged him enough to carry on, because that night Patterson once again was sitting in the darkness near the latest hospital site, this time in a goods wagon with Dr. Brock. The lions had been growing increasingly bold, walking into various camps — three in one afternoon — and attacking passersby. The traffic manager, from a passing train, had spotted one half-dead coolie up a tree. The stationmaster at Tsavo had seen a man-eater in the station yard, and some workers had spotted one stalking Dr. Brock as he was returning home from the hospital at sundown earlier that day. Patterson had ordered that some cattle be penned up inside some tents he had pitched near the wagon. The two men arranged some canvas padding beneath themselves and settled in to wait.

"We had the lower half of the door of the wagon closed," Patterson later wrote, "while the upper half was left wide open for observation: and we faced, of course, in the direction of the abandoned [hospital] *boma,* which, however, we were unable to see in the inky darkness. For an hour or two everything was quiet, and the deadly silence was becoming very monotonous and oppressive, when suddenly, to our right, a dry twig snapped, and we knew that an animal of some sort was about. Soon afterwards we heard a dull thud, as if some heavy body had jumped over the boma. The cattle, too, became very uneasy, and we could hear them moving about restlessly. Then again came dead silence." Silence, the familiar silence that Patterson and Brock feared would be interrupted by a desperate scream and a choked, muffled grunt.

As most house-cat owners know, felines mask their long list of shortcomings with ostentatious displays of patience; often a cat will lie motionless, figuring its moves in advance, waiting for the sweet moment when the prey blinks in the darkness. In their wagon, Patterson and Brock wondered what was up, and at one point Patterson was going to climb out of the wagon and investigate. But Brock suggested he was insane to do so and persuaded Patterson to stay inside. For the moment, his life was thus spared, as the lion was watching them all the time, "almost within springing distance."

Even before they begin serious dating, every human alive has spent a terrified night hour or two, maybe in the company of a cousin or a pal, maybe outside on a camping expedition or in a suburban backyard. The forest demon has been heard outside the tent; no earthly creature walks the way *it* walks. It's right *there*, just on the other side of the canvas, and any minute it's going to come inside and kill you. You sit there in your tent, holding your shoe in one hand and your penknife in the other, knowing full well you are defenseless, for the terror has already marked you and you are already near death. You *want* to see it, see its face, its eyes. And you hear every living thing, every beetle, every ant, every blade of grass that has been touched by the air. It is *there*, just out of sight.

So at last, Patterson, too, decided he saw something coming toward them. "I feared, however, to trust my eyes, which, by that time, were strained by prolonged staring through the darkness, so under my breath I asked Brock whether he saw anything, at the same time covering the dark object as well as I could with my rifle." But Brock did not answer, and Patterson turned just for a moment to catch the doctor's eye, when the huge beast lunged at them. "'The lion!' I shouted . . ." Both men fired at the same time.

▼▲▼▲▼

No matter what the stationmaster says, there must be a monument around here someplace, you say to yourself, maybe a stone marker that says something like "Near this spot, some horrible lions ate a bunch of Indians, R.I.P." But there's nothing, no marker, no souvenir hardware, nothing at all.

You can go to Tsavo and try to track the tale, okay, but there's no trail; the narrative disappears in the rocky soil and the treacherous scrub and evaporates in the unbearable heat. And you can hike through the brush and get to the bridge at Tsavo without too much trouble, but it's a bridge, so what?

Stalking the story so long after the fact is tough. The Tsavo Historical Society, you know, is a circumstantial sort of personal invention — a museum of whatever you happen to find. And it's always empty. On one end of the bridge, some worker, a later arrival oblivious even to gossip, let alone recent history, has scrawled some graffiti in Hindi that reads "1923 Lagwana Bhawan" — somebody bound for immortality, no doubt. As for Patterson, he left long, long ago — thrown out, I hear, after a scandalous mishap on a small safari outing sometime after his famous lion shoot.

So the spoor of the dead is easier to pick up far from the field. Here, for example, is a friend back from the library with a biography of John H. Patterson. No, different J. H. Patterson, not a colonel at all, but a bigwig at the National Cash

Register Company back at the turn of the century. He shows up again in '13, indicted for something. Wrong guy.

Pattersons are everywhere, like lions in the bush, all different, but with similar markings. Here, for example, is an obituary the *New York Times* ran on June 20, 1947:

> Col. John Henry Patterson, commander of the Jewish Legion in the first World War and a supporter of the Zionist cause, has died at the age of 80, according to word received here from Los Angeles by the United Zionists—Revisionists of America.

You think, "Oops." Another ranking Patterson, the third so far. How many can there be?

But hold it. The second paragraph:

> An engineer and a big game hunter as well as a military man, Colonel Patterson was best known perhaps for his efforts to establish a Jewish army to fight Hitler.

Can this be right? An Irishman starts out to build a bridge in Africa and ends up trying to form a Jewish army to fight the Führer?

> Born in Ireland of a Protestant family, he served with the British Army in Africa and India, participating in the Boer War, 1900 to 1902.
>
> Entering the service with the Thirty-third Battalion of the Imperial Yeomanry in South Africa, he was mentioned three times in dispatches and received the Queen's Medal, with four clasps, and the D.S.O. [Distinguished Service Order] in the first World War.
>
> Colonel Patterson was leader of the Jewish Mule Corps . . .

There it is, a life after lions. It gets better:

> Colonel Patterson was leader of the Jewish Mule Corps at Gallipoli, fought in Egypt and commanded the Royal Irish

Fusiliers, the Royal Dublin Fusiliers and the Thirty-eight Battalion, Royal Fusiliers.

A fighting companion of the colonel in 1921 was Vladimir Jabotinsky, Jewish writer and warrior, who was said to have been a founder of the Irgun Zvai Leumi, secret army of Palestine.

In 1940 Mr. Jabotinsky, the president of the New World Zionist Organization, appealed here for the creation of a Jewish army of 100,000. Colonel Patterson, as a former British officer, spoke in favor of the separate military force.

Two years ago at a dinner here sponsored by the New Zionist Organization of America, Colonel Patterson criticized the British Government's administration in Palestine.

As a big-game hunter Colonel Patterson brought down in the jungles of Tsavo in British East Africa during 1907 [*sic*] two lions that were said to have eaten 135 men. His feat drew praise from a fellow hunter, Theodore Roosevelt.

Well, it wasn't 1907, was it? And it was the *Zion* Mule Corps, right? And that count of 135 might well be high, but that's our man. John Henry Patterson, 1867–1947. Suddenly you find you've been stalking some really strange game — not what you thought at all, not just a bully bridge builder and part-time lion shooter, but also the hero of a couple of wars, a militant Zionist leader, a guy who sought to unleash 100,000 angry Jews on Hitler.

I first met Patterson in his guise as a literary muse. It seems that he might well have been involved in a little adultery, Kenya-style, back in '08. By that time, Patterson was a big man in the British East Africa Protectorate, as it was then called. He was married and well known. He had written a best-selling account of his adventures at Tsavo and had taken on the mantle of great white hunter, an impressive garment indeed, especially to the rising numbers of visitors coming out on safari.

Such a tourist was thirty-four-year-old Audley James Blyth,

son of the first Baron Blyth, who, accompanied by his young wife, Ethel Jane, arrived in Nairobi bent on taking a safari through the Northern Frontier District, up Marsabit way, where the earth looks brand-new, barren, and still full of volcanic zeal. Patterson was headed up that way on a surveying mission and agreed to guide Mr. and Mrs. Blyth on their expedition. Alas, thirty-five miles south of Marsabit, and more than 200 miles north of Nairobi, Mr. Blyth "accidentally shot himself in the head with a revolver," in the words of the official dispatch. "Death immediate."

Blyth had been ill for a couple of days, "suffering from fever and sunstroke," Patterson reported. The trio had enjoyed a good safari up to that point — or at least Mrs. Blyth had been having a good time, shooting lions, elephants, rhinos, gazelles, and warthogs, while Mr. Blyth nursed a sore foot. His limp apparently gave way to a feverish depression, during which Blyth took a revolver and, in the middle of the night, shot himself.

Patterson immediately buried the body, burned Blyth's tent — "I did not wish painful memories to be recalled," he wrote later in his book *In the Grip of the Nyika* — and suppressed the consequent mutiny by the safari's bearers and porters, all of whom were quite appalled at Patterson's actions.

Worse still, instead of returning immediately to Nairobi, Patterson and Mrs. Blyth continued toward Marsabit. By this time, Mrs. Blyth was sharing Patterson's tent, since the great hunter was complaining of a fever all his own, and nursed him through his ailment, which he later described as diarrhea. Patterson's book shows pictures of Mr. Blyth's body being borne away on a stretcher, along with a subsequent photo taken of Ethel Jane a few days later, perched cheerfully next to a dead rhino.

Patterson's report of the incident convinced none of the responsible officials, however, and the great hunter made his own position a little more shady by telling friends he was going to run off to England with Mrs. Blyth. Finally, the governor launched an investigation, and in 1909 the results were released.

Patterson apparently had quarreled steadily with Blyth over the ivory from an elephant kill. Further, it seemed he may have done a little covering for Mrs. Blyth, who was actually in her husband's tent at the time he got depressed and accidentally shot himself. According to the native witnesses, the porters had been instructed to bury Blyth's body deep in the earth, and while they were doing that, Patterson burned all the man's belongings, including his diaries and journals containing his account of the safari.

The natives also testified that Blyth's fever was responding well to the cold baths they had been giving him and that he was making a marked recovery. His anger with Patterson, however, had not subsided and in fact had been fueled by the growing closeness between his wife and their guide. Finally, according to the witnesses, Mrs. Blyth became afraid of her husband's jealous anger and "went and slept in Colonel Patterson's tent."

Early the next morning, she returned to her husband's tent, the natives said, "and directly she entered we heard a shot and the lady came running out." After Blyth's death, according to the witnesses, "Colonel Patterson and the lady occupied one tent."

The governor sent the report to Lord Crewe, the colonial secretary, who, in order to prevent a scandal, made a deal with Patterson: Lord Crewe would decline to use native testimony and exonerate the hunter if Patterson agreed to resign on a claim of ill health and leave the country.

The Blyth mystery captured the imagination of Ernest Hemingway after it was retailed by Philip Percival, the famous white hunter, during the writer's first hunting expedition in

East Africa in the thirties. The sordid triangle and the theme
of emasculation by cuckoldry marked the finished story, "The
Short Happy Life of Francis Macomber," which was published in *Cosmopolitan* in 1936.

So what had happened to Patterson between his lion hunt at
Tsavo and his scandalous safari? The Boer War, for one thing.
Patterson spent three years in South Africa commanding a yeo-
manry regiment, "and at times Regular troops of all arms,"
as he later wrote, and he apparently acquitted himself very
well. Certainly, the Boer War, one of the bloodiest fought on
African soil, was just his cup of tea: "Those were glorious
days — days when one could thoroughly enjoy warfare — a
wild gallop over the veldt, a good fight in the open, and the
day won by the best men." For despite his hunting and his
safariing, Patterson always considered himself a professional
soldier: "From my boyhood I have either been a soldier or
taken a keen interest in soldiering."

After he was tossed out of Kenya, Patterson took to traveling for recreation, but during the years leading up to World
War I, he became increasingly preoccupied by his passion for
soldiering. Even in his travels he couldn't keep his mind off
military matters, so his wanderings were really elaborate bus-
men's holidays. He routinely visited various detachments of
the British imperial armies — from the King's African Rifles
in Uganda to the "North-West mounted men of Canada away
in the wilds of the Klondyke." On a visit to America, he stayed
with Theodore Roosevelt in the White House, visited the infantry in Alaska and cavalry units in Yellowstone, loitered for
a while with the Seventh Cavalry, and marveled at the bread
served in the enlisted men's mess at Fort Riley — "cannot be
surpassed at the 'Ritz,'" Patterson noted.

He was an inveterate battlefield tourist and visited famous
sites from the Plains of Abraham to Waterloo to Gettysburg,

where he delivered himself of the predictable opinion that the South would have won if only General Longstreet had been on time and that losing Stonewall Jackson was a decisive event in the Confederacy's defeat. He met Mrs. Stonewall Jackson and Robert E. Lee's daughter and then spent some time touring Germany at the invitation of the general staff. According to Patterson, when he no doubt modestly told his guide of his rapid rise through the officer corps — like many officers, he had risen from lieutenant to lieutenant colonel after less than a year in battle in South Africa — the man, a German officer considerably older than Patterson but inferior in rank, "stopped short, in the middle of the pavement, saluted me gravely and said: 'You are Napoleon!'" Patterson also discovered three crucial, almost Napoleonically important, observations which, on his return to England, he duly reported to the German military attaché: "[First, that] I considered the abominable type used in German newspapers and books responsible for the be-spectacled German; that although their railway stations were wonderfully clean, yet they were without a decent platform, and my insular modesty had been shocked on many occasions by the amount of German leg I saw when the ladies clambered into and out of the carriages; and lastly, that I thought the long and handsome cloak worn by the officers might be greatly improved by making a slit at the side, so that the hilt of the sword might be outside, instead of inside the cloak, where not only did it make an unsightly lump, but was hard to get at in case of urgent need." In Belgium, he told the cavalry to get rid of its heavy sabers and instead use an infantry rifle and a lighter sword, "but above all I impressed upon them to be sure about the rifle, as the occasions for the use of the *arme blanche* in future would be rare. . . . I was of course looked upon as a Cavalry leper for expressing such heretical opinions." (Later, according to Patterson, after "poor little Belgium had been crushed," a

Belgian officer made a special point to call on him to tell him that the surviving Belgian officers "often talked" about Patterson and that they had decided he was right about the rifles after all.) During the war, when Patterson went to Mons, site of a devastating German victory only months before, he laid full blame for the defeat on the failure of the French and English intelligence services. In Madrid, he went "to see something of the Spanish Army," but he didn't like what he saw: "There was too much *"Mañana"* about it." Patterson was no diplomat.

By the time World War I came along, Patterson had thoroughly alienated those whose support he would later seek. In *With the Zionists at Gallipoli,* a book published in 1916, Patterson, who was, after all, only a lieutenant colonel, was often bitterly critical of the British war effort, especially in the Dardanelles campaign of 1915, suggesting massive incompetence among not only army commanders, but also among government strategists, including David Lloyd George, who became Prime Minister in December 1916, and Winston Churchill, who had pressed for the southern-flank policy. But the book was published after Britain had suffered some of her severest defeats, and the fact that Patterson was right only served to further irritate his superiors. Although he claims that up to that point of the war, "my relations with those with whom I came into contact were excellent, and on the very rare occasions when they were otherwise, it was not due to any seeking of mine, but, unfortunately, my temperament is not such that I can suffer fools gladly," including, especially, fools with a higher rank than lieutenant colonel. Our man Patterson had decorations for bravery, commendations for gallantry, enemies for arrogance, and an inability to tolerate views divergent from his own, especially if they pertained to military matters.

Normally, this sort of thing would have been dismissed by

readers as the rantings of an unhappy officer. But Patterson's *The Man-eaters of Tsavo* had been a best-seller, and he had an audience for his work and an image for himself, and the curmudgeonly attitude he took toward his peers and superiors and the intemperate way he discusses their perceived shortcomings in *With the Zionists at Gallipoli* gained him a great deal of animosity.

World War I really wasn't Patterson's idea of a good war, anyway. It was a war which, according to Patterson, was nothing compared to the Boer War. In *With the Zionists at Gallipoli,* he noted that warfare had changed. Where once it was a "wild gallop . . . it is now but a dyke-maker's job, and a dirty one at that."

Patterson's superiors probably thought they were punishing him by giving him command of something called the Zion Mule Corps — 500 unhappy Jews, many of whom were Russian or otherwise not British, and most of whom had fled to Egypt from Palestine to escape the Turks. If his superiors smiled at the thought of Patterson being ordered to take command of this ragtag outfit, he, in fact, was delighted. Patterson was a Pentateuchal sort of chap, fascinated since his childhood with the heroic Old Testament exploits of the Jews and very much in sympathy with the growing movement for a Jewish homeland in Palestine. Instead of seeing command of the Zion Mule Corps as a demotion, he was elated at the thought of leading the first all-Jewish fighting force since the Maccabees. He equipped his men with captured Turkish rifles, drilled and trained them in the art of the teamster, gave all of them shoulder flashes bearing the shield of David, and led them off to war at the bloody battle of Gallipoli, where they acquitted themselves well.

The Zion Mule Corps quite naturally became a focus for those who embraced the Zionist cause, most notably a zealot named Vladimir Jabotinsky, an Odessa-bred firebrand and a charismatic leader in the struggle to establish a Jewish "free state" in Palestine. Jabotinsky had fled Russia and established himself in Copenhagen, where, during the war, he published a pro-Zionist newspaper that was of significant propaganda value for the Allies. Determined to see the establishment of a Jewish fighting force in Palestine, he enlisted as a private in the Twentieth Battalion London Regiment and gathered around him a platoon consisting mostly of Mule Corps veterans. According to Patterson's account, "from his humble position in the ranks he bombarded the Prime Minister, and the secretaries of State for war and Foreign Affairs in this country; he sent emissaries to America, North and South, to Russia, Poland, the Caucasus, etc., and when, in July, 1917 [only four months before the Balfour Declaration, setting forth Britain's determination to help in the establishment of a Jewish homeland in Palestine], the Government declared their intention of creating a Jewish Regiment, he had everything in train for the formation of a legion at least 50,000 strong." Jabotinsky formed an instant and permanent bond of friendship with Patterson, who was given command of the Jewish Battalion in July 1917; by the following January, Private Jabotinsky was Lieutenant Jabotinsky and Patterson's aide-de-camp. And at the end of January 1918, the Jewish Battalion — a platoon of Mule Corps members and a large contingent of exiled Russian Jews, the vast majority of whom, according to Patterson, were tailors — were sent marching through London on their way to Egypt. Officially, they were the Thirty-eighth Battalion of the Royal Fusiliers, who, along with T. E. Lawrence's Arabs, fought Britain's battles in the Middle East against the Turks.

But the formal establishment of a Jewish "army" came to an end shortly after the war. By 1921, riots — pogroms, really — were tearing apart Britain's Palestinian mandate, as Arabs rampaged through Jewish settlements, murdering Jews by the dozens. Jabotinsky — with Patterson's clear collusion — in order to provide some safety to the Jews had changed the Jewish Battalion into the Jewish Legion, then into the Jewish Defense Corps, and, finally after Jabotinsky's arrest, into the Haganah, the predecessor of the present-day Labor Party.[8] Jabotinsky, Menachem Begin's mentor in militant politics, was supported throughout his career by Patterson. In fact, as Jabotinsky was cooling his heels in a British jail in March 1922, Patterson was addressing a mass meeting of Zionists at Carnegie Hall dedicated to establishing a Palestinian homeland: "The suggestion that there must be no failure in this movement reminds me that when the Jewish Regiment was about to be formed everybody predicted failure, and yet it was a great triumph," he told delegates. "We had all sorts of difficulties. A delegation of Jews went to the office of the Secretary of State and requested 'Do not call them Jews.' So they called us Fusiliers. And then the British Tommy called us 'Jewsiliers,' and they even found us a motto — 'No advance without security.'"

Patterson's next book, *With the Judeans in Palestine*, published in 1922, was much more pointed. He accused the British of abandoning the Balfour Declaration, of engaging in policies that were systematically anti-Semitic, and of encouraging the pogrom.[9] "It is a black page in our history," he wrote, "and those responsible should not be allowed to escape just punishment." Jabotinsky's dream, shared by Patterson, of having a large, well-armed Jewish force in place in Palestine to force the government's hand, was crushed; he was arrested for "banditism, instigating the people of the Otto-

[8] Later, as the violence grew, Jabotinsky, in defiance of leaders like David Ben-Gurion (who once called Jabotinsky "Vladimir Hitler"), broke with the Haganah and assumed the leadership of a right-wing faction called Irgun — today's Likud Party.

[9] Patterson pointed out that the rioters ran through the streets crying, "*El dowleh ma'ana*," or "The government is with us."

man Empire to mutual hatred, pillage, rapine, devastation of the country, and homicide in divers places." Jabotinsky was sentenced to fifteen years' hard labor. Patterson was incensed: "This trumping up of the preposterous charges mentioned is a disgrace to British justice, and the whole history of this atrocious outrage is a foul stain on our fair name." A public outcry in England and Europe forced the government to annul the sentence.

The British eventually appointed a Jew, Sir Herbert Samuel, as high commissioner to Palestine. In an effort to prove his fairness to the Arabs, however, he only made the situation worse. Jabotinsky and his followers went underground. Patterson went on the warpath, spending the next two decades stumping up and down England and across America for the Zionist cause, invariably speaking "as an English officer." In the years just preceding the Second World War, Patterson's name suddenly disappeared from *Who's Who,* despite his widespread fame, and when he died — at the home of his son, in La Jolla, California — little notice of his passing was taken in the British press, and no obituary appeared in *The Times.* Patterson had crossed the line once too often. A year after his passing, Israel was born.

Patterson, as a military man. An interesting career. After his Boer glory, never promoted. He led an imperfectly Victorian life about half a century too late. It would be imprecise to say that Patterson was to the Jews in Palestine what T. E. Lawrence was to the Arabs. But if there are important contemporary resonances, they aren't accidental. Patterson then, like Israel now, was the victim of the bad public relations he created for himself. Rarely since Patterson has there been so much wrong with being so often right.

In the summer of 1898, of course, all that scandal and adventure and politicking still lay ahead. In 1898, Patterson was not yet a best-selling author, or a famous hunter, or an adulterer, or a soldier, or a Zionist partisan. He was just a supercilious young man with lions in his front yard and lots of work to do.

▼▲▼▲▼

Both Brock and Patterson fired simultaneously, just as the lion was nearly on top of them. They missed, but "probably blinded by the flash and frightened by the noise of the double report," the lion missed, too, swerving at the last moment off into the darkness. It was a wash, but another sleepless night for our hero. With uncharacteristic candor, Patterson wrote, "The next morning, we found Brock's bullet embedded in the sand close to a footprint; it could not have missed the lion by more than an inch or two. Mine was nowhere to be found. Thus ended my first direct encounter with one of the man-eaters."

You may think that all Mr. Patterson had on his mind were a couple of lions crazy for Indian food. But it would not do to forget that Patterson was also in charge of constructing a very important railway project. Remember? The bridge at Tsavo?

If his nights were spent awake waiting in ambush, his days were spent plotting the blasting of rock and the spanning of small gullies. While it's true that Patterson was the only full-time lion hunter in his camp — a policeman's role, inherent in his position and consistent with his character and very much in line with the representation of his prior experiences in India, where he was said to have shot very many tigers — he also had been charged with the construction of the bridge and with other permanent railway fixtures fifteen miles either side of the Tsavo. So to him, the lion patrol was strictly moonlighting; in fact, Patterson did most of his serious lion hunting at night, although he would occasionally go out by day to hunt the lions, mostly to please his men. His most pressing work was urging on his crew, most of whom were distressed to distraction by the presence of the man-eaters.

Patterson's chores must have seemed endless. He found that he not only had to take up temporary track and eliminate the expeditiously laid diversions required by the military, he also had to establish a water supply at Tsavo — for both his men and his machinery. He spent many evenings dispensing justice among disputatious coolies, fielding complaints from his jemadar, reading reports, and studying Kiswahili so he could converse with the local tribes. In his book, Patterson describes the work undertaken just with the bridge itself: "Cross and oblique sections of the river had to be taken, the rate of the current and the volume of water at flood, mean, and low levels had to be found, and all the necessary calculations made. . . . I marked out the positions for the abutments and piers, and the work of sinking their foundations was begun. The two center piers in particular caused a great deal of trouble, as the river broke in several times, and had to be damned up and pumped dry again before work could be resumed. Then we found we had to sink much deeper than we expected in order to reach a solid foundation. Indeed, the sinking went on and on, until I began to despair of finding one [a solid base] and was about to resort to pile-driving, when at last, to my relief, we struck solid rock on which the huge foundation stones could be laid with perfect safety."

In addition to sinking the foundations of the bridge, Patterson had a great deal of difficulty finding suitable building stone in the area. "It was not that there was none to be found," he wrote, "for the whole district abounds in rock, but that it was so intensely hard as to be almost impossible to work." Patterson was about to give up and use iron columns for the bridge piers when he accidentally found a source of good building material while out hunting with Dr. Brock. To get the stone to

TO CONSTRUCT A BRIDGE WITH THE NEW STONES HE HAD FOUND, PATTERSON REQUIRED "FIRST CLASS PATHAN ARTISANS."

the bridge site, he built a small tramway and rolled the rocks down to the rough ravine. But to get the rocks down the ravine, he first had to span the Tsavo with a temporary bridge made from palm trees and logs. The bridge was not a triumph of his craft, however: Coolies and trolley loads of stone regularly tumbled off the little structure.

Still, finding the building stone was a major accomplishment for Patterson, since using iron columns would have caused a considerable delay. And if Patterson thought he was lucky finding the right kind of stones for his bridge, he was even luckier that the lions backed off the camp for a while. When it came to industrial relations, however, his luck ran out.

To construct the bridge with the new stones he had found, Patterson had sent down to Mombasa for some masons capable of working and dressing the rock. He stipulated in his requisition that he required "first-class Pathan artisans," men capable of doing the necessary stonecutting without undue instruction or supervision. It was not that Patterson was unusually demanding; to the contrary, to his men he seemed a quiet, placid, even undemanding man, if somewhat punctilious and overstarched.

In his behavior toward his men, he was a more or less typical colonial man: aloof and superior, but fair and insistent on fairness in those over whom he held power. While he almost certainly would rather have been building bridges in Buckinghamshire, given a choice, like most of his countrymen, his overwhelming sense of duty would have swamped those kinds of concerns. They would not, however, have masked his ambition. Like many others who came out to Africa, India, and the other imperial territories, Patterson was deeply competitive; for a brief time, for example, he vied with Preston to be seen by the laborers and by other Europeans as the best hunter. Fortunately for Patterson, Preston, as railhead engineer, had other, more pressing problems, so the field was left clear enough.[10] If Patterson was occasionally preoccupied with the trappings of his role, he paid the price for those preoccupations — while deeply worried about the lions, his countless nights in trees and his time-consuming daylight hunts were as much for show as for effect. Yet the way his subordinates saw him was not as important to him as the way he saw himself, and on that count he was heroic, indeed. It would simply never occur to a man like Patterson that his position was assailable.

Patterson quickly discovered that his "good Pathan artisans" were useless featherbedders. They "had not the faintest notion of stone-cutting" and were just working a scam to enable themselves to pick up the masons' wage of forty-five rupees each month instead of the twelve earned by ordinary workmen, which is what they were. "On discovering this fact," Patterson wrote, "I immediately instituted a system of piece-work, and drew up a scale of pay which would enable the genuine mason to earn his forty-five rupees — and a little more if he felt inclined — and would cut down the imposters to about their proper pay as coolies." Patterson called all the men together and presented his plan. While the men all smiled and nodded, the newcomers were already plotting their countermove. "Now, as is often the case in this world, the imposters were greatly in the majority; and accordingly they attempted to intimidate the remainder into coming down to their own standard as regards output of work, in the hope of thereby inducing me to abandon the piece-work system of payment. This, however, I had no intention of doing, as I knew that I had demanded only a perfectly fair amount of work from each man."

[10] Vic Preston told me that his father, Ronald O. Preston, sometimes questioned Patterson's description of his one-man man-eater mission. "My father felt that a lot of people were involved . . . including him. After all, my father shot lions, many people shot lions there [in the Tsavo district]. But who knows whether or not it was this lion or that lion?"

The pseudomasons were a troublesome crowd anyway. Patterson frequently found himself in their camp, breaking up quarrels and separating the Hindus from the Moslems. Following on the heels of the lion attacks, the plotting and scheming was spreading discontent among the workers and Patterson found that in addition to the practical problems of building the railway facilities, he also had his hands full of angry Indians.

One evening, Patterson was reading alone in his hut when he heard a ruckus coming from the nearby masons' camp. Soon, one of the native officials came running to him with a tale of murder and mayhem. "I ran back with him at once," Patterson recalled, "and succeeded in restoring order, but found seven badly injured men lying stretched out on the ground, These I had carried up to my *boma* on *charpoys* (native beds); and Brock being away, I had to play the doctor myself as best I could, stitching one and bandaging another and generally doing what was possible. There was one man, however, who groaned loudly and held a cloth over his face as if he were dying. On lifting this covering, I found him to be a certain mason named Karim Bux who was well-known to me as a prime mischief-maker among the men. I examined him carefully, but as I could discover nothing amiss, I concluded that he must have received some internal injury, and accordingly told him I would send him to the hospital at Voi . . . to be attended to properly. He was then carried back to his camp, groaning grievously all the time.

"Scarcely had he been removed, when the head jemadar came and informed me that the man was not hurt at all, and that as a matter of fact he was the sole cause of the disturbance. He was now pretending to be badly injured, in order to escape the punishment which he knew he would receive if I discovered that he was the instigator of the trouble. On hearing this, I gave instructions that he was not to go to Voi in the special train with the others; but I had not heard the last of him yet. About eleven o'clock that night I was called up and asked to go down to the masons' camp to see a man who was supposed to be dying. I at once pulled on my boots, got some brandy and ran down to the camp, where to my surprise and amusement I found that it was my friend Karim Bux who was at death's door. It was perfectly evident to me that he was only 'foxing,' but when he asked for *dawa* (medicine), I told him gravely that I would give him some very good *dawa* in the morning.

"Next day at noon — when it was my custom to have evil-doers brought up for judgment — I asked for Karim Bux, but was told that he was too ill to walk. I accordingly ordered him to be carried to my *boma,* and in a few moments he arrived in his *charpoy,* which was shouldered by four coolies who, I could see, knew quite well that he was only shamming. There were also a score or so of his friends hanging around, doubtless waiting in the expectation of seeing the 'Sahib' hoodwinked. When the bed was placed on the ground near me, I lifted the blanket with which he had covered himself and thoroughly examined him, at the same time feeling him to make sure he had no fever. He pretended to be desperately ill and again asked for *dawa*; but having finally satisfied myself that it was as the jemadar had said — pure *budmashi* (devilment) — I told him I was going to give him some very effective *dawa*, and carefully covered him up again, pulling the blanket over his head. I then got a big armful of shavings from a carpenter's bench which was close by, put them under the bed and set fire to them. As soon as the sham invalid felt the heat, he peeped over the edge of the blanket; and when he saw the smoke and flame leaping up round him, he threw the blanket from him, sprang from the bed exclaiming "*Beiman shaitan!*" ("Unbelieving devil!"), and fled like a deer to the entrance of my *boma*, pursued by a Sikh sepoy, who got in a couple of good whacks on his shoulders with a stout stick before he made his escape . . . and I never had any further trouble with Karim Bux. He came back later in the day, with clasped hands imploring forgiveness, which I readily granted, as he was a clever workman."

Patterson hoped incidents like that would have an instructive value for the surly Indians, but the workers seemed determined to undermine his authority any way they could. One morning, as he was returning to his hut after spending another fruitless night in a tree somewhere, he came upon a group of coolies playing cards and lazing about the quarry where they were supposed to be turning stone. Patterson watched them through the undergrowth for a while, then, to scare them, fired his rifle in the air. "On the report being heard, the scene changed like magic: each man simply flew to his particular work, and hammers and chisels resounded merrily and energetically, where all had been silence a moment before." Patterson broke into the quarry, fined the coolies a few rupees each, and demoted the foreman who had allowed the crew to goof off. He then continued to his hut. He had just arrived when "two of the scoundrels tottered up after me, bent almost double and calling Heaven to witness that I had shot them both in the back. In order to give a semblance of truth to an otherwise bald and unconvincing narrative, they had actually induced one of their fellow workmen to make a few holes like shot holes in their backs, and these were bleeding profusely. Unfortunately for them, however, I had been carrying a rifle and not a shot gun, and they had also forgotten to make corresponding holes in their clothing, so that all they achieved by this elaborate tissue of falsehood was to bring on themselves the derision of their comrades and the imposition of an extra fine."

Far from deterring mischief by his workers, Patterson's insistence on work for pay galvanized the worst element of the labor force. All of the masons and many of the coolies were determined to put him "quietly out of the way," and, on September 5, 1898, several days after the quarry incident, after a long meeting, it was decided by the Indians to murder Patterson. The plan called for him to be killed when he went down to the quarry; his body would be thrown into the bush, and, after the local carrion had their way, the coolies would claim Patterson had been eaten by one of the lions. "To this cheerful proposal," Patterson wrote, "every man present at the meeting agreed, and affixed his finger-mark to a long strip of paper as a binding token." Unhappily for the conspirators, however, Patterson was tipped off by an informant an hour after the meeting broke up. Patterson thanked the man, but decided to make his usual visit to the quarry anyway, since, following the dictates of his own self-image, he didn't believe them capable of carrying out such a plot.

So the next morning Patterson jumped on board a trolley for a ride to the quarry. "As I reached a bend in the line, my head mason, Heera Singh, a very good man, crept cautiously out of the bushes and warned me not to proceed." Heera Singh wouldn't give Patterson a specific reason for his warning out of fear for his own life, but he did tell the colonel that twenty other masons were staying away that day because they were afraid of trouble at the quarry. Patterson dismissed the warning with a laugh and continued on his way.

"On my arrival at the quarry, everything seemed perfectly peaceful," he recalled later. "All the men were working away busily, but after a moment or two I noticed stealthy side glances, and felt there was something in the wind. As soon as I came up to the first gang of workmen, the jemadar, a treacherous-looking villain, informed me that the men working further up the ravine had refused to obey his orders, and asked me if I would go and see them. I felt at once that this was a device to lure me into the narrow part of the ravine, where, with gangs in front of me and behind me, there would be no escape; still, I thought I would see the adventure through, whatever came of it, so I accompanied the jemadar up the gully."

Patterson seemed about to be a victim of his own arrogance. His failure to take seriously the treachery of the masons was about to land him in great jeopardy. "When we got to the further gang, he went so far as to point out the two men who, he said, had refused to do what he told them — I suppose he thought that as I was never to leave the place alive, it did not matter whom he complained of. I noted their names in my pocket-book in my usual manner, and turned to retrace my steps. Immediately a yell of rage was raised by the whole body of some sixty men, answered by a similar shout from those I had first passed, and who numbered about a hundred. Both groups of men, carrying crowbars and flourishing their heavy hammers, then closed in on me in the narrow part of the ravine.

"I stood still, waiting for them to act, and one man rushed at me, seizing both my wrists and shouting that he was going to 'be hung and shot for me' — rather a curious way of putting it, but that was his expression. I easily wrenched my arms free, and threw him from me; but by this time I was closely hemmed in, and everywhere I looked I could see nothing but evil and murderous-looking faces. One burly brute, afraid to be the first to deal a blow, hurled the man next him at me . . ."

This sort of excitement will do you no good in the middle of the night. Tsavo is far behind you now, and the gradual climb to Makindu is a long one. The train, as you may have noticed, moves very slowly up this long grade, so slowly that you might,

if allowed, jump from the train, stroll alongside the carriages
for a while, and observe the dark silhouette of the distant
Yatta Plateau off to the northeast; Chyulu ridge is the abrupt
range to the south-southwest. Beyond lies Kilimanjaro. So
slowly does the train move that you might sit and reflect on
the broad Kenyan night sky, then rise and step back aboard
the train as it passes.

At the rate we're going, we'll be able to keep pace with
Preston's work, and even slow a bit for Patterson's trials. In
fact, so slow is this journey that, for now, it might be good to
roll to a stop for a moment here in this textual siding and reflect on the role of the Indian laborer in constructing the infrastructure of the empire.

The Uganda Railway was just one of dozens of such projects
underway at the turn of the century. Railroads, highways,
buildings, telegraph lines, dams, schools, docks, hospitals,
and prisons were being built in all parts of the empire, not just
in East Africa. From Suez to Sarawak, huge public works
projects occupied the attention of the Colonial Office as well
as a whole raft of entrepreneurs, advocates, merchants, missionaries, and military men. Railroads, of course, were most
vital to the development of each colony and, generally, preceded other projects. Canada, India, Australia, South Africa,
and many lesser colonies and dominions were bound together
by rail. By 1907, there were just over 600,000 miles of railway in the world, almost half of which (some 240,000 miles)
were in the United States. The bulk of the rest were in British
colonies or in the British Isles: In Africa, five of every six of
the 18,516 miles of track on the continent were used by railroads operated by Britons; more than half of the Asian total
was in India; naturally, all 20,000 miles of rail in Australia
were British-built; and the Canadian system, with nearly
23,000 miles of track, was the second-largest in the Western
Hemisphere. In all, more than one third of all the rail tracks

in the world outside the U.S. were in Britain or in British possessions. And almost every mile was laid by Indian crews. For most of the eighteenth, nineteenth, and a part of the twentieth centuries, Indian labor was a precious exportable commodity. While wages paid Indian coolies were low by European standards, they were high enough to draw thousands of men away from their homes and villages to work in fields in far-flung corners of the empire. Compared to indigenous laborers found in most colonies, Indian workers were dependable, easily trained, and very plentiful. So when a dam was needed in British Guiana or when a telegraph line was needed in Nigeria, Indians were brought out to do the job.

The effect of this labor emigration from India created predictable problems: A subclass of fatherless families was created, and while money flowed back into India from workers abroad, the coolies themselves were housed and fed in barely adequate conditions. They were often cranky. Ask Patterson.

▼▲▼▲▼

We left Colonel Patterson, you will recall, standing unarmed in a coolie-filled ravine surrounded by a bad labor problem. Hundreds of angry men, sworn in blood to each other to kill him, were coming at him, brandishing crowbars and hammers. A solitary British officer faced what seemed to be certain death at the hands of a multitude of malicious, mutinous masons. One man has rushed forward, and the rest seem eager to follow.

Patterson's narrative resumes: "I quickly stepped aside [and] sprang onto the top of [a] rock, and before they had time to recover themselves I had started haranguing them in Hindustani."

Patterson told them he knew all about their plot, but that it was a lousy one and that their story would never be believed and many of them would be hanged. "I said that I knew quite well that it was only one or two scoundrels among them who had induced them to behave so stupidly, and urged them not to allow themselves to be made fools of this way. . . . were upright, self-respecting Pathans going to allow themselves to be led away by men like that?" Besides, Patterson told them, even if they succeeded in killing him, he'd just be replaced by another sahib and probably one not as patient and fair with them as he had been. Sensing he had the sympathy of the majority, Patterson said he'd send the malcontents down to Mombasa, while the rest could continue their work. If he heard of no further plotting, he would forget the whole thing. "Finally I called upon those who were willing to work to hold up their hands, and instantly every hand in the crowd was raised . . . after dismissing them, I jumped down from the rock and continued my rounds as if nothing had happened. . . . They were still in a very uncertain and sullen mood, however . . . so it was with feelings of great relief that an hour later I made my way back, safe and sound, to Tsavo."

But as soon as he left the quarry, the plot was hatched anew, and this time Patterson wasted no time in telegraphing for help from the railway police and Mr. Whitehead, the district officer (not, please note, Mr. Whitehouse, the chief engineer). The D.O. promptly led a detachment of askaris twenty-five miles overland, arriving in the nick of time. "I have no doubt," Patterson later wrote, "that his prompt action alone saved me from being attacked that very night." A couple of days later, the railway police arrested the ringleaders and took them to Mombasa, where they were sentenced to hard labor — a fine deterrence, no doubt.

About the time the mutinous masons were deported, the lions reappeared, stalking the camps by day and night. Patterson, sick of camping in trees and trying to second-guess the beasts, decided to try a trap, a real Rube Goldberg contraption made from wooden sleepers, tram rails, pieces of telegraph wire, and lengths of chain. The trap itself was divided into two compartments. In one compartment, Patterson planned to lodge a couple of Indians as bait. The other compartment was for a trapped lion. "The whole thing was very much on the principal of the ordinary rat-trap," Patterson observed, adding, no doubt to the relief of the Indians, "except that it was not necessary for the lion to seize the bait in order to send the door clattering down."

The technical description of Patterson's lion trap is worth a little examination. According to his notes, it was a large box with a lot of rather awkward mechanical engineering applied as a sort of add-on. "A heavy chain was secured along the top part of the lion's doorway, the ends hanging down to the ground on either side of the opening; and to these were fastened, strongly secured by stout wire, short lengths of rails placed about six inches apart. This made a sort of flexible door which could be packed into a small space when not in use, and which abutted against the top of the doorway when lifted up. The door was held in this position by a lever made of a piece of rail, which in turn was kept in its place by a wire fastened to one end and passing along to a spring concealed in the ground inside the cage. As soon as the lion entered sufficiently far into the trap, he would be bound to tread on the spring; his weight on this would release the wire, and in an instant down would come the door behind him; and he could not push it out in any way, as it fell into a groove between two rails firmly embedded in the ground." The whole thing was enclosed in a tent and surrounded by a thick *boma* to provide the necessary challenge.

The lions, amazingly, paid Patterson's trap little heed, opting instead for a couple of coolies housed nearby in a more conventional manner. So nonplussed had the lions become by this time that they didn't even bother carrying their prey into the bush, eating them instead by the light of the victims' campfire, despite the fact that a jemadar, apparently frightened blind, was firing shots at them while they ate.

Patterson left the remains of the coolies where they were, hoping the lions would return, and once again went up a nearby tree. The only visitor was a hyena; the lions had attacked another camp some distance away.

After that, Patterson sat in a different tree every night for a week. But he might as well have waited in his trap: "Either the lions saw me and then went elsewhere, or else I was unlucky, for they took man after man from different places without ever once giving me a chance of a shot at them. This constant night watching was most dreary and fatiguing work, but I felt that it was a duty that had to be undertaken, as the men naturally looked to me for protection."

The process was beginning to wear on him. "In the whole of my life I have never experienced anything more nerve-shaking," wrote Patterson, who was not yet married, "than to hear the deep roars of these dreadful monsters growing gradually nearer and nearer, and to know that some one or other of us was doomed to be their victim before morning dawned. Once they reached the vicinity of the camps, the roars completely ceased, and we knew that they were stalking for their prey. Shouts would then pass from camp to camp, 'Beware, brothers, the devil is coming,' but the warning cries would prove to no avail, and sooner or later agonising shrieks would break the silence and another man would be missing from roll-call next morning.

"I was naturally very disheartened at being foiled in this way night after night, and was soon at my wits' end to know what to do; it seemed the lions were really 'devils' after all and bore a charmed life."

Tsavo and Patterson's bridge are enveloped by the two giant national parks at Tsavo East and West. The two parks are divided, approximately, by the Mombasa-Nairobi road and by the railway. Despite what would seem to be a prime roadside location, the still, hot, dry days at the Man Eaters are too rarely punctuated by commerce. But hold on — here's a convoy of zebra-striped minibuses filled with tourists.

The Man Eater comes to life, Samuel gives up his chair, where he has been napping, voices fill the staircase, and presently a score of Orientals tumble into the dining room. We all know that the Japanese are good tourists, fiends for photo-documentation, the cultural paraphernalia of the world a series of hazy backdrops behind their brides, their sisters, or their aunts.

They had just emerged from the game park and were making their way northwest to Nairobi. I had visions of them lining up in front of charging buffalo while some oblivious cousin snapped the photo. But I was wrong. They had had a bad day.

"No animals," one man said when I asked him how his safari was going. "Yesterday, we had a good day. But today no animals, you know, except the lions."

Tourists can find lions. If Patterson had had his thinking cap on, he'd have imported a boatload of sightseers. They'd have led him to his lions.

Not me, though. I'm a bum tourist. I spent *weeks* driving through game parks and rough country looking for lions and never found any. I'd pass a minibus like this one bearing the Japanese visitors, ask the driver, "Any lions?" and he'd say, "Sure, just around the next corner," but they were never there. I found lions on buildings and on signs, on buses and trucks and *matatus*, the queer-looking Japanese pickups that serve as a casual bus service, and I found lions on candy wrappers and T-shirts. I'm sure, however, that if I'd asked

LIONS OF KENYA

LIONS OF KENYA

Corfield or Archer or Dyer to show me lions, they'd have
said, "Eh? Lions? Right, mate, just over there behind that
rock." And when I came back, they would have shrugged and
said, "Funny, they were there just a *second* ago." To find
lions, you need enthusiasm, luck, and experience, and I had
only one of these.

Patterson had two out of three, but even that wasn't enough.
And, as time passed, he also had a lot of help — mostly un-
welcome — arriving from the coast. By late in the fall of
1898, the lions at Tsavo had become a subject of great speculation among the British colony on the coast, and civil, naval,
and army officers began showing up, determined to find and
kill Patterson's nemeses. But they fared no better than Patterson, while the lions grew more fearless and more accomplished. One night the lions ate dinner within earshot of Patterson's camp: "I could plainly hear them crunching the bones,
and the sound of their dreadful purring filled the air and rang
in my ears for days afterwards." Patterson says he decided to
stay in bed, he says he figured the dinner guest was dead by
that time, and, besides, he says it was too dark to see anything. What really happened, I suspect, is that he got the
willies and pulled the blankets up over his head.

Shortly after that episode, the lions switched their tactics in
an effort to increase their efficiency.[11] Where before one lion

---

[11] Aelian claims that in addition to his strength, "the Lion shows intelligence. For
instance, he has designs upon cattle and goes to their folds by night. . . . And he
strikes terror into them all by his strength, but seizes only one and devours it."

Unless he is starving, a lion will not charge about, running furiously after his
prey. In fact, it is the female of the species that is the hunter. All lions, however,
are experts in terror: They formulate rough strategies before a kill, and their
strategies can sometimes be devious.

The late Joy Adamson, in *Born Free* (New York: 1960), recorded the way her
favorite lioness, Elsa, loved to roll about in elephant and rhino droppings and
supposed that this was done instinctively to disguise her natural scent.

had done the dirty work while the other waited in the bush, now both lions were gate-crashing and taking off their victims together, one and two at a time. Once, the lions burst into the largest camp, situated, for security's sake, near the station and the railway inspector's quarters. "Even from my *boma*," Patterson wrote, "I could plainly hear the panic-stricken shrieking of the coolies. Then followed cries of 'They've taken him; they've taken him,' as the brutes carried off their unfortunate victim and began their horrible feast beside the camp." The inspector, a Mr. Dalgairns, was roused from his sleep by the shouts and, grabbing a rifle, fired more than fifty shots in the direction of the lions' growls. That happened on the last day of November 1898. The next morning, Patterson and Dalgairns went to examine the spot, but instead ended up following the trail of what they assumed was a wounded lion. "There was a trail on the sand like that of the toes of a broken limb," Patterson noted. "After some careful stalking, we found ourselves in the vicinity of the lions and were greeted with ominous growlings. Cautiously advancing and pushing the bushes aside, we saw in the gloom what we at first took to be a lion cub; closer inspection, however, showed it to be the remains of the unfortunate coolie, which the man-eaters had apparently abandoned at our approach. The legs, one arm, and half the body had been eaten, and it was the stiff fingers of the other arm trailing along the sand which had left the marks we had taken to be the trail of a wounded lion."

That did it, as far as the coolies were concerned. They went on strike, demanded an audience with Patterson, and told him that they'd come from India to build a railroad, not serve as simba chow, and that no amount of money and no person could convince them to work another minute as long as the lions prowled, and that they'd like to go home, thanks. Just as they presented their side of the labor negotiation, a goods train passed from the railhead camp down the line toward Mombasa. The coolies threw themselves on the tracks, stopping the train, and as many as could swarmed on board and went back to India.

The construction of the railway came to a halt for nearly a month. Patterson praised those workmen who had "sufficient courage to remain," but the coolies made it plain that they were there because Chief Engineer Whitehouse was afraid to allow any more trains to come down to the coast and it was too far to walk. To protect themselves, the workers developed some interesting defensive housing arrangements, putting up camps on top of water towers and beneath their tents, digging pits into which they could slip in the event of a lion visitation. There were coolies sleeping in beds lashed to trees and coolies sleeping on girders stacked high off the ground. "I remember that one night when the camp was attacked," wrote Patterson, "that so many men swarmed on to one particular tree that down it came with a crash, hurling its terror-stricken load of shrieking coolies close to the very lions they were trying to avoid. Fortunately for them, a victim had already been secured, and the brutes were too busy devouring him to pay attention to anything else."

Patterson finally sent for help. He had already asked District Officer Whitehead, the same man who had rescued him from the mutinous masons, to come with a detachment of askaris to help him hunt down the lions. When the coolies jumped ship, Patterson pressed Whitehead yet again, and this time the D.O. replied that he would arrive on the train early the next evening, December 2, and to hold dinner for him.

That evening, Patterson sent his camp boy to fetch Whitehead from the station, but the poor chap rushed back into Patterson's camp and said there was no train at the station and no railway staff at the station and no district officer at the station. The only thing at the station, he reported, was a lion on the platform.

Patterson says he didn't believe "this extraordinary story," since, by this time, all the coolies were prone to overexaggeration. But in his account, Patterson uses that excuse over and over to justify his own inaction, and I think the idea of walking a mile or so through the bush alone in the dark struck him as ill-advised. I don't blame him.

Patterson waited for Whitehead anyway, but after several hours he decided to eat alone. As he was starting to doze off, he heard a terrifying sound. From someplace nearby in the scrub he could hear the low, guttural sighs of the man-eaters and he could hear them crunching the bones of some new victim. Suddenly worried about Whitehead's fate, he fired a rifle in the general direction and thought about going out in the darkness after all. Fortunately for Patterson, the lions obligingly took their meal elsewhere.

The next morning, he went to where the lions had been to investigate. Instead of finding the customary head-and-toes corpse, he found Whitehead, "looking very pale and ill, and generally dishevelled," but, remarkably, intact. Patterson was clearly surprised and asked Whitehead why, if he was in the neighborhood, he had stood him up for dinner the previous night.

"That infernal lion of yours nearly did it for me last night," said Whitehead.

For some reason, Patterson thought Whitehead was joking. "Nonsense," Patterson said, "you must have dreamed it!"

Instead of bothering to answer him, Whitehead simply turned his back on Patterson. "That's not much of a dream, is it?" he asked.

The clothes on his back were demolished: One huge tear went from his neck down to his waist. In fact, Whitehead himself was nearly torn in two. He showed Patterson "four great claw marks, red and angry through the torn cloth.

"Without further parley, I hurried him off to my tent, and bathed and dressed his wounds . . ."

Poor Whitehead, it turns out, had arrived late on the train (the sound of which Patterson *must* have heard quite clearly). Accompanied by his lamp-bearing sergeant, an askari named Abdullah, Whitehead decided to take a shortcut through the bush to Patterson's camp. Together, they made their way through the darkness, Whitehead, admitting his fear, occasionally drawing closer to his sergeant than protocol normally allowed. But since Abdullah was even more afraid than Whitehead, Whitehead's closeness must have seemed somehow encouraging. When they were about halfway there, they heard a low grunt and froze in their tracks. It was too dark to see anything beyond the ring of light provided by the lantern, but they heard one or two small noises and at first, full of hope, thought it was only small game. They began moving forward again, when out of the night a man-eater jumped them. Whitehead had a very close shave; he was sent reeling as the lion swiped at his back. He fired his carbine, but missed the lion, who was making his escape, dragging Abdullah behind. Whitehead fired again, but it was too late. The lion had bounded off into the dark bush, and all he could hear was its growl in the darkness. At one point, he heard Abdullah screaming, "Oh, master, a lion!" Then there was nothing. Whitehead hid as best he could and waited for first light. As it happened, it was Abdullah's bones that Patterson heard being chomped in the night.

The next day, December 3, 1898, the train from Mombasa brought some additional railway officials, along with the superintendent of police, a Mr. Farquhar, and twenty of his sepoys, all arrived to help kill the lions, "whose fame," Patterson noted, "had by this time spread far and wide." Sepoys and railway officials alike were planted in trees near each camp. Whitehead and Patterson took up a place inside a steel crib on a girder near the station. Despite a lot of sarcasm from the Europeans and near hysterical fear from the sepoys, Patterson insisted that his lion trap be hauled out again and the police superintendent dutifully ordered some terrified sepoys to stand inside as bait.

In the darkness, the men at their stations — in trees, on water towers, behind rocks — waited nervously. According to Patterson, nothing happened until about nine o'clock, "when, to my great satisfaction, the intense stillness was suddenly broken down by the noise of the door of the trap clattering down."

Patterson rejoiced. "'At last,' I thought." Along with Whitehead and the others, the men rushed toward Patterson's improbable bait box.

Inside, the bait-sepoys were armed with Martini-Henry rifles and plenty of ammo and they had a lamp burning inside their half of the cage. They had been ordered to shoot the lion immediately, the moment one entered the trap, but "instead of doing so," Patterson reported, "they were so terrified when he rushed in . . . that they completely lost their heads and were actually too unnerved to fire. Not for some minutes — not, indeed, until Mr. Farquhar, whose post was close by, shouted at them and cheered them on, did they at all recover themselves. Then when at last they did begin to fire, they fired with a vengeance — anywhere, anyhow."

Patterson, Whitehead, and the other sentries ran for cover, ducking the sepoys' rifle fire as the men blasted blindly away. While they completely missed the lion — which was standing only inches away from them — they did succeed in blowing away part of the cage, allowing the lion to escape.

Patterson was dejected: "How they failed to kill him several times over is, and always will be, a complete mystery to

me, as they could have put the muzzles of their rifles absolutely touching his body."

Whitehead, Farquhar, the visiting officials, the sepoys, and
the askaris spent two more days like this, then went home.

On the morning of December 9, a native coolie came running
wildly into Patterson's *boma*, shouting, "Simba! Simba!" He
explained that the lions had tried to nab a worker down by
the river, but had decided on a donkey instead. According to
the coolie, the lions were in a nearby thicket calmly eating the
animal. This, the Indian pointed out to Patterson, might be a
good time to go lion hunting.

Patterson grabbed a heavy rifle lent to him earlier by Farquhar and started a careful stalk of the lions, the coolie acting as guide. Alas, at the last minute, the worker broke a twig
and alerted one of the lions, who made for the bush. Patterson quickly armed a band of workmen with tin cans and
other noisemakers and formed them into a nervous semi-
circle around the thicket. Patterson crept around to the other
side and gave a signal. The workmen started their racket,
as Patterson took cover behind an anthill in the middle of a
wide path that he judged to be the lion's most likely route of
escape.

"Very soon I heard a tremendous din being raised by the
advancing line of coolies, and almost immediately, to my intense joy, out into the open path stepped a huge maneless
lion. It was the first occasion during all these trying months
upon which I had had a fair chance at one of these brutes, and
my satisfaction at the prospect of bagging him was unbounded.

"Slowly he advanced along the path, stopping every few
second to look round. I was only partially concealed from
view, and if his attention had not been so fully occupied by
the noise behind him, he must have observed me. As he was
oblivious to my presence, however, I let him approach to

within about fifteen yards of me, and then covered him with my rifle. The moment I moved to do this, he caught sight of me, and seemed much astonished at my sudden appearance, for he stuck his forefeet into the ground, threw himself back on his haunches and growled savagely. As I covered his brain with my rifle, I felt that at last I had him absolutely at my mercy, but . . . never trust an untried weapon! I pulled the trigger, and to my horror heard the dull snap that tells of a misfire."

The lion was distracted anew by the racket made by the coolies, and, happily for Patterson, jumped off into the bush instead of on him. As it leapt, Patterson pulled the other trigger, wounding the animal as it disappeared. Patterson thus escaped with his life, but not with his honor. The coolies thought he was a jerk, that he'd blown his best chance at ridding them of their predator.

▼▲▼▲▼

Open your door to no one. In moment of extremis, we seek solace in companionship, and in desperation we entertain all callers, including our deepest doubts, as if they were old friends come to visit and chat for a while. How often they surprise us by coming with all their belongings; they greet us at our own door and, as we stand muttering apologies, instantly they move in to stay. What dreadful houseguests; for they never sleep and insist on having us join them in their late night amusements. And they leave us poor, having robbed us of our most precious possession.

The coolies were absolutely right; there was nothing for Patterson to do but spend the night alone in a small elevated platform near the body of the partially eaten donkey. It was a dark night, and Patterson, afraid the lions would drag away the donkey carcass before he could get a shot off, secured the bait with wire. "Everything became extraordinarily still," he wrote. "The silence of an African jungle on a dark night needs to be experienced to be realised; it is most impressive, especially when one is absolutely alone and isolated from one's fellow creatures, as I was then." Patterson strained against the black silence until he fell into a sort of "dreamy mood" from which he was startled by the breaking of a twig. Patterson began imagining other noises, too, including a sigh from a man-eater — "a sure sign of hunger." For hours, Patterson sat there in his rickety tower, dreaming of lions.

Finally, his dream came true. A lion came out of the silence of the night through the bushes. But then it stopped and growled angrily, apparently spotting Patterson, whose disappointment soared at the prospect of the lion's going away.

"But no," wrote Patterson, "matters quickly took an unexpected turn. The hunter became the hunted; and instead of either making off or coming for the bait prepared for him, the lion began to stalk *me*!"

For two hours the lion slowly circled Patterson's "crazy structure," and with each circuit, it came closer and closer. Patterson fully expected that at any moment, the beast would rush his flimsy platform, bringing his vigil to a bloody conclusion. The contraption was quite poorly engineered, considering it was erected by a bridge builder; it was held up only by four very flimsy poles, and the whole thing swayed dangerously with even the slightest shift of Patterson's weight. If even one of the poles gave way, he would quite literally become dead meat. He quite rightly feared, too, that the lion could easily jump to the twelve-foot-high plank of wood that served as his platform. The intense anxiety of the silent, dark stalk began to rattle him severely. There was nothing Patterson could do, of course, except watch and wait and wait. In the darkness, the lion waited, too, with a cat's patience and with a cat's eyes. "He horrified me," Patterson admitted.

"I began to feel distinctly 'creepy,'" he wrote, "and heartily repented my folly in having placed myself in such a dangerous position. I kept perfectly still, however, hardly daring to even blink my eyes: but the long-continued strain was beginning to tell on my nerves, and my feelings may be better imagined than described when about midnight suddenly something came flop and struck me on the back of the head. For a moment I was so terrified that I nearly fell off the plank, as I thought that the lion had sprung on me from behind. Regaining my senses in a second or two, I realised that I had been hit by nothing more formidable than an owl, which had doubtless mistaken me for the branch of a tree. . . . The involuntary start which I could not help giving was immediately answered by a sinister growl from the ground.

"After this I again kept as still as I could, though absolutely trembling with excitement; and in a short while I heard the lion begin to creep stealthily towards me . . ." Finally, the lion came into view, a murky figure in the deep black of a Tsavo night. "I took careful aim and pulled the trigger."

▼▲▼▲▼

One of the best places found in East Africa to discover the truth about the mysterious ways of the lion is at one of the tables next to the swimming pool at the Norfolk Hotel in Nairobi, where a patient man can sit quietly and not only learn something, but also drink something at the same time, and where he can talk about lions without the slightest risk of actually being distracted by the presence of the animals.

"Lions study each other," Tony Archer said during one highly spirited lesson. "Obviously, cubs learn from the mother and watching others. I've often seen cubs give away a hunt completely by being too damned eager instead of staying put until the zebra are within striking distance. They can't wait and spoil the whole thing, and the entire pride sulks for hours.

But when they are in better form, they will work together well. From the front, a lion — particularly a lion lying down with a bit of grass for cover — is almost invisible. From the rear, they keep an eye on one another. That's why a lion has black spots on the back of the ear and a black tip on the tail. A lot of information is passed from one lion to another by watching their hunting party. From an angle, from the rear, it's easier to know what's going on. But from the front, the animal is extraordinarily well camouflaged from its prey."

Sir Alfred Pease notes that lionesses bear more distinct markings than the male. Since the females do much of the hunting, this perhaps makes good sense.

Sometimes, lions scheme to increase their indolence. According to Sir Alfred, they can locate game already killed by watching for carrion birds. "I once witnessed an undoubted case of this," he wrote. "I had killed a roan antelope on very open country, and when about a mile from the spot I turned round to watch the vultures dropping down to feast on the remains. Two lions were slouching across the open plain, making a bee-line for the carcass. . . . They were approaching down wind, and as the carcass had not been there an hour before, they could not have known of its position except by the vultures. I have seen jackals follow the birds in the same way."

"If I'd been in Patterson's shoes, I would want some good trackers with me," Archer told me. "It's much better to trap a lion than to put up bait and have a lion feed on it, and stalking the thing and shooting it." Patterson, Archer said, was lucky to have survived as long as he did in view of the methods he used.

Patterson had in fact pressed his luck many times in his obsessive search for the lions of Tsavo, but never quite to the ludicrous extreme he reached on that plank twelve feet above the man-eater on a dark, quiet night. As Archer said, "Didn't they ever hear of box traps?"

Even so restrained a voice as that of Frederick Selous, one of the most famous white hunters in the history of Africa, thought Patterson stretched the limits of probability once too many times, "especially on that one occasion when whilst watching from a very light scaffolding, supported only by four rickety poles, he was himself stalked by one of the dread beasts." Selous, writing in the foreword to Patterson's book on the episode, considered that Patterson just didn't realize the strength and agility of his opponent: "In my own experience I have known of three instances of men having been pulled from trees or huts built on platforms at a greater height from the ground than the crazy structure on which Col. Patterson was watching that night of terrors."

But Patterson took a shot in the dark. There was a roar and a vicious thrashing below the wobbly platform. Finally, the lion leaped crazily into the bush; in an adrenaline-fed frenzy, Patterson blazed away in the general direction he thought the lion had gone. He heard a series of deep groans, then some deep sighs, then nothing. *Nothing.*

Softly at first, hesitant and questioning, voices began floating across the bush. Patterson shouted that he was safe and that one of the lions was dead, "whereupon such a mighty cheer went up from all the camps as much have astonished the denizens of the jungle for miles around." Lights came on in the camps, and, with tins beating and with happy shouts, the men came and surrounded Patterson's platform and fell to their knees, calling him a saviour.

Patterson sensibly refused to allow the men to search for the body of the beast until there was enough light to ascertain that it was really dead; he knew that even a mortally wounded lion could still easily kill a healthy man. "Accordingly," he wrote, "we all returned in triumph to the camp, where great rejoicings were kept up for the remainder of the night, the

Swahili and other African natives celebrating the occasion by an especially wild and savage dance."

Patterson spent a sleepless night, and even before it was fully dawn, he was out looking for his trophy, followed by dozens of coolies. When he found the body and determined the lion was quite dead, his followers "crowded round, laughed and danced and shouted with joy like children, and bore me in triumph shoulder-high around the dead body." He found two bullet holes in the lion — one behind the left shoulder, which had probably gone through its heart, and another in a hind leg. The lion was nine feet, eight inches from the end of its tail to the tip of its nose.

By sunup on December 11, telegrams were streaming in, congratulating Patterson, and within a few days, "scores of people flocked from up and down the railway to see the skin for themselves."

The first half was the best half of the battle. The weeks leading to Christmas 1898 were marked by skirmishes — all notably unsuccessful — with the other lion. At one point, Patterson set a trap using goats as bait, but when the lion obligingly showed up to eat the goats, Patterson fired and killed the bait.

The second man-eater was finally killed four days after Christmas in a stalk that involved a Rasputin-like series of charges by the lion, during one of which Patterson found himself scurrying up a tree in the nick of time.

When word got down to the coast that the second lion had been killed, the Indians returned to work and Patterson was presented with an inscribed silver bowl from the coolies. The incident was mentioned by Salisbury, the Prime Minister, in Parliament, and was the subject of numerous magazine articles.

The man-eaters had eaten a total of twenty-eight coolies and uncounted natives. The generally accepted total is 128.

Patterson's lions are mounted and on display in the Field Museum of Natural History, Chicago.

A fast reader will still have some time to nap in the dawn before breakfast, which, by the way, will be a hearty one, with plenty of eggs, rashers of bacon, lots of toast and tea.

Eat. An hour or so after breakfast, the twilight plains of Kenya will turn into Six Flags Dark Continent, and you'll be in Nairobi, along with thousands of tourists and plenty of tourist-trappers. Even if you're traveling on to Kisumu, the train won't leave until tonight. You'll have at least one day to pound about in Nairobi. So eat.

PART THREE

NAIROBI AND EVERYPLACE ELSE

WHEN THE TRAIN ARRIVED IN NAIROBI IT WAS AN hour late, and I had made plans to meet a friend at a local hotel. There was one taxi parked in front; another was just rounding the corner, but it was ten seconds away at least, so, *as luck would have it,* I grabbed the waiting cab just ahead of my French nemesis and his girlfriend. Getting in, I hesitated just a second, just long enough for her to perhaps painfully ignore me and for him to pass me another dose of animosity, then I jumped in the backseat.

Ten seconds later, I was out again, pushing the cab across the parking lot while the very fat taxi driver sat inside yelling, "Please, faster!" The battery was flat. The Frenchman had got another cab, of course, and as he pulled away he gave me a warm and friendly smile. We never saw each other again, so I'm glad we parted on such cheerful terms.

▼▲▼▲▼

Yet another journalist, this one young and American, has arrived in Nairobi on the trail of a hot story. He's traveling light — no bulky history, no awkward anthropology — and he's looking for big game: He wants to find some white person he can make look really stupid.

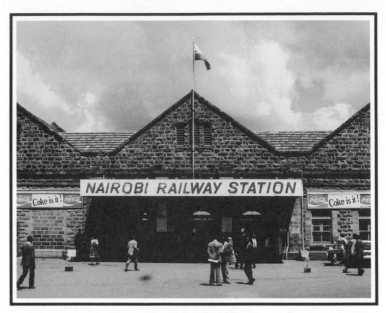

AT THE NAIROBI STATION

It's his first time in Kenya, and he has brought along not only his own fresh perspective on whites in Africa, but also his Yankee sense of rectitude. And besides, he has already spent some time in South Africa, where he saw the face of the beast and it was white.

To stalk his prey, he asked around town a little bit. He approached an elderly white woman running a souvenir stand at one of the hotels at one point and asked her to turn in a few of her friends, but he frightened her. So she put him on to me, and I invited him to dinner.

We met at a gambling casino in Nairobi that was only days away from bankruptcy. Tourists, it turned out, didn't come to Kenya to gamble, so the biggest losers in the gaming rooms had all been Kenyans. To save the citizens from themselves, the government had issued an edict that gambling could be conducted in hard currencies only, and since the Kenya shill-

ing is a currency of decidedly local interest, and since even ob-
taining hard currency is a gamble for most Kenyans, the government's new policy had the effect of excluding all residents
of the country. Hundreds of people were going to lose their
jobs. Consequently, service in the casino restaurant was a trifle
nonchalant. Along with a visiting French photographer who
seemed to know everyone ("He's a drug dealer, I think . . ."
"That man makes documentary films . . ." "Ah, there's my
friend the ambassador, excuse me . . ."), we sat and watched
a few middle-class Kenyans and a lot of white foreigners meet
to discuss travel plans or autoinflated deals over plates of cool
chicken and pasta. The young journalist was trying to make a
deal, too. He gave me that look — that half wink exchanged
by the brotherhood of politically correct thinkers, the equivalent of a secret handshake — and told me his plan, to find a
white person and make him look stupid. He said he thought I
might know where to look.

Well, in Kenya, as in the rest of East Africa, knowing where
to look for the wildlife is half the game. Zebra and antelope
are a cinch: even the Taru desert is overpopulated at the moment. Elephant? More difficult, especially now that not even
tourists are safe from the guns of poachers and bandits.

But some species are more endangered than others, and,
compared, for example, to tracking rhino or elephant, finding
stupid-looking white people in Kenya is definitely no problem. We were, for example, sitting in a restaurant where half
the clientele were imported white folks, most of them wearing
clothes that wouldn't be allowed on a golf course. Right next
to us, at a neighboring table, four chatty, happy tourists sat
sucking spaghetti; two men, dressed like Italian waiters, wore
tight-fitting shirts left unbuttoned to reveal their hormonal
exuberance. One woman wore a native dress and an olive-
drab floppy cloth cap bearing the word "*Jambo!*" — the

Swahili word for hello — while the other woman wore a
T-shirt across the front of which was emblazoned the legend
"Bitch." To them, and to most tourists, they were well within
the limits of propriety. More than any other country on the
continent, Kenya, with its well-oiled tourist industry, is Afri-
caland for those who wish to illuminate the heart of darkness
with the flash of a million Nikons. Last year, hundreds of
thousands of tourists came to Kenya, and during the endless
high season, from July through the following March, they are
everywhere. In the game parks, fist fights break out between
tourists in minibuses and rented cars jockeying for camera
position next to a bored and drowsy lion. Scarlet tourists flop
beached and greased for roasting along the Mombasa shore,
and in Nairobi, they strut through the Norfolk Hotel — the
best hotel in East Africa, and an important landmark for both
visiting and resident whites — in suburban military garb,
with Stewart Granger and Karen Blixen on their minds. They
all look pretty damn odd, if you ask me.

But, as I told the young journalist, to spot the real thing,
the rare white African, you have to narrow your search a
little. "Perhaps you should try to catch them at a social gathering of some sort," I said. "Maybe you can get somebody to
invite you along to a private club." I was trying to be helpful,
really. There were, I said, plenty of weddings and cocktail parties at the Norfolk. I wanted to describe to him the time I met
two native-born white women at a function at a local hotel
and accompanied them to a party, where I drank white Kenyan gin and watched them dance their white Kenyan dances
until they passed out and I fell asleep. I woke up in the backseat of a taxi parked in front of the hotel. Everyone concerned
had looked exceptionally white and definitively stupid. But I
could see that he was looking for a more profound, more
searching kind of foolishness, something that he thought

would capture the truly evil nature of the white man in Africa, and it seemed likely that polite self-destruction would just not be good enough.

Later, after the young American had lost his patience with me and left in a bad mood, the French photographer, who had quietly watched our conversation, intervening at the last moment to preclude any overt unpleasantness, wondered aloud about the journalist. "He's after colored people," he said, "but the ones he's after are white."

If white Kenyans are now a rare species poached nearly to extinction by visiting journalists with an ax to grind, it wasn't always so. Africa before Europeans, like England before Romans, has more anthropology than history, and whatever story the past has to tell in Africa is described in tribal migrations, conflicts, and usurpations. Before there were Kikuyu in Kenya, there were Portuguese, and before there were Portuguese, there were Omani Arabs. Once, white people ("Europeans," as they are generically known, no matter their origin) were everywhere in Kenya, building schools and hospitals and roads, but also institutionalizing patronization and suppression and generating enormous jealousy and resentment.

But that was long before most of the citizens of Kenya were born. This planet is littered with people who have become the hostages of their own history, and the white tribe, now the smallest and most vulnerable tribe in Kenya, is no exception.

If history is a crime, then I suppose the railway is an accomplice. Even before its completion in 1901, the railway began attracting large numbers of settlers more or less typical of the kind of men drawn by frontier life: undercapitalized farmers, indolent cadet sons of aristocratic families, bourgeois wanderers with a romantic streak, writers, con men, and mission-

aries. By the mid-twenties, parts of Kenya had come to resemble a more temperate Shropshire, complete with Gothic
revival churches, quiet country inns, and a thin slice of aris-
tocracy, led by Hugh Cholmondeley, the third Baron Delamere, who had hocked his family estates in England to pay
for his agricultural adventures on the equator. The arrival of
Europeans in Africa was a probably good thing from a contemporary point of view — disease was reduced, tribal warfare was suppressed, slavery was eliminated, schools were
built, and the colony-nations of Africa were brought into the
global community. From a modern point of view, however,
we despise the good intentions of the Victorians, and the colonial era is now seen as an ugly exercise of racial dominance,
one that has engendered not only the somewhat understanda-
bly excessive antiwhite bias of African nationalism, but also
the impassioned, sometimes poorly reasoned reaction to history on the part of those who live outside the continent. On
sight, most Americans or Europeans can't tell a Nigerian Ibo
from a Rwandan Hutu, but nobody has trouble spotting an
African of Dutch or English descent. Consequently, bloody
tribal oppression and personal power, the principal compo-
nents of political life in Africa, go everywhere unnoticed, except where the players can be easily distinguished and their
wicked deeds rightfully noted. The reason for this is simple:
Invariably, power, during the process of decolonization, was
passed with tremendous expediency from the colonizing government to whomever had the next most power, despite the
fact that the recipient of power without exception represented
only a single tribe's interests and was bound to put those interests ahead of all others — except, perhaps, important personal ones. Thus was born the traditional rule of the Big
Man, the embodiment of the cult of "nationalism." The biggest crime in the history of colonization in Africa is the way in
which it was abruptly brought to an irresponsible end.

But if white Kenyans are uncomfortable from time to time, they should recall that nobody ever intended to create a white Kenya in the first place. A British government white paper, published in 1923 — only three years after Kenya received full colonial status — reminded settlers that "primarily, Kenya is an African territory, and H.M.'s Government think it necessary definitely to record their considered opinion that the interests of the African natives must be paramount." So, stranded in a world created by their fathers, but one which was mandated to disappear from the beginning and which now no longer exists, white Kenyans go about their business quietly, nervous in the knowledge that among all the tribal groups in the country, they're the ones that stand out.

Their ranks have grown thinner since the zenith of empire, and some of the favorites from my personal pantheon are now gone. No more Patrick Shaw, who was called "The Gunner." Shaw helped run a boy's school all day and drove around chasing criminals all night, shooting first and not bothering with questions later. Shaw weighed well over 300 pounds, slept ten minutes at a time in a straight-backed chair, and struck fear into the heart of every dishonest Kenyan. It was assumed no crook would ever kill Patrick Shaw, and, despite rumors to the contrary, no crook did. Shaw died of heart failure in late 1986,[1] and according to many Kenyans, the recent surge in lawlessness is due in no small part to the knowledge among criminals that they will not be visited in the night by Patrick Shaw.

And no more Hugh A. W. Pilkington, heir to millions, who came to Kenya in 1969 as part of the European youthful revolt program, stayed to run the Nairobi Classical Society, and lived in a suburban Nairobi mansion, where he devoted a

---

[1] Patrick Shaw, along with several other white Africans, is profiled in a previous book of mine, *African Lives* (New York: 1988).

room filled with needlepointed cushions to the dog that saved him from an angry buffalo and where he took in youngsters from Uganda and Ethiopia, educated them, then sent them off to universities in North America and Europe.

And no more Diana, Lady Delamere, whose beauty and wit seduced a generation of colonists, and whose peripheral involvement (as Diana Broughton, at the time the young wife of the elderly Sir Jock Delves Broughton) in the murder of her lover, Josslyn Hay, the Earl of Erroll, in 1941, became the focus of much rich speculation, and whose exploits formed the basis for James Fox's book, *White Mischief,* and the popular film based on that book. If gossip is a measure of immortality, then Diana Delamere will live forever; nearly half a century after Diana's then husband killed her lover, the neighbors — and the neighbors' grandchildren — are still talking.

But the survivors of empire are no less colorful, and there are still enough "vanilla gorillas," as they are sometimes called, to put together a pretty decent social scene in the middle of a continent that is frequently marked by indecency of one kind or another. Michael "Punch" Bearcroft, who helped fight Jomo Kenyatta's Mau Mau uprising by founding the famed Kenya Flying Police, stayed around to run the police wing for his former adversary, and is undoubtedly the only commercially licensed one-armed helicopter pilot in the world. Or Jan Hemsing, the extraordinarily prolific historian of Kenya's white landmarks, including the venerable Norfolk Hotel. Or Anthony Seth-Smith, whose father came to Kenya in 1904 and who, after reading for a degree in geology at Oxford, returned to East Africa to pursue a career as a professional hunter. Or Rupert Watson, who only a dozen or so years ago was a young British lawyer, but who's now a Kenya citizen — much to the astonishment of his family — and a writer who practices law barefooted, perhaps the very last settler in a long line of emigrants from England. Or Ted Goss, now retired after a lifetime as one of the best-known game-park wardens in Kenya; when last seen, Goss was in Tsavo, working on a rhino census for the World Wildlife Federation and advising a squad of antipoaching rangers. Or John and Elli D'Olier, proprietors of an extraordinary vineyard on the shores of Lake Naivasha. Or Tony Archer, whom we have already met, once one of Kenya's most sought-after white hunters and now a guide for extremely wealthy clients seeking the luxury of an old-fashioned tented safari.

▼▲▼▲▼

Like odd species in the wilderness, white Africans have their favorite haunts. It's obvious, for example, that you'll never find them in places like the districts out along the Naivasha Road beyond Kinoo, where Nairobi becomes an urban emergency, as thousands of new arrivals set up corrugated homes, then wait for the regular appearance of government bulldozers so they can start city life anew once more, scratching ad hoc neighborhoods out of the red clay soil. And it's safe to assume that you won't find many in the Northern Frontier District, home of Somali raiders, Ugandan bandits, man-eating lions, and endless army convoys.

On the other hand, one might think a cricket match might be a good place to run across a few dreamy, nostalgic ex-Brits. Cricket, after all, is a game of exceeding subtlety and mystery and resembles another English passion, gardening, more than any other team sport. But the Nairobi Gymkhana Club, the site of a really pleasant pitch, where I went one Sunday to watch the finals of the Southern Credit Tournament, is an Asian enclave. I watched Swamibapa, a brilliant Asian side, take on the Nairobi Jaffreys, whose coolly energetic team sported lots of Martins and Stevens and Alfreds, all with

Kenyan surnames that started with two or more consonants. All morning I waited for at least a token white, but there was only me, smiling and shuffling and trying to look a part of the scene, as Indians and Kenyans played an odd English game in the middle of Africa.

The Europeans, of course, were all at the track, a hallowed place where members of Kenya's white tribe perform elaborate risk-taking ceremonies while bedecked in their colorful, traditional native dress — the men in blue blazers, the women in their white frocks and important hats.

The Jockey Club at Ngong is fifteen minutes from the center of Nairobi, but only a step away from English country life. The exquisitely beautiful racetrack provides a weekly venue where white people gather to gossip about each other and well-dressed squires bet their tailor-made shirts on country nags. Situated at the foot of the Ngong Hills, the track is a haven of genteel vice and consequently an ideal Caucasian habitat, one that has the casual architectural ambience and artificial verdancy that reflects the affection its patrons have for their environment — especially its climate. It reminded me more of a Southern California hotel than a racetrack in Africa.

There is, you know, an air of unfortunate optimism at most horse-racing tracks, where anything is possible until the very last moment, when the magnificent creature that has been an object of intense anticipation becomes a despicable beast that has betrayed genetics. At the Jockey Club in Ngong, however, the atmosphere is somewhat thinner, resembling nothing so much as a country carnival, where old friends greet each other and talk about business and horses. The compere for these proceedings is a tweedy gentleman of impeccable geniality, Sir Charles Markham, who in addition to managing the affairs of the Jockey Club's Ngong racetrack, also serves as chairman of the exclusive Muthaiga Club and is therefore per-

haps the most socially prominent white man in the country. At
Ngong, Sir Charles, looking every bit the distinguished elder
statesman, is in his element, glad-handing old friends, hand-
ing out ribbons and gold cups to horse owners and trainers,
and making highly amusing small talk in the manner of A. E.
Mathews, but with all the affable ease of a game-show emcee.

I spent the afternoon dogging Sir Charles, eavesdropping
on his conversations, watching him perform perfectly the rituals of polite society, and waiting for him to give me a good tip
on a horse. It occurred to me after only a few minutes that at
least to Sir Charles the white Kenyans with whom he passed a
word or two were not just fellow countrymen or acquaintances. Rather, they were guests of his, participants in a wonderful party given by a very generous host. Everyone was
having a pleasant time, thanks to the extremely efficient exer-
tions of the man most white Kenyans must consider to be the
leader of their pack.

In fact, Sir Charles was once a political figure in Kenya and
more than anyone else represents whatever is left of the old
colonial order in the country. In a quiet conversation, I sought
to encourage a bit of volatility for the sake of a pithy quote or
two, and so I asked him about the end of British rule in Kenya
and whether he thought independence had come too quickly.
I don't know what sort of answer I expected, but what I got
was the mild observation that while the British are often accused of pulling out of Africa too quickly, according to Sir
Charles and contrary to my point of view, if the decolonization process had gone on much longer than it did, "You'd
have had massive bloodshed. You'd have had thousands of
British soldiers here. Can you imagine some mother in Derby
losing her son to maintain a colonial regime? If it had dragged
out, there would be no Europeans left.

"What saved those of us with a white face," Sir Charles

continued, "was [Jomo] Kenyatta's famous speech in Nakuru when he made his promise 'not to forget, but to forgive.'" The protective shadow of Kenyatta still hangs over the white tribe in Kenya, and Kenyatta's decision to try to maintain white skilled workers, along with white wealth, has been used as a model for other postindependence leaders — most recently by Zimbabwe's Robert Mugabe — with varying amounts of sincerity and success.

The secret for white survival, according to Sir Charles, is to foster a certain talent at camouflage. As he told me, "If you keep a low profile, you can stay here [Kenya]," although his profile is anything but low. His mother, Gwladys, figured prominently in the scandal that followed the murder of Lord Erroll; she was conducting a very public affair with the aristocrat before Diana Broughton caught his eye. These days, Sir Charles is a highly visible and extremely personable symbol of white Kenyans. He is accosted so frequently by visiting journalists, he told me, that "a friend of mine, a journalist in England, says I should charge for corkage."

There are some 50,000 whites resident in Africa, and, according to Sir Charles's analysis, they all conform to one of three types: The first group — and the smallest — are "the British or ex-British" — by which he also meant those Kenyans of British ancestry. This group, numbering no more than five or six thousand, he said, includes those who have made a long-term commitment to Kenya and who make their permanent homes in the country. They are known widely as "settlers," and Sir Charles is certainly part of their caste. The second and largest group, he says, are called "two-year wonders" — contract workers for multinational corporations, airlines, and the like who are sent to Nairobi on two- or three-year contracts and who will leave on the expiry of their working agreement. The third group is "a peculiar tribe, all part of

these 'agencies' — the UN and God-knows-what." A lot of
those in the third group, Sir Charles wildly suspects, "are involved in rackets in duty-free and all that," although I felt that
my acquaintances in the United Nations Environment Programme, based in Nairobi, would be surprised and alarmed
to learn of this accusation. Most of the UNEP people I know
have spent careers on the edge of acceptability in precarious
political climates and seem to me to be unlikely suspects to
fleece the local customs office.

But according to Sir Charles, "The first group are a little bit
frightened about what happens to their children. There is, at
the moment, a slightly hostile attitude of the authorities toward the Europeans — not from those higher up, but from
the petty officials, the police and so forth." He cited the case
of a woman arrested for conducting a meeting without a permit when she decided to invite some friends into her home for
tea and the arrest of a trial advocate of the high court for
crossing a yellow line. (If, to Sir Charles, white Kenyans are
"a little bit frightened," another long-time Kenyan disputed
Sir Charles's characterization. He told me the whites in Kenya
"were scared out of their skins.")

I asked Sir Charles the question that every visiting white
journalist asks every resident white Kenyan: Why did he stay?
He looked at me as if I were an imbecile. "I have been here
since I was a boy, and my wife was born here. I love this country." He added with a flat certainty: "I have nowhere else to
go. I hope to be buried here."

In the movies, it looks great to be young, white, and in Africa:
There's Meryl Streep as Karen Blixen, the melancholy Dane,
stalking her front porch, surrounded by houseboys, a huge,
red, shimmering sun setting in the dark green Ngong Hills behind her. She is worrying vaguely about her coffee crop, but

worrying even more about when Robert Redford, as her imaginary lover, Denys Finch-Hatton, the aristocratic white hunter, will show up with a gramophone and a bottle of bubbly. And maybe the fiction wasn't far from the fact: "We lived lives of great charm," one old-timer told me over tea in Nairobi. "We worked all day to build up this country, then we drank all night tearing ourselves down." At least, he added, "That's how I remember it."

But the drama in Kenya these days is in black and white, and white Kenyans find little charm and less comfort in the romance of Africa. As a third-generation white citizen told me, "The government definitely wants us out. But they don't know how to get rid of us" — although it sometimes appears that the present government is trying to figure out a way. According to one anxious white Kenyan, "There's a lot of prejudice against us." He said he had always expected a certain amount of popular reaction against whites, but instead he felt prejudice was more policy than conviction. "[Prejudice exists] not on the personal level — not as much in the shops or in the street — but in the [lower and middle levels of the] government." While the South Africans are the masters of racially determined policies, some whites complain that the Kenyan government is trying to come up with some home-grown policies of its own that apparently are intended to reduce the influence not only of Europeans, but also of the most reviled Kenyans of all — Asians, particularly those of Indian descent.

The sense of growing antiwhite sentiment is often tangible. If you ask a white Kenyan about local fishing spots, he'll take you fishing, and if you ask him about local beer, he'll get you drunk. And ten years ago, if you asked about the local whites, you got an earful of highly personal gossip and a full-blown political exegesis couched in terms both hopeful and skeptical. These days, the subject is discussed in whispers and in

fear. Two weeks after I returned from my most recent visit to
Kenya, I received three letters from white citizens I had inter-
viewed during my recent visit. All of their letters began with a
pretense for writing — one wanted the address of a photographer, another wanted the name of the publisher of a book I
had mentioned, the third wanted just to "keep in touch." But
they all ended with a common request: Would I please not
quote them by name if I wrote about white Africans. "We're
just a bit nervous," one man wrote. "In fact, my wife was angry
that I had even talked to you about the subject [of race]."

Actually, most white Kenyans are much happier talking
about the sexual predilections of their neighbors than they are
about race. Voices lower, eyes wander whenever the subject of
the government's racial attitude is mooted. One man grew
quite angry when I asked if he felt the government was treat-
ing all its citizens fairly. "That's a foolish question," he said.
"We have made our deal. We get left alone, provided we cause
no trouble." It was people like me asking those kind of questions, he said, that caused difficulties. Another wrote to me
after my departure begging me not to quote him by name,
since he had "serious misgivings" about associating himself
with "possibly unpopular views."

It's difficult to turn up the numbers necessary to determine
exactly how much Kenya's white tribe has to lose, but despite
the government harassment and the greed of petty politicians,
it must be said that the majority of whites in Kenya live in far
better conditions than the majority of black Kenyans. There
are many reasons for this relative affluence, but one of them
must be that whites generally have easier access to wealth;
there seems to be a global financial prejudice against blacks,
and if a banker had to choose between lending money to a
white man or a black man of equal worth, the black man
would likely walk away empty-handed. On the other hand,

it's certainly true that black politicians of humble backgrounds own the largest estates and the most profitable businesses in Kenya. This anomaly is the reward, no doubt, of working hard in the public's service, the fast track to wealth in most of Africa, where corruption is often breathtakingly brazen. Jomo Kenyatta, the country's secular saint, once berated one of his ministers for not lining his pockets sufficiently, and the present problem with poaching can only be attributed to corruption in the highest levels of the military and the government.

Yet while prejudice may breed corruption, corruption can also help ameliorate prejudice, and, in general, the whites don't do badly in Kenya. Many still have substantial holdings in the country, and their homes are often among the largest and best dwellings in Nairobi's exclusive northwestern suburbs. Most white families enjoy the help of domestic servants, and most lead lives of quiet prosperity, many engaged in businesses that were started by their fathers or grandfathers. Indeed, whites in general are held in some esteem by many blacks, and even those white Kenyans most anxious about the racial attitude of the government agree that among the *mwananchi* — the Swahili term for a black citizenry — there's a polite sympathy for the white man. One chap, a white safari guide, recalled once being rushed to a rural clinic with a serious wound. "There was an enormous queue of people in front of the clinic," he remembered, "many of whom must have had emergencies as grave as mine. Without hesitation — and without discussion or formal agreement — I was passed to the front of the queue and seen to at once. It was remarkable. It just didn't seem right to them that I should wait at the back until it was my proper turn."

Another white Kenyan claimed that he had "never felt such a thing" as antiwhite prejudice. "In fact," he said, "if I am sitting at a café, there's a good chance that I'll be served before anyone else." He thought one reason for such deference was that "if you're white, you're more likely to have money," a widespread assumption that causes many whites to be the targets of street thugs and panhandlers. "But," he added, "if I didn't believe the government of this country was going to treat me fairly, I would never live here."

The bottom line, as some Kenyans suggested to me, is that whites just don't take well to minority status. As a retired academic in Nairobi told me, "We [whites] don't do very well in social environments where we are both in the minority and have relatively little power." He felt that the real threat to Kenyans of all stripes was from government corruption, instability, and the general trend away from democratic traditions. Recently, the government of President Daniel arap Moi banned local publications and began imprisoning their editors for running pieces that discuss corruption or other shortcomings; at the same time, crackdowns have resulted in the frequent detention of political opponents. The recent murder of a potential Moi rival, Robert Ouko, an influential leader of the Luo tribe, provoked serious disturbances both in Nairobi, where, as a consequence of antigovernment demonstrations, the university was closed for a time, and in Kisumu, Ouko's hometown, where a protest by 5,000 people was finally broken up by the army. Ouko's murder was the fourth case since independence — beginning with the murder of another influential Luo, Tom Mboya, in 1969 — of a potential presidential rival meeting death under mysterious circumstances. Jomo Kenyatta was widely assumed to have covered up the first three. Moi is suspected of covering up this one: Ouko was taken from his home at three in the morning and found days later having been shot in the head and set afire. The government at first sought to claim it had been a suicide.

When Kenyatta, Moi's predecessor and a member of the

dominant Kikuyu tribe, ruled Kenya, it was widely assumed
that the Kikuyu would continue to dominate Kenyan politics
and other Kenyan tribes. And, in a way, they have, insofar as
Moi's ability to survive, as a member of the minority Kalenjin
tribe, has been based on his ability to keep the Kikuyu squab-
bling among themselves, especially after the murder in 1975
of Josiah Kariuki, a powerful Kikuyu opponent. But now,
more than a decade after Kenyatta's death, Moi seems to have
rewritten the political rules in Kenya. Tribalism has begun to
give way at last, but instead of leading to a multifaceted democracy of some sort, it has devolved to the politics of personal power, but with an old-fashioned Stalinist flavor. The
single party in Kenya, the Kenya African National Union, or
KANU, provides the basis for the wide-ranging powers of
the President. The secret ballot was outlawed more than two
years ago, so troublesome political upsets are scarce. Every
member of the rubber-stamp legislature is a KANU member,
so debate in the Kenya legislature, which once enjoyed a reputation for colorful and vigorous forensics, is now limited to
personal attacks on other members and speeches in praise of
the President. Typically, legislative seats are passed from a father to other members of his family and as personal power
increases tribal loyalties are gradually becoming less important than family ties.

Dissent — even apolitical protest — is suppressed quickly
and in harsh and personal terms. Recently, for example,
KANU decided to destroy a large portion of the city's principal park, Uhuru Park, to build a sixty-story skyscraper, the
tallest in Africa, complete with two adjacent ten-story towers,
a huge convention and conference facility, and parking spaces
for 2,000 cars, despite the huge convention and office facility
that already exists only a few meters away. A four-story-tall
statue of Moi is planned to grace the front of the complex.

The building and the statue will cost almost US $200 million and, despite the availability of other, more suitable building sites elsewhere in town, will destroy much of the park — a monument to civic pride when it was opened by Kenyatta shortly after independence. I have never been near Uhuru Park and seen it less than crowded, and with good cause, since the park provides the only inexpensive recreation in a city that not only provides little for the poor, yet seems willing to spend $200 million on a skyscraper and a statue of the local Ozymandias. In Uhuru Park, there is a small pond with rowing boats, pathways provide sheltered places for strolling, and the tiered landscaping of the park provides a pleasant view of the city. The KANU building proposal for Uhuru Park is similar to giving away most of Hyde Park or the Jardin du Luxembourg to office-block developers. Quite naturally, the plan was denounced by most white Kenyans and many liberal black Kenyans.

But one influential Kenyan, Mrs. Wangari Maathai, a dedicated environmentalist and the popular leader of Kenya's Greenbelt Movement, took the matter to court. Not only was it dismissed, but Mrs. Maathai's personal life and her marital record were brought up in parliament. She was roundly and very publicly ridiculed, even by the President himself. Her movement was branded "subversive" and thrown out of the offices given to it by the government, and she was held up to the nation as an example of a troublemaker. Her suppression was complete and final: The High Court, once a symbol of the integrity of Kenya's independent judiciary, but recently seen as a casualty of the government's drive toward thorough authoritarianism, refused even to hear her case.

Not only do individuals face ruthless retribution at the hands of an apparently nervous government, but so do whole groups of undesirables. The Kenyan government recently instituted an official policy of racial oppression directed against the Somalis, an ethnic group that has become a scapegoat for most of Kenya's ills. The Somalis of Kenya were ordered to report to government screening centers to determine if they were Kenyan Somalis or Somalis from neighboring Somalia. Despite possessing birth certificates and passports, most were summarily imprisoned or deported. Children were left alone when army units swept through Somali neighborhoods, and Somalis were pilloried in racist terms as lazy, or dishonest, or primitive, or prone to senseless violence in the press and elsewhere. Those who have been allowed to remain are forced to carry pink ID cards, similar in every respect to the odious passbook system once employed in South Africa. One Asian Kenyan I know well is terrified: "We [Asians] have always been hated by the blacks here," he told me. "We think what they are doing to the Somalis, they will do to us next."

The director of one important international humanitarian agency told me that Moi's government is "among the worst, among the most paranoid" in Africa and that he is forced to travel into and out of the country using false or deceptive travel documents. When Kerry Kennedy, Robert F. Kennedy's daughter, came to Kenya in 1989 to give the humanitarian award named after her father to a political opponent of Moi's and to urge the government to stop the detention of political dissidents, she was roundly lambasted by government officials, members of parliament, and the local press.

According to one Kenyan, the government was using its white population as a resource to bolster its international image. "We will soon see whites appointed to positions of high visibility in ministries that are troubled," he predicted, and sure enough, within three weeks of our conversation, Dr. Richard Leakey, the son of Louis and Mary Leakey, Kenya's most accepted white family, was put in charge of the wildlife ministry, where inefficiency and corruption until recently had combined with increases in the price of ivory to create a poacher's paradise in Kenya. (Another Leakey son, Philip, has been a member of the Kenya parliament for years. He dutifully trots out for ceremonial events and generally serves as the government's exemplary white man — and certainly the only one sitting in any legislature anywhere in black Africa. But as a Kenyan journalist told me and as Mr. Leakey would no doubt dispute, he's there for show, a token honkie.)

But it is the long-term stability of the government, and not the country's short-term issues, that have most white Kenyans nervous. "Kenya wants to be a multiracial society," one up-country Kenyan told me. "They [the government] want to build a country that is stable. And we, the whites, want that, too, even more than they do. For us, stability is survival. So they must accept what we have to offer. If they don't, they'll decline into racialism, and they can't be seen to do that."

"There is a future in this country, but only as long as the present regime is in power," a white businessman in Nairobi told me. He was worried, he said, about the rising discontent among young black Kenyans, who, even after receiving university training, found there were no jobs. Every year I heard coup rumors from sources of varying reliability from everywhere between Mombasa on the coast to Kisumu on the shores of Lake Victoria, and by 1990 demonstrations in support of a multiparty democracy were routine, despite the increasing ruthlessness of the government in suppressing them. "This country is in the middle of a tremendous population boom," said the businessman, "and there are a lot of young school-leavers who have very high expectations. They see Western television, and they see government ministers riding about in big cars. The government must adjust to these people, because if the government goes, if the radicals get power, we go, too."

For some white Kenyans, whether the government stays or

goes, there's little point in making grand plans for their future in Kenya. "I would never suggest that a young man come to Kenya to make his future," one woman told me. "There is no future for the whites in this country. *Period*. We may have something to contribute, but it won't be accepted, not as long as the politicians can use us as an explanation for their cock-ups.

"I was born in this country, and so was my mother. But if the government changes or if there's trouble, I'll be tossed out without a moment's notice."

We were sitting on the terrace of the Norfolk Hotel, which, perhaps more than any other enterprise in Kenya with the exception of Lord Delamere's pioneering ranching efforts, best represents the success of postcolonial white enterprise in Kenya. For most of this century, the Norfolk has been one of the most important gathering places for white Kenyan society; its terrace bar provides a Saturday-night playground for young white Kenyans, much as it did for their ancestors — people like the remarkable early famed aviatrix Beryl Markham; the self-styled "White King of the WaKikuyu," John Boyes; and Berkeley Cole, another aristocratic pioneer — and other colorful characters who helped settle the country. Almost every important East African safari, including Teddy Roosevelt's famous 1909 expedition, has used the Norfolk as a jumping-off point.

Built in 1904, just after the railroad's arrival, by an eccentric English adventurer named Major C. G. R. Ringer, the hotel was purchased in 1927 by Abraham Block, who originally had come to Kenya as part of Joseph Chamberlain's refugee resettlement program and whose family operated the hotel until 1989. In March 1989, the Norfolk, along with a number of other old-line Kenyan hotels, including the Aberdare Country Club, was sold to a subsidiary of Lonrho, the

British conglomerate. Old-timers in Nairobi fear the worst for the Norfolk, but changes have been modest so far. Despite rumors of a high-rise block, the new owners seem determined to keep the hotel's modest scale and to emphasize its personal service, the secret to its success. Throughout the year, weddings, receptions, cocktail parties, and corporate bashes are held at the Norfolk; resident Kenyans of all types jam the lobby and crowd the banquet rooms or, from seats at the tables along the rear wall of the terrace bar, amuse themselves by watching the antics of the tourists. Generally, the mood is the same a guest would encounter at any typical British provincial gathering.

The Norfolk is irretrievably a part of the story of whites in Kenya, an institution. In fact, as I sat chatting with the woman, her fears and pessimism seemed to be betrayed by the sudden appearance of some familiar local whites, showing up to celebrate a birthday. We watched them for a moment, and as she acknowledged her acquaintances, she told me that last year twice as many people had been around for the same occasion. She seemed almost pleased to be making the point, but when she claimed that if things turned nasty in Kenya, the Norfolk would be among the first places to go, I was doubtful. The hotel seemed such a permanent fixture that it seemed to me highly unlikely it would fold under the pressure of change. And I said so.

She only shrugged. "There's something we always know here," she said as she rose to join her friends. "It's something we always remember: If things go wrong, you're a white man in a black man's country."

▼▲▼▲▼

Africa is a continent rich with the possibility of high adventure, a place full of perilous exploration and surprising dis-

IN THE NEIGHBORHOOD OF NAIROBI

coveries, which is why I was on my hands and knees in the damp, steamy night, brushing back thick spiderwebs and straining against the blackness looking for my guide, a local chap named Walter. It was one of those situations in which we seasoned correspondents find ourselves now and again, where any loud noise, any sudden movement could lead you off the narrow ledge of safety and into the yawning abyss of anarchy and trouble.

I had forgotten to bring a flashlight. In fact, I didn't own a flashlight. Walter had a flashlight he had borrowed from his cousin, but the batteries were low and the dark night swallowed its dim, yellow beam. I was ready to give up, to retreat in failure, to join the long list of those defeated by Africa's inexplicable ways, when suddenly I heard Walter whisper urgently. I couldn't make out what he was trying to say, but I heard him carefully moving the full, glass bottles and I knew we'd finally found what we'd been seeking: the last nineteen bottles of Diet Coke left in Kenya.

We carefully wrapped newspaper around each bottle, stacked the wrapped bottles in a cardboard box, and made for the door, just ahead of the bottling plant's smiling watchman, Walter's cousin, who had warned us he could get yelled at if his boss found out anything about all this and that we should beat it before the other watchman caught on. Walter tossed him the flashlight, and we were gone.

Our dark world is illuminated in flashes of scandal, some big, some small. The lapse in production of Diet Coke in East Africa is a small scandal indeed, but one not without irony. In a country that less than ten years ago depended on the fluctuations of the international coffee market for its fortune, tourists have become the new cash crop. Little more than twenty-five years ago, tourists in Africa were so rare they commonly wrote books about their experiences. Last year, the 700,000 visitors to Kenya wrote of their experiences on postcards. In the course of two lifetimes, Kenya has gone from tribal warfare, famine, and pestilence, through colonialism, past independence to discount wholesale tour marketing. Men whose grandfathers had never seen a white man are now entrepreneurs in a booming souvenir economy, where almost every nuance of cultural experience can be dummied up in a hurry and staged for the benefit of a busload of Belgians.

The fact that, thanks to me, Kenya, at least for that moment, was a nation bereft of Diet Coke was perhaps the one concession to tourism Kenyans had not been willing to make. Maybe it was the line they had drawn for themselves; maybe Coke Classic is the point to which they will move and they will move no further. I retired to my air-conditioned hotel room to eat potato chips, drink ice-cold Diet Coke, and watch *Jaws III,* that night's video offering, just as I had planned. But I couldn't help thinking that something had changed in Kenya, something small in scale maybe, but large in implication. There was a new wind blowing across the dark continent, and it smelled to me like Obsession and Old Spice.

I could barely follow the movie — same old fin, same old water. The next day, I figured, if it wasn't too hot, I'd jump into my rented Suzuki and see if I couldn't find a little bit of Africa someplace in the neighborhood of Nairobi and maybe even take a snapshot or two.

There was a *squadra* of Lancias lined up next to the Norfolk Hotel, Kenya's quintessential settler inn, and the lobby was chock-full of Italians in town for the Marlboro East Africa Safari Rally. Great, gasping crowds of tourists swarmed over the Lord Delamere Terrace Bar to get to the sightseeing buses clustered out front; Americans stood elbow to elbow with French tourists; a platoon of binocular-draped, olive-drabbed

Germans maneuvered into a couple of Land-Rovers, and in
the background I spotted a canceled TV star, the blond cop
from "Cagney & Lacey," I think.

There's something about boys and jeeps and Africa that
makes a movie. I shoved a Dutch cheroot in my mouth,
flipped down my shades, mounted my 4WD Suzuki, and, in
the company of Alan Rose, a redheaded, well-mannered photographer, pulled out into traffic. Twenty minutes later, I
turned left, and thirty minutes after that, I turned right and
pulled in behind a van that was painted with black zebra
stripes and filled with holidaymakers from the profitable side
of the Pacific rim. Out the window, I watched the colorful pan-
orama of East Africa unfold. Obsessively neat Indian shop-
keepers stood behind counters in arcaded blocks built to
Bombay standards by their fathers, whose own fathers had
been brought over at the turn of the century to lay track for
the railway through Kenya, the railway that had resulted in
the invention of Nairobi; neatly dressed panhandlers lined the
sidewalks, each guarding his four-foot turf, and men in Peter
Max-width bell-bottoms and bearing plastic elephant hair
bracelets chased wandering groups of tourists; I saw an American girl turn on her Timberlands and indignantly tell a bracelet
vendor that she "didn't buy products made from elephants."
So he asked her if she wanted to change some money. Then he
asked her to give him some. I took his picture out the window; he disappeared down an alley next to the market and
next to a warren of stalls, each selling identical hand-carved
artifacts, some all the way from Taiwan. On a corner, I saw
two disco-dressed Kenyans bearding a pair of backpacking
coeds and an earnest-looking young man wearing an Aussie
outback hat, and as I inched forward I heard one of the men
say "from South Africa," and I knew the the rest of the story:
a friendly greeting from an exile from South Africa, a ques-

tion about where you're from, a question about the American Indians (or Australian aboriginals or whatever fits), a question about why blacks have to live in poverty, a question about colleges and universities, and, after a cold drink, the long tale of woe — how they narrowly escaped from South Africa, how the white racists took everything they had, how the poor folks at home are trying to send them money, how the problems with the South African rand made exchange ridiculous, how so many kind people have helped, how they have to catch a midnight freighter to Djibouti on their way to Boston (or Adelaide or Toronto or wherever fits), and finally a request for a loan — three, four hundred dollars, that's all. For education. For justice. For the future. Ask for proof, maybe an identity card, ask to take a photo, and, with a farewell volley of accusations of racism, they're gone. Last year, it was Ethiopia. Year before that, Uganda. There's a bumper crop of outrage everywhere in Africa — it's a renewable resource — and a good con man can take his pick and reap a harvest nurtured by guilt and good intention.

Students, businessmen, workers, Nairobi's employed citizenry whose shy politeness is often mistaken for passivity, clogged pedestrian crossings and wove their way around Nikon-laden students, businessmen, workers from the rude north who blocked traffic while they took pictures of cute African women and funny African beggars. Busy civil servants made their way toward the government offices, often dodging hurtling *matatus*. Each *matatu* is fitted with a camper shell, bad brakes, faulty steering, and bald tires, and each *matatu* carries a phenomenal load of compacted passengers, many of whom are diverted from their destinations and sent instead nonstop to heaven when something breaks down or when their pickup swerves into oncoming traffic.

Nairobi's no Mexico City or Calcutta, but it's no Pleas-

EACH *MATATU* IS FITTED WITH BAD BRAKES, FAULTY STEERING, AND BALD TIRES.

antville, either. The city's services are crumbling under the pressure of an unprecedented population explosion and a concurrent boom in the unemployment industry. The city is ringed by temporary neighborhoods, rambling districts of corrugated mayhem that are thrown up overnight each night by thousands of newcomers from the economically depressed countryside, each hopeful of finding work and each likely to find only disappointment. The capital's highways disintegrate as they thread through these grim precincts; the heavily cratered tarmac is marked by precipitous edges, reducing the space on the road to just enough room for a single file of traffic on which two constant streams of trucks, buses, *matatus,* and automobiles confront each other at high speed. The object of the game is to see if you can just touch the side mirrors of oncoming vehicles with your own mirror. A soft "tick" is good, a "crack" can be very dangerous, but a miss can be catastrophic. There's double fun at night, when the motorists of Kenya demonstrate the efficacy of their high-beams — the better, no doubt, with which to see you.

Out beyond the Hilton, on the other side of the tracks and past the freight yard, around the bend from the National Stadium and just down the road from The Bomas of Kenya, where Africans in native garb dance the wild dances the tourists dream about, is Nairobi National Park, the capital's own drive-through zoo. The park is home to a small pride of sleepy lions, a few giraffes, a mess of antelope, some brazen baboons, a penned-up black rhino, and an animal orphanage. It's the smallest park in the country and backs up onto the runway at Wilson Airport, the terminal for all tourist flights to other, outlying game parks. I had been out there several times before, but it was always during the off season — the period between March and July, when the prices fall with the seasonal rains. Now, however, tourists were in season, and

NAIROBI NATIONAL PARK, THE CAPITAL'S OWN DRIVE-THROUGH ZOO

Nairobi National Park was my goal. I followed the creeping trail of traffic out the Langata Road until I saw the park entrance, an imposing gate very similar to the entrance to Adventureland in Anaheim.

The place was jammed. Minibuses, rented cars, and Range Rovers with diplomatic plates filled the parking lot. Off to one side, a small kiosk sold ice cream and straight ahead was the ticket window. A tail of cars and vans waiting to enter the park stretched out through the parking area almost to the main road. I parked the Suzuki, bought an ice-cream sandwich, and watched the vehicles slowly inch forward toward the entrance gate, while Rose wandered off in search of the photo of a lifetime.

Once, I watched Ringling Brothers unload a circus train in California. The roustabouts and the performers all worked together dragging the animals off the train in small cages with the wheels attached. The bigger animals — llamas, elephants, three dozen horses, some camels, and the like — pretty much took care of themselves, but the big cats came in boxes. They looked angry. I remember that I sat on the loading dock of a warehouse and watched the animals pass on their way to what I imagined was the big top, but what was really a downtown convention center surrounded by motels.

Same deal, different wildlife, and after twenty minutes watching angry people in cars, and after a serious sunburn on *top* of my head, I was ready to go back.

The Amboseli plain: the lazy circling carrion birds.

No sure horizon here, only the liquid images of heat, the pervasive heat, shaping a sea out of dust that breaks against the flanks of distant Kilimanjaro.

If I were going to find a little Africa in an ocean of tourists, I thought, it might be useful first to find somebody with a

little navigational skill. So I'd enlisted the aid of my friend
Tim Corfield, a pro safari guide, and, along with Rose, we'd
gone off to look for big game. Elephant, to be exact, since
Corfield is an elephant expert.

You'd think spotting an elephant would be easy. And sometimes, it is. In your bathtub, for example, or down your
girlfriend's blouse. But Africa's big, bigger than Michael Jackson, and an elephant can simply disappear into the continent's vast, well-mapped tracts. Corfield was the man for the
job, I thought. He was the author of an incredibly useful
handbook, *The Wilderness Guardian,* which covered most
facets of life outdoors, from ambushing poachers to tran-
quilizing a rhino to getting a Land-Rover out of a raging river.
He had studied elephant behavior for years in Tsavo, and he
had been one of the most active antipoaching experts in
Kenya. Besides, Corfield looked right for the job: rugged cotton shirt, chinos, high-topped boots. In the movie of his life,
Corfield is the glamorous star, with perfect brown hair, perfect straight teeth, perfect manly jaw. In fact, Tim Corfield
looks the way you *think* you look when you feel great and
aren't looking at yourself in a mirror. He's redeemed only in
that he has as much trouble with women as the rest of us. He's
better with elephants.

So when I called Corfield, I knew what I was doing. I figured we'd go down to Tsavo or out to Amboseli, spot a dried
flake of elephant spoor, get down on our bellies, and slide behind a rock while we watched elephants go through all their
secret, almost human rituals. Instead, we went up a dirt track
to the west until it gave onto a small rise so we could watch
the plain below us. A dense copse in the distance marked a
tourist lodge; you could see the swimming pool of another
nearby to the south and an airstrip just beyond them both.

"We look for elephant, right?" I said as I whipped out my
binoculars. Rose, a study in scarlet after a few days in the

equatorial sun, screwed on his five-foot telephoto lens and said nothing. Neither did Corfield. We stood on the rocky outcropping for maybe five minutes, the hot wind blowing gently, all of us leaning forward, me looking through my binocs, Rose telephotoing the plain below, and Corfield holding his hand over his brow, like Cochise, to shield the sun. We looked damned statuesque. "It's too hard to look for elephant," Corfield finally said. "Look at the way the cars and minibuses are moving." I didn't get it, but Corfield had already made his find: "There!"

He pointed at a distant part of the plain, a convergence point for what looked like a white minibus demo derby. Isuzu Troopers, Land-Rovers, and dozens of passenger vans were flying across Amboseli's dusty, rutted roads. "Come on," Corfield said. "Let's go."

We jumped into the car, and Corfield roared off in pursuit of a trail of various vehicles. "The guides get bigger tips if they find lion or elephant," Corfield explained as he struggled to keep control of the wildly bouncing Suzuki. He explained that while there are still clients who expect intimate, sometimes luxurious old-fashioned tented expeditions like the ones he customarily leads, most tourists who come to East Africa come with certain well-defined, limited expectations. "It's just a quick guided tour and checking off animals on a checklist," he said. "Once you've seen animal A, you move on to animal B and check it off, and so on. When they [the tourists] get back to camp they feel satisfied with what they've checked off on their lists. They've seen what they came to Africa to see." According to Corfield, the better way is to "spend some time when you spot an animal. Let the silence soak in. Try to understand what you're seeing. I mean in the old days, you'd never conceive of going on a safari and taking less than a month over it. You'd have to take the country as it came. If you came across a flooded river, you'd wait. You might be away for months."

For most of the first half of this century, most tourists who came to Kenya came well armed. Almost all the safaris that left Nairobi were hunting expeditions: large, expensive paramilitary operations, with lots of porters and trucks and good china and a decent chef. Allen Spaulding, who went to Kenya in 1930 on an expedition with the Buffalo Museum of Science in Buffalo, New York, told me that in three months he put 2,600 miles on his hunting vehicle — an old automobile. "There weren't any roads, and there weren't any bridges. It was just across open country with a good, heavy rope. When we came to to a river or a stream, they tied the rope around the car and twenty-five or thirty men went on the end of the rope and pulled it through. It was strange, in a way. Imagine me, a nineteen-year-old, having two servants and a tent attendant who waited on me at the table; he washed all my clothes and generally took care of things — made the bed, of course, that sort of thing. After breakfast, the gun bearer would come in and pick up my binoculars — you lived with binoculars. I've still got them, a Zeiss pair. Cost me twenty dollars, the best in the world. We left two days before Christmas and came back just before the rainy season in the spring."

The exploits of early settlers, like Karen Blixen, and hunters, like Hemingway, helped create a market for travelers looking for a little romance off the usual tourist trails, and, gradually, as the number of nonhunting visitors increased, local businessmen started selling more streamlined holiday packages. Shenti Sheth, now a senior executive of Nairobi's giant United Touring Company (UTC), described to me the way tourists were treated by early entrepreneurs. As a young man, Sheth had come to Nairobi in 1942 and gone to work for Gibbs, a car-hire company that had gradually moved into the safari business and eventually merged with other tour operators to form UTC.

"When you decided to take a safari in those days," he told me one day, "you wrote us and we corresponded about the sort of itinerary you required. When you arrived, we met you at the airport. We took you to your hotel and then we discussed cars and drivers. In those days, a hotel room at a good hotel — the Norfolk or the Queens [now defunct] — was about twenty shillings [$4.00, in the 1940s] a day. Car hire was about fifty cents [about a dime] a mile." A first-class safari cost less than $500 — about the same amount a modern visitor would pay for a quick visit to a place like Amboseli. "But," Sheth added, "in the early days that was quite a lot of money." Gibbs, he said, didn't cater to budget travelers, but it did offer quality service and efficiency. Sheth recalled an incident in 1942 when "two Italian gentlemen" reserved a car for a private safari and paid for the vehicle in advance. Sheth duly delivered the car to the men at a prearranged site. The men drove the car away into Uganda. Only later did Sheth learn that the two men were escaped POWs from a prison camp in the Aberdares.

Budget safariing in the early days of tourism was a much more casual proposition. Karl Pohlmann, the founder of one of the country's largest minibus tour operations, told me he started his business in the midfifties driving tourists through the countryside in a secondhand Ford Fairlane: "Never once got stuck, either," he said. He would raise clients at the local hotels and was among the first to try to attract cost-conscious vacationers who were interested mainly in sightseeing and photography.

According to old-timers like Sheth and Pohlmann, two principal factors changed the nature of tourism in Kenya. The first was the introduction of low-cost jet travel. "It used to take two or three days to come down from London," Sheth recalled, "and our customers were never middle- or lower-class people. They were people who had a very good idea of what they wanted when they came to Kenya. It was relatively expensive." By the early 1960s, BOAC and other carriers were offering two-week East African holiday packages and the safari companies had to develop new strategies for dealing with a more democratic clientele.

The second major factor was the abolition of hunting in Kenya in 1977. "Now that there are no hunters out there to provide feedback on poaching and the like, the government has a pretty free hand," one former professional hunter told me. "The month after hunting was abolished, thousands of elephant were killed, hundreds of rhino. It was a bloodbath. Still is."

The half dozen or so professional hunters with whom I spoke all agreed that organized hunting helped control the animal population and provided a sort of police force that most poachers feared. "Now the poachers don't even fear the [Kenyan] army," one retired hunter told me. "And why should they? The military's behind a lot of the poaching anyway." In fact, the head of Kenya's army was recently asked by two visitors how long it would take him to end poaching if he *really* had to. "Two or three days," he replied.

After a decade of corruption in Kenya's wildlife management agencies, the final straw came in 1988, when tourists started getting killed by poachers in game parks. The U.S. government imposed a travel advisory, tour bookings started declining rapidly, and suddenly the big-zoo aspect of African safariing was scaled back to something more in line with the historical overview, which is to say to an Africa where roaming about the countryside can be quite dangerous to man and beast.

The Kenyan government responded by overhauling its wildlife department and installed Leakey, chairman of the East African Wildlife Society and a vocal critic of the government's previous policies, at the top, despite his open assertions that senior government officials were involved in poaching and his long-established habit of publicly discrediting the government's artificially low poaching figures. One of Leakey's early comments following his appointment suggested his interest in reintroducing controlled hunting as a way of monitoring poaching in the game parks.

▼▲▼▲▼

We are getting thoroughly off the track here, but those arriving in Nairobi with the idea of exploring parts of Kenya not accessible by rail could do worse than hiring a plane or car and simply aiming for the more isolated parts of the country. At least by visiting the unlikely destinations it might be possible to escape the tourist crush.

In exactly such a frame of mind, I went one day to see Kenya's oldest game-park warden and perhaps its most famous: George Adamson, perhaps the greatest lion tamer since Daniel, who lived in rugged isolation in the middle of the Kora National Reserve, surrounded by a hundred miles of scrub and a handful of lions. Adamson, the husband of the murdered Joy Adamson, author of *Born Free* and other books, occupied a simple, thatched lean-to from which he solicited donations for his famous lion research project and, in turn, donated his own services — along with his petrol, and, from time to time, his new Land-Rover — to the rangers in charge of policing Kora and keeping it free of poachers.

Without a week or so to spare, one can't just drive over to George's house. His camp — called Kampi ya Simba — was one hundred miles or so from the nearest small settlement. To see Adamson, you have to fly, and to fly, you have to ingratiate yourself with the fearsome Seton family — dad, uncle, kid.

The Seton son was a wonderful fellow and a very good pilot to boot. I had flown with him out to Timau once and I
planned on flying with him to Kora. I made arrangements
with dad Seton, who told me that Adamson had no provi-
sions for visitors, so I'd be more welcome if I brought along
some food. I dutifully showed up at the airport with a half-
dozen cooked chickens and sandwiches supplied by the Norfolk's kitchen.

That's when I met uncle Seton. He didn't just suggest that
maybe something more substantial would be in order, he
screamed it. Since I had no way of knowing what was expected of a visitor to Adamson's except what his brother had
told me, I felt somewhat embarrassed. With one of the Kenyan mechanics, I made a grocery run and returned with a
carload of vegetables, eggs, fruit, bread, and whiskey. That
seemed to mollify uncle Seton, who then okayed his nephew
for the flight.

I was met at the airstrip by Georgina Edmunds — known
as Doddie to Adamson — who had seen our approach and
driven several miles out to the airstrip to pick me up. She took
me back to Adamson's camp, where I chatted with the naturalist, watched him play with three new cubs he'd just adopted,
and ate a few of the eggs his cook had scrambled into an
omelet.

We talked a little about the trouble he was having attracting sponsors and how his presence had helped keep poachers
at bay. "They seem to keep away from here," he said of the
Somalis who had been threatening Kora. "They know how
much attention we get here."

Adamson was sanguine, and with cause. He had been
working in the Kenyan bush for a generation and more. He
was well known, often discussed, and personally liked by
many. "We survive," he said.

A few months after my visit, Adamson was gunned down

by Somalis as he went to the airstrip to greet another batch of Seton-delivered, grocery-laden visitors.

By mid-1989, the poaching problem in Kenya was out of control. The army, perceived publicly to be so deeply involved in the banditry, was not likely to be challenged by President Moi, who, like Jomo Kenyatta — and, for that matter, like most other African presidents — has spent most of his political career balancing the army against various factions in his government. And few members of the top echelon of the military are involved in the tourism business, so a drop-off in that sector is a matter of small concern to them. One thing is certain: Moi will not allow his grip on government in Kenya to be loosened for the sake of stopping poaching. By the middle of 1989, poachers had killed two tourists from Germany and an Audubon Society member from Connecticut. They had wounded three others. And they had murdered Adamson.

Following a pattern established when warnings about the ubiquitousness of AIDS in East Africa were widely published, instead of taking firm action, the government accused the Western media of biased reporting. "It's War Against Slanted Reports," said a headline in the *Kenya Times,* as if that would do the trick and end the problem.

Not likely. Poachers have killed nearly 50,000 of the 65,000 elephants that roamed Kenya's plains a decade ago, and the escalation in the value of ivory will hasten the end of the rest. Then Kenya will lose the $350 million tourists bring to the country each year, and President Moi will pray for a rise in the price of coffee, Kenya's second-largest cash earner.

Corfield thought the solution to the poaching problem was more likely to be found abroad than at home anyway. He had earlier described to me his work with wildlife management groups to promote a grass-roots effort in Europe, America, and the Orient to boycott all ivory products. "Only if we eliminate the demand can we stop the destruction of the elephant," Corfield had said. It seemed optimistic to me, especially in view of Japan's curious record of insensitivity on whaling and other similar issues. Nevertheless, in the summer of 1989, the wife of photographer Ian Douglas-Hamilton was dispatched to America to spread the word, the government of Kenya put together a big tusk-burning show in which they put the torch to their stockpile of seized ivory, and the U.S. joined other nations in banning ivory imports, thereby removing the responsibility for poaching a convenient distance from Kenya, at the expense of countries like Zimbabwe that had husbanded their wildlife resources more responsibly.

We were tearing along a dusty trail, flushing the guinea fowl out of the weeds, and, I thought, generally wreaking havoc on the local biosphere. I asked Corfield about the effect of tourism on Kenya's wildlife. "Almost none," he said in a hoarse vibrato. I was surprised. I had assumed that rampant tourism would have a horrible effect on the animal population, but Corfield claimed that poaching and the population explosion caused much more harm. "As long as tourists obey the rules, I really can't see they can cause much damage. In fact," he added, "when people come to places like Kenya in great numbers to see the wildlife, the financial impact of tourism can only be of ultimate benefit to the animals."

After a quarter hour or so, we came upon a huge, jostling herd of minibuses, all surrounding a massive bull elephant. We maneuvered our way into photo range. Corfield was a bit of a photo buff, so he and Rose exchanged f-stop information and aperture lore while the elephant hammed it up for the traffic. I was looking out the back window at another Suzuki approaching at high speed. As it drew closer, the driver suddenly swerved off the road and stalled briefly in the tall grass. There was another man in the front seat. He looked

THE ELEPHANT HAMMED IT UP FOR TRAFFIC.

at me and tilted his head almost imperceptibly toward the passenger in the back, a young woman with very important hair and a black bustier. We made eye contact, and she sort of smiled almost. I swear I recognized her. I swear it was Madonna. Really. Then she was gone.

▼▲▼▲▼

I guess I feel a little sheepish acknowledging the fact that I've spent a good deal of time in Africa and I haven't killed any animals there yet.

I tried once, quite recently, actually. I woke up one morning with a certain blood lust, a kind of cruel gleam in my eye, and set out to "murder some fish," to use a phrase favored by the current American President, a thin man who looks like a responsible grownup, like a banker, maybe, but who has demonstrated his inability to outwit seafood much more publicly than I. When it came time for me to play foil to fish, I went to a little fishing hole in the shadow of Mount Kenya. Nobody saw me fail except my colleague, Alan Rose, and he failed, too, so it's a wash, bar-tale-wise.

When I was twelve or fifteen I saw a picture of the Prince of Wales fishing for trout in Scotland. He was wearing a tie. I decided then that trout fishing was the way to go. Not only do I dress well for my intended meetings with great fish, but I also exercise considerable humanitarian restraint, insofar as I almost never catch anything. Sure, some awkward pubescent fly-chaser will sometimes bump into my caddis and weave itself a tale of entangled grief, but it's rare. So I fish often, and with great affectation, and with a high degree of ritual, and I almost never get my hands wet.

To kill trout in Kenya requires some malice aforethought, and, to be honest, except by begging a ride on a Nanyuki-bound freight out of Nairobi, it's not likely that a train passenger will find himself near a good fishing spot. Once, not too long ago, one could escape Nairobi by train and not be forced to confront either Mombasa or Uganda as a consequence. The line to Nanyuki, now used only for occasional freight runs and rare tourist trains, leaves the capital and runs north through Thika and Nyeri, where Baden-Powell is buried, to Nanyuki on the northern side of the mountain. That neighborhood — between say Nyeri and Naro Moru — is an angler's dream. Once, the train from Nairobi would pull into a pleasant, shady station like the one in Nyeri. A passenger with a certain disposition toward fish would alight, and he would be met by a vehicle from one of the lodges. He would be housed, fed, licensed, and given a stretch of water to beat and then directed to a bar full of liars who might listen impatiently to his complaints.

But something happened to trout fishing in Kenya. It remained, of course, a pleasant pastime for those who lived there. I knew a man who worked as a scientist at the United Nations Environment Programme in Nairobi; he had skin cancer on the back of his hand from holding a pole on too many sunny days.

Trout fishing as a pursuit of the casual traveler, however, declined in the 1960s and '70s. Today, very few tourists choose to forgo drives though game parks long enough to wade a stream. As a result, many of the lodges just aren't prepared when an angler shows up.

We stayed at the Aberdare Country Club, mostly because Tony Seth-Smith, who had told me a good many stories about lions, mentioned the place when I turned the subject to fish. Thinking back, I now realize he had mentioned it just after he had hesitantly broached the subject of his own favorite place, then, perhaps alarmed at my Waltonesque demeanor, needed an out. So it was the Aberdare Country Club for me and Alan Rose.

Once the Aberdare Country Club was, well, a country club. Wealthy people played golf and tennis there; a little engineering inspired a riffle or two in the stream that runs a mile or so below the golf links and an angling club was launched. But when the number of local wealthy types diminished, the club tried to compensate by bringing in tourists, and that was that. Finally, the country club was relegated to base-camp status for tourists bent on sleeping in a tree at the nearby Ark. Tourists would come in off the road and check in at the Aberdare Country Club. At a certain time, they would be packed into a minibus or two and taken off into the Aberdare National Park, where they would be lodged in an unusually uncomfortable wood-frame motel on stilts next to a watering hole of sorts. The idea was to stay up all night and watch warthogs and the like come and drink water and roll in the mud and fight with each other. This sort of thing goes on to this very day, and tourists are charged a pretty penny for it, too. I tried it once at

A STREAM THAT RUNS A MILE OR SO BELOW THE GOLF LINKS

the competitor's place, Treetops, but I guess I didn't get it or something. It reminded me of camping out, and as far as I'm concerned, camping out and hiking are the penalties assessed to the losing side in war. Anyway, they sleep in the trees, like zealous Druids. Maybe you just have to be in the mood.

Besides, the long-range view is just as good from the Aberdare Country Club or from the garden at the nearby Outspan, a truly great country inn, by the way, with a fine kitchen, a serviceable wine list, but no fishing. From either place you can sit in a sun-filled garden and look up at the snow atop Mount Kenya or far away at the Aberdare range.

The Aberdares rise beyond the country club's golf course, newly refurbished by the hotel's new owners, the Lonrho hotel subsidiary. Nobody seemed to want to go golfing when we were there, but there was a volley of activity around the tennis courts, the special province of the new manager, who admitted he knew little about fishing, but who nevertheless wished us luck.

Rose and I fished the Aberdare's stream for three solid days at the beginning of the rainy season. At first, the flow suggested a kind of trout nirvana, with plenty of rapids, runs, riffles, seams, and holes and a series of perfect-looking pools. Our sources in Nairobi had encouraged us to use a variety of gaudy wet flies or something called a "Mrs. Simpson," a peculiar fly that resembles the North American Montreal pattern. A couple of local chaps, though, said to go with a Royal Coachman. Two other Kenyans stood for a while observing us; they told us we were doing it exactly right and left laughing. We covered and re-covered the stream using about four different patterns and a few different sizes at various depths. When nothing worked, we tried nymphs, then streamers. Just to cover the gamut we even floated a few dry flies across the water.

By the third day, the water was high and muddy and we were high and dry. I stood in a place that I had claimed for myself on the first day, only to notice somewhat tardily that it was a lair for some animal; a freshly killed rat was on the doorstep. Normally, a fisherman likes to absorb his surroundings; in Africa, however, that can be risky. Huge tropical plants, like mutant escapees from a radioactive terrarium, dangled in the water; large, four-engine insects dived and strafed, while mosquitoes sucked blood from my neck. The thick bush was alive with unseen mammals. Rose suffered more than I did; I chain-smoked little Sumatra cigars, especially during the later hours of the day, when the lower end of the food chain woke up.

To make a long fishing story a short, truthful one, we didn't catch anything. Here's why: It was the wrong time of the year; the water was high and muddy; we had the wrong flies; we used incorrect presentation; we fished the wrong streams;

we crashed through the brush, making lots of racket and scaring the fish; after the first day, the weather was often rainy; the fish weren't hungry; there were no fish; we were lousy fishermen.

Most of all, we were in the wrong place. A few days later, we stopped by the Naro Moru River Lodge, best known, perhaps, as a base lodge for Mount Kenya climbs but boasting a guide service that will gladly put together fishing treks to streams higher up on the mountain, where the seasonal rainfall problem is relatively inconsequential.

So after three days trying to catch trout in Kenya, we thought the best use for our experience was to simply make a fishing story out of it. To try it out, I told my fishing tale to an elderly waiter in the railway station restaurant in Nakuru. He had grown up near Nyeri, he liked to fish, and he knew the Aberdares well. When I got halfway through my story, he started laughing, and the more I went on, the harder he laughed.

So I stopped. "I get it," I said. "There are no fish there, right?"

He couldn't stop laughing.

"Come on. Is that it? Nobody's caught fish there in years, right?"

"No, no," he said, gasping. "The stream below the country club is a very easy stream." He stopped to laugh again. "So. You must be a terrible fisherman."

I saw nothing funny in that.

PART
FOUR

———————

THE END
OF THE LINE

If YOU WANT TO SEE AFRICA GALORE, IF YOU WANT TO GET to the heart of it all, get to Kisumu, only four or five hours from Nairobi. If you're driving from Nairobi, take the road west out past Naivasha, scene of so much preindependence white mischief, and out past Elmenteita, where the soda lake is pink with flamingos. Then over a range of cloud-covered mountains, through lush green countryside, and down into the equatorial basin, down through the rain and thunder to a malarial backwater on Lake Victoria, to Kisumu.

But the better way to go, of course, is by train. You pass by what was once the highest station in the empire, but is now the highest station in the Commonwealth, and you'll pass the station at Equator, which is on the equator, and where the village children provide the most polite, pleasant company in the country.

But be careful when you pay your fare: If you're looking for a cheap and exceptionally pleasant way to go to hell, Kenya Railways has your ticket, since, true to its original purpose, for less than thirty dollars the railroad will transport you in considerable comfort from the lap of seaside luxury in Mombasa to a frightful stop at Malaba on the Uganda border, where those unfortunates bound for Kampala have to

**THE STATION AT THE EQUATOR, WHERE THE VILLAGE CHILDREN PRO-
VIDE POLITE, PLEASANT COMPANY**

get off the train and hitch a ride down the road to Tororo,
where, in theory, a Ugandan trail will be waiting to take them
to what in recent years has become a real dead end.

I was in Kampala once not too long ago as a crew member on
a freight flight. It wasn't charming there, so Uganda wasn't
some place I wanted to revisit, although I had inadvertently
flirted with circumstance and nearly wound up there despite
my best intentions. It had happened when, in the course of
writing a piece on Kenya for a magazine, I had decided to fly
along the route taken by the railway northwest from Nairobi
and Nakuru, along the Mau Escarpment, the dramatic eastern edge of the great Rift Valley.

It was a wonderful flight, very much out of a postcard. The land gradually rose below us as we flew over the deep crater at Susua, a holy place to the Masai, past the peculiar American-built satellite tracking station at Longonot, over the rift lakes of Elmenteita and Nakuru, and finally out over the great equatorial forests that cover the escarpment.

Past Njoro, the roads disappeared beneath the thick vegetation and we flew through squalls of rain. Out the window, I glimpsed occasional waterfalls and dark jungle pools. Africa is more plains and desert than jungle, but the heart of the continent seems to beat beneath that menacing green canopy, and it captured my attention, as it might yours. Suddenly, as if a line had been drawn by an impatient man, the forest gave way to fields thick with cane and tea, and in the distance was Lake Victoria, an endless, gray sea, disappearing along the horizon into an Africa far more brutal and far more complicated than the Africa that exists in Kenya. Here, along the shores of the great lake, Kenya took on more of the trappings of its neighbors. Villages seemed threatened by rampant vegetation, and the farms below us were small. In a valley, a circle of huts surrounded a single cow, and there a group of half-clad children waved to us from a grassy clearing on a flowery hilltop. Along the swampy shore of the lake, great flocks of waterfowl prowled the muddy flats, while hippos floated offshore. Small fishing boats were sprinkled across the lake, and from nearby Uganda, a huge cargo ferry made its way toward Kisumu. On the plains, the birds of death had circled slowly in the heat; here, noisy gulls swooped and floated on the air. Generally speaking, Nature seems to have a better sense of humor near the water.

We flew over Kisumu, where a trio of ancient, once glorious lake steamers sit rusting in the mud. We left the railway behind and turned north toward the invisible seam that divides Kenya and Uganda. We were aiming for Busia, scene of a re-

A TRIO OF ONCE GLORIOUS LAKE STEAMERS RUSTING IN THE MUD

cent cross-border incursion by rampaging Ugandans, who, as one Kenyan border guard told me, "want to be here, not there."

Like many such isolated settlements, Busia is a one-street town; the main highway is the main street. But you can go too far in Busia if you aren't careful. For in Busia, when you're out of town, you're out of luck and you're in Uganda. We circled the southern edge of the town, found the overgrown landing strip some five or six kilometers back along the highway, and landed. Dozens of children, all anxious to see inside the cockpit, converged on the airplane, terrifying me and the pilot, narrowly missing the spinning prop.

I left the pilot guarding the aircraft and hitched a ride into town on the back of a gravel truck, much to the amusement of the driver, who merrily tooted his horn at every opportunity and pointed up at the white man struggling to keep his balance atop a load of loose gravel. People laughed, children waved, and, eventually, the police stopped us, fined the driver twenty shillings, and told me to walk the remaining half kilometer into town.

I wandered through Busia's busy clutter of small shops and taverns, then out again to the road, where an endless queue of trucks — most driven by the hard-pressed Somalis who seem to dominate the East African transport industry — waited to cross from Kenya into Uganda. Two-man police patrols were everywhere. Occasionally, I stopped to chat with various drivers; the Ugandans seemed anxious to tarry; the Kenyans seemed anxious to leave. A small man brandishing a Coca-Cola waved to me from a storefront, and I sauntered over.

"You are a journalist." He was certain.

"Yes. Right."

"You must write that the Ugandans are animals."

"All right. But why?"

"Because they want to come here, to Kenya. And we hate them."

He escorted me along the dusty boulevard, pointing out bullet holes in walls, telling me stories of cross-border invasions and near atrocities embroidered with his disgust and introducing me to people who also spoke with great passion, but always in a language other than those I understood.

Finally, I reached the border. My escort fell away. I was alone.

Border guards armed with automatic rifles lounged against the gate that blocked the road; behind them, a small customshouse provided shelter for a few uniformed clerks. In the distance — maybe fifty meters or so — was the Ugandan border. Beyond, I could see a great crowd of people, all lined up beneath the Ugandan flag flying from a crooked pole alongside the road.

I loitered but a moment before a guard approached. "Where are you from?"

"Sorry?"

"You are not Kenyan. You must go to immigration." He pointed to the customs office.

"Why?" But he was already guiding me by the arm, past the gate, into the customshouse, and finally up to a short counter behind which a woman sat eating what appeared to be a sandwich. She asked to see my passport. I placed it on the counter and waited.

She looked idly at the passport, sitting there, eating slowly, pouring a cup of tea. Finally, she finished her meal, stood, stepped up to the counter, looked at the Kenyan visa in the passport, and said, "This is a single-entry visa."

"Yes?"

"You must go back and get another visa."

"Back to Nairobi? No. I have no wish to proceed to Uganda."

"No." She corrected me. "Back to Uganda." I felt suddenly very tired. She turned and poured another cup of tea.

"I haven't left Kenya since I arrived," I said. "My visa is still valid."

"How did you get here?"

"I flew."

She snorted, then went to another small office, where she chatted in Swahili with an unseen man. She came back once, took my passport, then disappeared again. I could hear her talking, and the man seemed to be agreeing. Then they both left out a rear door. I sat waiting for an hour, two, three. Occasionally, someone would wander in, look around, wait fifteen minutes or so, then leave. It was hot and dry, and my initial anxiety at being caught up in some weird immigration folly at last gave way to fatigue, and I nodded off from time to time.

Suddenly, a door slammed, and I heard the man and woman reenter the back room. Both of them were talking loudly, boisterously. I heard some papers being shuffled, and a telephone call was made. Then, at last, the woman returned, smiling broadly.

"Yes," she said, cheerfully. "You must return to Kampala for the proper visa." I tried to protest, but she only waved me off.

I felt dizzy. I took my passport, walked out the door, looked to my left and into Uganda. My previous visit over that border had been during a particularly turbulent Ugandan episode, and I didn't want to go there again. The hideous excesses of Idi Amin — now encamped on the Zaïre-Ugandan border, waiting for Ugandans nostalgic for a president that not only killed them, but also cared enough for them to actually eat them, to rise up and demand his return — have segued into the hideous excesses of Yoweri Kaguta Museveni and his bloodthirsty crusade of national salvation. Only a month or so earlier, I had had dinner with a chap just returned from an assignment in Kampala. He had met with the man who ran the Ugandan government's commission investigating human rights abuses, but had had to leave early when the man unexpectedly and without provocation began first insulting his visitor, then declaring that his visitor's mother enjoyed a hefty measure of carnal eccentricity. Uganda is racked by disease, including an epidemic of AIDS, and in the eastern provinces, people following the dictates of a crazy woman who claims divinity are dying at the hands of the army, for she has convinced her followers they cannot be killed. In February 1990, Museveni canceled the permits of all foreign journalists in the country and had two Ugandan journalists imprisoned after

the two men "defamed" visiting Zambian President for Life
Kenneth Kaunda by asking why, after twenty-five years in
power, he wouldn't step down and by asking him why Zambia's national airline provided service between Johannesburg
and New York when Kaunda was in the forefront of Africans
demanding sanctions against South Africa. (On the same day
in February, Malawi withdrew the credentials of its foreign
journalists for unexplained reasons, while in South Africa,
American TV star Ted Koppel, participating in the hoopla
that followed Nelson Mandela's release, expressed indigna-
tion that his TV crews hadn't been given free rein in the country because of emergency restrictions. Western journalists are
routinely harassed by African governments, which object to
unflattering stories that appear in newspapers and on television in the West.)

Uganda was once the colony of choice in British East Africa. But then came independence and the bloody reigns of
some of Africa's most vicious madmen — Milton Obote,
Amin, Obote yet again, now Museveni. These days, Uganda is
everybody's favorite African worst-case, although many other
countries rival Uganda in mass criminality. The Ethiopian
government, for example, has killed far more of its citizens
than the Ugandan crackpots have. Still, it's astonishing there
are any Ugandans left for their government to kill. At any
rate, I had no Ugandan visa — mine had been summarily
stamped "Cancelled" in Nairobi after I had asked the passport official there an apparently touchy question. I had wanted
to know if the train was still running between Tororo and
Kampala. So I stood outside the small customs office, where
I envisioned the smiling Ugandan immigration officer pointing to the smiling Kenyan immigration officer, and I saw myself shuffling between the two gates for eternity.

Then I noticed that the Ugandan border post, to my left,
was shaded by a large tree and surrounded by purple bougain-

villea and that, despite the dust kicked up by the ragtag group
of would-be emigrants, the far side of the border looked almost festive. I could hear people laughing; someone had a ra-
dio and I could hear the tin-can sound of syncopated African
guitars. To my right, the Kenyan post was surrounded by
sandbags; a military truck was blocking the road. The distance separating the two border posts was less than 200 meters, such a short distance.

I turned and retreated into the office. The woman was reading a magazine and sipping from her cup. There was nothing
I could say to her, so I walked back out into the sunshine,
smiling as if nothing were wrong. Then I turned right, toward
Kenya, nodded cheerfully at the border guard — the same one
who had sent me inside to immigration. This time, he saluted
and gravely waved me through without so much as a glance at
my passport.

▼▲▼▲▼

So if you take the train from Nairobi, avoid Uganda, if you
can. Kisumu, formerly Port Florence, is close enough.

Unlike the dry and dusty ride up from Mombasa, the route
to Kisumu meanders first through the Rift Valley before
climbing the Mau Escarpment, but like the trip from Mombasa to Nairobi, the ride to Kisumu is in darkness most of the
way — a pity, really, since much of this route is ostentatiously
floral. The trip is slow going, cars on the road that more or
less parallels the track will reach Kisumu three times faster
than the train, which takes twelve hours to complete the journey. There is a downside to travel by automobile, of course.
Several times, just outside Nairobi, the railway crosses the
busy, narrow, potholed highway, where trucks, cars, and
buses merge metal in the middle of the night.

Long after dark, the train skirts the first of the three Rift
Valley lakes, the one at Naivasha, where large homes like the

NAKURU, AN ODD, MODERN-STYLE STATION BUILT IN 1955 DURING
THE TWILIGHT OF THE COLONIAL PERIOD

Djinn Palace flank the lake and where John D'Olier makes a
white wine that has, in the course of only a few years, gone
from the weird and fruity to what is now sold as Naivasha
White, a fine, dry wine, infinitely superior to the local papaya
wine that constitutes its only real competitor and better than
all the white plonk sold at my local state-run wine shop. Just
down the road is the excellent lodge at Naivasha, and nearby
is the home of Guy D'Olier, John's half brother, who is the
proprietor of a large and, owing to the great number of period
films now being made in Kenya, much used antique auto collection.

Much later, the train rolls into Nakuru, an odd station
built in 1955 in the most modern style during the twilight of
the colonial period. The station's dining room is my favorite
railway restaurant, but you'll get no service there in the middle
of the night.

Nakuru was a fabrication of Lord Delamere's, who lived

nearby. The town is an important regional center, one of the largest in the country, and while it's no metropolis, the station at least reflects the town's self-importance: vast, unused waiting rooms, platforms that stretch nearly back to Nairobi, railings to control the surging crowds. In fact, the crowd is out in front of the station, milling and gossiping in the pleasant open-air marketplace. In the town, there's a certain Old West charm, with an abundance of shops and stalls. I encountered an intriguing scam at Nakuru: Three kids point out a mystery liquid under your car. They inspect it, pronounce the situation perilous, and either offer to repair the damage themselves or take you to a reliable cousin who will do the work. If you leave the train in Nakuru, you'll find a couple of hotels — the Nakuru Inn, near the market, or, better, the Tropical, near the intersection of Moi and Kenyatta. But the accommodation of choice for tourists like us is Lion Hill, situated on the shores of Lake Nakuru, a national park where bird-watchers can watch more birds than they knew existed.

So a stop in Nakuru isn't a bad deal. From the station restaurant, you can see most of the town; from the lodge on the lake, you can see most of the park.

On the other hand, if you stay aboard the train, by morning, you'll be in Kisumu, and Kisumu, the original terminus of the railway, is trouble enough for most people. You'll find few tourists in Kisumu. But there is a Peace Corps office, a great deal of brightly painted, tumbledown colonial architecture, and, moored at the very end of the railway on the dock, three elderly steamers, including the S.S. *Nyanza,* which was assembled and launched in 1909, once in service on Lake Victoria.[1] Thieves have ransacked the old ships, and their brass fixtures ornament the town's bars and clubs.

You can meander down to a small amusement park that

[1] The *Nyanza* is the second-oldest ship on the Victoria service. The oldest is the S.S. *Victoria,* launched in 1907, which is, unbelievably, still in service in Tan-

KISUMU, THE ORIGINAL RAILWAY TERMINUS

has been set up in the center of town and check out the Ferris wheel, then walk over to the bar at the Imperial Hotel. That's where I went the last time I was there. The clientele is amusing and varied, and you'll have something cold to drink. Good food, too. Out by the pool, where I noted one of the *Usoga*'s brass telegraphs planted in cement, I encountered one of the other white people in Kisumu — a very blond American girl who was talking intensely to a local Lothario: "So, I go '*Shiiiit*,'" she was saying. "I mean, I'm like, 'Oh, *fuuuuck*,' you know?" He asked her how long she had been in Kenya, but I missed her answer. She had a peach of a sun-

zania. The other ships at Kisumu are the *Usoga*, launched in '13, and the steamer tug *Kavirondo*.

THE END OF THE LINE

burn, so I reckoned either she wasn't Peace Corps, or she was, but hadn't unpacked yet.

There are six noteworthy bars in Kisumu. One is at the New Victoria, a hostelry favored by the backpack set, and unless you want a lot of youthful, solipsistic sincerity with your beer, skip it. One is at Sam's Hotel, but the place is a Nemo-class dive. Two are at the Imperial Hotel, one is at the old yacht club, and the other is at the Nyanza Club, which is private.

I went to the Imperial to see if I could run down somebody who would go out on a limb and invite me to the Nyanza, but it looked like a bust. There was one Euro-type sitting at the bar, and while he didn't look very clubby to me, he at least looked miserable enough to have an interesting gripe, so I sat down and offered to buy him a beer.

"I'll buy you one," he said, introducing himself as someone other than Robert, the name I have given him, and explaining that he was living on the largess of the taxpayers of a European country. He was a development man, he explained, interested in finding new and improved ways of irrigating the local crops. I suggested he pump some water out of the ocean-sized lake outside, but he only grunted. "It's not so easy," he said, and then explained why at great length and in technical detail.

Robert had a lot to say. Throughout his conversation, he complained bitterly about the local bureaucracy, explaining that the local officials were incurably corrupt. At one point, he said that after seeing as much as 80 percent of donated funds go unaccounted for, his government now insisted on spending its development grants itself. "These people don't know how to run a country," he said.

I looked up at the bartender, who was glowering at the man as he continued to condemn the Kenyan government in personal terms, quite oblivious to the enmity he was generating. Nearby, a waiter was silently counting ceiling tiles.

Finally, I managed to change the subject to the local hangouts, and he allowed that the Nyanza Club had the best bar in town, and, after some really clumsy manipulation, he volunteered to take me there as his guest.

On the way over, he explained that all his friends would be there. The members of the club had once been mostly British expatriates, he said, but these days the membership roll was filled with Britain's social surrogates in Africa, the Indians, because there weren't that many Europeans left in the neighborhood and because most blacks didn't have the money to join. Robert was, he said, one of the few white members left.

By the time we arrived at the Nyanza Club, I was starting to regret my good fortune. Robert was driving me nuts. I had made a mistake by asking him about irrigating with lake water and opened a floodgate of tedious conversation. He talked nonstop about water flow and pressure valves, and all his similes and metaphors were expressed in hydraulic terms. I felt as if I were drowning.

And when he wasn't talking about T joints and gravitational flux, he was talking about Africans or Indians. On the subject of Africans, he vacillated between bigotry and patronization, and on the subject of Indians, he obsessed on the potential seduction of their wives. The guy was blind white and from a country with one of the worst colonial records to boot. A half hour in a car with Robert made Julie Andrews seem like a soul sister.

It started raining heavily, and Robert had put away more than a few publicly subsidized drinks, and, since he'd been buying, I had put away even more than he had. With well- and cistern-chat filling the car, we careered through the empty streets, turning down one that was quiet and residential and into the club parking lot. The place was empty. As we clattered through the rooms, Robert pinpointed the obvious: "Dart room. Billiard table. Loo. Bar." A sleepy barman sat on a cooler reading a newspaper. Above him was the ship's clock from the *Nyanza*. I ordered a brandy and soda and maybe one or two more and maybe one after that, and soon I was outside in the dark, stumbling through the rain, trying to see how close the club's golf course was to the lake and whether hideous amphibious creatures really did crawl out of it at night like the barman had said. I couldn't figure it out, and I was getting lost. I wandered around until I could barely make out the light in the barroom, where Robert sat drinking and upbraiding the bored barman. I made a beeline for the window and almost tripped over some crates stacked next to the wall.

Alone in the dark, I felt I had stumbled across some resource more precious to me than any of Africa's riches, some miraculous booty from a place closer to home, sent to me, I thought, as a sort of divine memo, a hearty handshake from heaven. Somehow, three cases of Diet Coke had been sent halfway to hell and ended up stacked in the rain outside a sleepy lakeside bar in the heart of Africa. I had kicked the crates with my foot, then looked down to see the familiar logo, the red-and-white oriflamme of refreshment. It is, as I think J. P. Donleavy once wrote, the random accumulation of unexpected victories that makes life worthwhile, and I suddenly felt full of life, full of wonder at the possibilities life afforded. I reached down to pull a bottle out of the top crate. A beer bottle. I pulled out another, and another. Three crates of beer bottles, all jammed in crates meant to contain Diet Coke. All empty.

DID HIDEOUS AMPHIBIOUS CREATURES REALLY CRAWL OUT OF THE LAKE AT NIGHT?

APPENDIXES
INDEX

A Lion Primer

Of all our sins and transgressions, to none do we attach more shame and to none do we confess more reluctantly than to Ignorance. Yet it is a shortcoming most readily absolved. For we may seek our Solace only in Absolution, and our Absolution in Illumination, such as that which might be obtained surveying the word of God and the works of man. If therefore you brave but untaught lads would know about lions, then you would know some of these things which with constant regard to your welfare have been set down here.

Habitat of the Lion

First, be comforted that *Felis leo* is not the largest of the big cats. The biggest tigers are bigger than the biggest lions, but admittedly it's a matter of inches, sometimes mere fractions. Like the average tiger, the average lion weighs 450 to 500 pounds. Zoologists can barely distinguish between the skeletons of the two animals — something in the skull, around the nose.

Disregard their similarities, for their differences are great.

"The characteristics of the Lion and the Tiger have been of late considered perfectly similar," wrote the French naturalist Baron Georges Cuvier.[1] "This assertion, contradicted by the ancients and early moderns, has wholly arisen from some remarks made by travellers to the Cape. No doubt, where similar appetites, similar propensities, similar means, and similar circumstances occur, a great similarity of character must be found. Although individuals are observed to be more undaunted and ferocious, in proportion to the increased distance at which they may be found from the habitations of mankind, more especially the civilized races, yet the Lion, we should submit, when compared with the Tiger, is a noble animal; he possesses more confidence, and more real courage; he likewise differs in his permanent attachment to his mate, and protection of his young."

In any case, lions are the most familiar to us. They have, it might seem, been with us almost from the start, raiding rude dwellings all over southern Europe, killing mothers and carrying off babies. At one time, people who lived on the northwestern coast of the Mediterranean couldn't leave their homes without concern for prowling lions. Lions appear in bas-relief and on artifacts from regions as widespread as Russia and Mesopotamia, often with depictions of them killing bulls or other powerful animals, as in Cretan pieces from 1500 B.C. More frequently, lions were enlisted in the cause of propaganda. Lion hunts were favorite motifs, especially in Egypt and Assyria, from the twelfth through the ninth centuries B.C. Invariably, lions were depicted as victims of some king out to prove the superiority of his majesty over the king of beasts. Finally, lions went international. Han Dynasty emperors in third century A.D. China are seen thwacking lions,

[1] *The Animal Kingdom* (London: 1828).

and in sixth century A.D. India local kings are shown throt-
tling the beasts. Lions were a favorite, if imaginary, prey of
youthful aristocrats through the Middle Ages,[2] and until the
turn of the century lions were hiding in the very cradle of
civilization, that is, in the swamps along the banks of the Tigris
and Euphrates; they were also found in southern Asia. Once,
long ago, there were lions in Israel. By the end of the first century A.D., according to Pliny the Elder, lions were "found in
Europe only between the rivers Achelous and Mestus [on the
northwestern Aegean coast], but that these far exceed in
strength those produced by Africa and Syria," perhaps because they were closer. As a result, lions have always enjoyed
the kind of cultural notoriety of which other species can only
dream. Ancient Greeks were routinely bothered by lions.
A youthful Herodotus (485?–425? B.C.) might have been a
potential victim. (Although not a particularly observant one;
working with old science at his disposal, he wrote that "a
lioness . . . the most bold and powerful of beasts, produces
but a single cub, once in her life."[3] Not true, of course; two or
three is the conventional litter size, and four is not wildly
anomalous. A lioness has a lengthy career of litters. But see
"Cub Myths.")

Were there lions also roaming the streets of Rome? Not since
at least 500 B.C. That's not to say that Romans were unfamiliar with lions, the martyr-eating stars of ancient amphi-
theaters. Pliny the Elder, a victim of the eruption of Vesuvius
in 79 A.D., claims to have put down 20,000 facts worth
knowing in his *Historia naturalis,* and many were borrowed
from Aristotle. Aelian[4] did the same a hundred years later.

[2] Jessica Rawson, *Animals in Art* (London: 1977).
[3] Herodotus, *The Histories,* Aubrey de Sélincourt's translation (Penguin).
[4] Aelian, *On the Characteristics of Animals,* translated by A. F. Scholfield (Loeb
Classical Library, 1959). Claudius Aelianus was born in 170 A.D. Aelian and

Plutarch wrote about lions, and so did Aesop. Until very recently, our science was our literature, our religion, and we invented it over and over again until it sort of made sense. We should not easily dismiss what might be called classical zoology.

Now, lions live only in Africa, and perhaps in a small corner of northwest India.

Lions prefer the tall grass country; they don't live in the jungle, as a rule, because life in the jungle is hard and lions are immensely lazy. On the grassy plains, a pride of lions will take the high ground, lie in the sun on a rocky redoubt, and watch their prey below in the valley.

MAN-EATING LIONS VS. MAN-EATING TIGERS

We have it on the authority of Denis Lyell, writing in *Memories of an African Hunter*,[5] that "the difference between a man-eating lion and tiger is that a lion may pass from game to man as opportunity offers, whereas a tiger usually sticks to humans once he has found how easy they are to kill. Another distinction is that man-eating lions have no hesitation in break-

---

Pliny the Elder share a wide-ranging encyclopedic interest in natural history, and despite the fact that Aelian, a Roman who was very proud of his skill at writing in Greek, never cites a Latin writer — preferring instead to claim that his miscellany of facts has been gathered from Greek writers only — some of his accounts in *On the Characteristics of Animals* also appear in Pliny (*Historia naturalis*, VIII, xix, 51). Of course, Pliny, along with Plutarch (*De sollertia animalum; On the Cleverness of Animals* to me, but translated as *Whether Land Animals or Sea Animals Are the Cleverer* in the Loeb Library series) and Aelian, among many others, mined the same sources. A particularly rich one was Aristotle's *History of Animals*, a special favorite of Aelian's.

Aelian had a journalist's sense of self-preservation: "True," he wrote, "these phenomena appear far from conformity to nature, but I have reported what I myself have seen and heard."

[5] London, 1923.

ing into native huts; whereas the tiger nearly always lies in wait for his victims near much-used roads or paths."

LION-EATING MEN

In a portion of *The Golden Bough* entitled "Homeopathic Magic of a Flesh Diet," Sir James Frazer remarks that among the tribes of central and southern Africa, it was common practice to eat the heart of a lion in order to gain the beast's strength and courage. Some of these same tribes would abstain from eating a rabbit in case the animal's timidity might be transmitted to the diner.

According to Paul Hoeffler,[6] natives on the shores of Lake Victoria hunt lions in order to harvest their fat, which they regard as a cure-all. Rubbing the grease from the fat on sore joints, for instance, is supposed to be a cure for rheumatism.

LIONS ON THE LINE

Here are two messages sent by alarmed stationmasters on the Uganda Railway to the railroad's traffic manager shortly after the line's completion.[7]

The first was telegraphed from Simba in August 1905:

"Pointsman [by "points" are meant "switches"; a pointsman's duty is to make sure the incoming train is put on the correct track as it approaches the station] is surrounded by two lions while returning from distant signal and hence points-

---

[6] *Africa Speaks* (Philadelphia, 1931).
[7] Both are quoted by Sir Alfred Pease in *The Book of the Lion* (New York: 1914; reprinted 1987).

man went on top of telegraph post near water tanks. Train to stop there and take him on train and then proceed."

The second was sent from Tsavo eight months later:

"2 down driver [meaning the engineer of the train bound for Mombasa] to enter my yard very cautiously points locked up. No one can get out. Myself Shedman Porters all in office. Lion sitting before office door."

According to Sir Alfred, the Uganda Railway was an attraction for local lions, who would come to drink from the spill around the water towers; at Simba station alone, one man shot three lions in a single night from the station's water tower, and "it was by no means rare" for lions to wander through the station buildings early in the morning.

DIFFICULTIES IN LOCATING LIONS

Aelian says that "the Lion when walking does not move straight forward, nor does he allow his footprints to appear plain and simple, but at one point he moves forward, at another he goes back, then he holds on his course, and then again starts in the opposite direction. Next he goes to and fro, effacing his tracks so as to prevent hunters from following his path and easily discovering his lair where he takes his rest. . . . These habits of the Lion are Nature's special gifts."

HUNTING AS SPORT

"In reflecting upon the constituents of field sports," wrote Sir Alfred Pease, "I have come to the conclusion that there are four principal ones, and that when all these are present the sport is entitled to be true sport: —

"1. Absolutely wild game the object of pursuit.

"2. Nature's field for the action.

"3. Physical exertion.

"4. Exercise of skill.

"By this standard there is no true sport in attacking or pursuing any animal anywhere, save when it is absolutely free in its natural haunts. . . . To fish fairly in river, loch, and sea; to hunt fairly with hounds or rifle or gun on foot or on horseback; to stalk and climb after wild sheep, goats, chamois, mouflon, and deer; to pursue big game — all these satisfy the conditions laid down."

"The actual killing," according to former professional hunter Tony Archer, "is less than ten percent of the sport. It's the actual being out there, it's watching an excellent tracker working, it's getting close to animals which could be dangerous under certain circumstances, it's that build-up of a certain amount of adrenaline. Mostly, it's completely alien to what a person is used to doing. However much hunting an American or a European has done, Africa is completely different.

"But actually being on the ground, that, I believe, is what hunting is all about."

Mr. Archer's perspective, of course, is that of a man who used to roam from Uganda to Kenya to Tanzania — all countries where hunting is either outlawed or severely curtailed — in search of trophy animals. But as that's all gone now, in the course of a conversation he fell to talking about alternatives.

"Somebody came up with an idea which might catch on," Mr. Archer said, "and it could be really quite fun. You can do a hunting safari with a rifle that has got a camera rigged up with a telescopic sight. You have to stalk [an animal], pull the trigger and take a snap, which would actually record how you did." He also toyed with the idea of shooting animals with little balloons filled with water paint, then photographing them. Or his favorite possibility: A hunter plays tag with his prey. The object is to touch the animal he's been stalking — say a bull elephant or a lion. That, he thought, ought to result in a "buildup of a certain amount of adrenaline."

LION-HUNTING EQUIPMENT

Do go well dressed:

BOOTS: RUBBER-SOLED AND LIGHTWEIGHT
TROUSERS: HEAVY COTTON OR DENIM
BINOCULARS   HAT
ONE LIGHT RIFLE   ONE SHOTGUN
EXTRA AMMUNITION   BANDAGES AND ANTISEPTIC
A HUNTING KNIFE AND A CAMPING KNIFE

LASSOING LIONS

Sir Alfred Pease saw this done and recorded it thus: "This extraordinary feat has been performed in British East Africa by Buffalo Jones and a party of American cowboys, who brought over their horses from the States for that purpose. They astonished the world with what they accomplished, for not only did they rope a lioness, but a very large rhinoceros, as well as other game, such as giraffe, eland, zebra, cheetah, etc."

LIONS AND THE DEAD

Since lions are not reluctant to eat from an old kill, even if the meat is quite rank, not a few observers of Patterson's toil — including Anthony Dyer — thought they must have enjoyed the funeral rituals of the Indians building the Uganda Rail-

way. Open-air burials, they thought, such as those favored by
the Parsees and other groups, must have contributed to a siz-
able glut of dead men left out along the roadbed, and it was
suspected that the lions at Tsavo developed a taste for human
beings after repeatedly eating the bodies of men killed by acci-
dents and illnesses and left behind by Indian true believers.

Other observers, such as A. L. Butler, the superintendent of
the Sudan's game department, quoted in Pease,[8] suggests that
it was "owing to the immunity from retaliation" after their
first round of man-eating that encouraged the lions at Tsavo
to keep coming back for more. Butler says this is because Africans are more courageous than Indians. That ignores the
fact that at least one hundred African natives were also eaten
at Tsavo during the time Patterson was there.

LIONS AT REST

Lions often hunt at night and sleep all day and may be un-
conscious for twenty of every twenty-four hours. Not infre-
quently, they will lay about for days between kills. Hunters
and photographers have noticed that a recently fed pride can
be approached with some measure of safety. This is not rec-
ommended, however.

Some witnesses say it's almost impossible to wake a sleeping lion. Sir Alfred Pease, in *The Book of the Lion,* tells of the
time in 1902 when a Nile steamer stopped in the Bahr el
Ghazal to gather wood for the boilers. For two or three hours,
the crew worked in the forest hacking down trees and dragging them back to the bank of the river. Finally, an elderly
tribesman came to the ship's engineer to warn him that a lion
was sleeping nearby. Taking the story with a good deal of salt,

[8] Sir Alfred Pease, *The Book of the Lion.*

the engineer grabbed a .303 and tromped off with him to look at the sleeping lion. After a short walk, the tribesman pointed to an anthill and told the engineer that the lion was sleeping near it. "There was nothing visible as he approached the anthill," wrote Sir Alfred, "and, with a little run to gain impetus, he scrambled on to the top of it, by no means noiselessly. To his astonishment, a full-grown lion lay fast asleep just below him." He shot and killed it.

THE PARTS OF A LION

Lions come equipped with tremendously strong jaws. Their canines are long, with sharp edges and points; the upper canines are nearly twice as long as the lower ones. The rest of the teeth in a lion's mouth are inconsequential, since lions don't grind their food, preferring instead to swallow huge mouthfuls of flesh without chewing. The function of the canines is to seize and hold large, struggling animals and to rip flesh from bone. But teeth are not the only tools available to the lion, of course. The tongue of the lion has a very coarse surface, with short, sharp, spiny protuberances that allow it to lick the skin off a dead animal, while its claws are like steel needles. After a kill, a lion will suck the blood from the meat of the animal, leaving a treasure of pale pink flesh from which the pride will eat briskly. Lions are designed to kill and eat their prey quickly. Lions never play with their food.

BLOOD LUST AMONG LIONS

Unless they are very hungry, lions are slow to anger. Once they are motivated, however, they do enjoy killing and, unlike most other animals, will kill for the pleasure it gives them. In

March 1988, a single lion got into the sheep on a ranch in northern Kenya; it killed four men and over sixty sheep in a few hours. It also ate one ewe. It was not an isolated incident.

CUB MYTHS

The reproductive process in lions was a source of early confusion: "I notice [wrote Pliny] that there used to be a popular belief that the lioness only bears a cub once, as her womb is wounded by the points of its claws in delivery [Herodotus; see "Habitat of the Lion"]. Aristotle, however . . . gives a different account. . . . [he] states that a lioness at the first birth produces five cubs, and each year one fewer, and after bearing a single cub becomes barren; and that the cubs are mere lumps of flesh and very small, at the beginning of the size of weasels, and at six months are scarcely able to walk, not moving at all until they are two months old."

MAN AS THE MEAL OF LAST RESORT

As a rule, lions turn to eating humans when they can't hunt and kill much of anything else. Hence, most man-eaters are old and infirm or crippled. Polybius (died ca. 120 B.C.), a Greek statesman and historian and the author of the *Universal History,* quoted in Pliny, claimed that in old age the favorite prey of lions is a human being because the lions' strength is "not adequate to hunting wild animals; and that at this period of their lives they beset the cities of Africa." Consequently, Pliny added, when Polybius was with Scipio Aemilianus (died 129 B.C.; Scipio was a victorious general in the Third Punic War and later the leader of a group of senators who avidly pursued the study of Greek historical and philosophic texts;

Polybius, though nominally a political hostage at Rome because of his efforts on behalf of the Greek Achaean League against Rome, was their mentor), he "saw lions crucified because the others might be deterred from the same mischief by fear of the same penalty."

Man-eaters often have broken or dull teeth, and frequently they have badly injured limbs, usually caused by deeply embedded thorns and infection. Once they get the hang of it, lions must find men easy prey; they simply wander into a village, browse confidently among the huts, and walk away with food, with no tiresome lunging and leaping, no desperate death struggles. While most man-eaters are damaged lions, there are some healthy prides that include humans among the repertoire of their prey, especially after they find how easy it is to kill a man.

WITH RYALL AT KIMA STATION

As promised, a shorter story for a shorter night.

My dear lads: —

To-day I send you this tale, full of death, disfigurement, murder, scandal, cowardice, blood lust, and especially deceit, with the fervent hope that you will be amused and edified by it, and see in it parallels with the horrors that lurk in our own modern lives. For these are terrible times, when the deadly beasts of fashion and rhetoric lurk unseen everywhere waiting, waiting in the camouflage that our poor educations have provided them — see, there! the petty politician disguised as civil libertarian. And look! the valet of totalitarianism wearing the cloak of compassion. When they are on us, we are dead. Dies Irae, O tempora, and all that.

Of all the tales I know, the most entrancing are those in which men of certainty meet their monsters. This should not be surprising, since there is something both terrible and compelling about stories of beasts who eat men who have long considered themselves inedible. There is good cause for this fascination, I believe; for in these stories we learn that we are betrayed by those whom we fear most, yet most often seek to befriend. In short, we can be undone by our most noble and reasonable intentions. As my old friend Henty nearly said, we are more often misled by a plausible impulse, even more often perhaps than by an evil one, but the consequences may be just as serious in the one case as in the other.

Should you be so misled and find you are in the thick of trouble, you should always go to the most distant corner of the brain, where sleep our constant fathers — objective thought and difficult reasoning — wake them and ask their counsel. Hide nothing, for in most cases, cowardice lies at the bottom of concealment, and cowardice of all vices is the most contemptible. Remember always that should you have to face their temporary displeasure, it will be a small thing in comparison with the permanent injury that may arise from acting without thought. So lay the case frankly and honestly before them, my boys. You will there obtain such good advice as that which would have saved the life of poor Charles Henry Ryall, a dreamer.

Dreams are there in our handshake with sleep; we meet them when first we enter. Who has not had the experience of eating a large roast, then sitting politely while a particularly long-winded and emphatically incorrect uncle pontificates on neighbourhood politics of small consequence? It is then, at the first moment your eyes close and your head nods, that you see the other side, where your dream lives, and when the dream is over, a deeper sleep begins. Then, as a rule, you awaken.

Now, the end of the dream of Charles Henry Ryall, only twenty-five years old, early in the morning of 6 June 1900, unfolded perhaps like this: a soft, low moan, almost like the sigh of an old man; then the gentle rocking. Perhaps in his dream he is at sea with his ancient grandfather. Next, the warm, wet air. He conjures the tropics. He is floating on the soft swells. The waves lap gently on the shores of paradise. Mr

Ryall at that moment was dreaming a dream so sweet it should have never ended. A disappointment, really, that it wasn't about dentistry, for if he had opened his eyes in time, the last thing Charles Henry Ryall would have seen was teeth, for he died face-first in the mouth of the beast.

Now, dear lads, we come to the part of our tale that although succinct yet will supply the grout necessary to bind the mosaic that is all these pieces, for the story of the Uganda Railway is a story of peril and politics, and politics in our day passes by the name of history and to-day history largely passes unnoticed.

The danger of discussing history is that it is too easily demonstrated that history seems to have nothing to do with us. All of us have a personal history, yet we all live well apart from all our histories; none of you lads, for example, can name all your great-grandparents. Do you know even where your grandparents were born? Can you say the names of a single one of your great-uncle's children? So we can see that in a way even our own history is hidden from us; and because the most remarkable events in our lives have occurred so recently, it is only natural to assume that the most pertinent portion of our histories begins with our first truly memorable experiences. In that way, we each reinvent the world as we pass through it, and, without the information that a knowledge of history provides, we can gaily declare that all our ideas are the best ideas because they are the very latest ideas.

So we may say that if the history of our own lives holds so little interest for us, it is unlikely that the history of other events in which we have played no role at all will strike us as compelling. Perhaps, however, you will stop solely for the pleasures such stories provide, for if history is politics, perhaps it is also well-organized journalism and journalism is nought but gossip with witnesses; or, more likely, history is just the improbable come to pass. Take, as a pertinent illustration, the idea of building a railway to Uganda.

As I said, it was the year 1900, when the Empire was still in robust health, when a full quarter of the world's peoples were given fair government by a British monarch, and when British ingenuity in response to both the highest calling and the burden of our race was engaged in many wonderful things which it was hoped ultimately would be of great benefit not only to England but also to those countless unfortunates who lacked much and who desperately needed our help and counsel. In Africa, where slavery, pestilence, and war had evoked a profound darkness, it was decided that to open the country to commerce and civilization would be the means best suited to halting the cruelty and despair that surrounded the lives of the people there and also to ensure the Nation's security and the security of India by bringing the headwaters of the Nile, Egypt's blessing and its curse, under the provident protection of England. And so Lord Curzon begged parliament to build a railway stretching from Mombasa on the Indian Ocean to Lake Victoria and the headwaters of the Nile in Uganda, and eventually they assented, eventually the railway was built, and eventually a curious incident occurred as a consequence of the building of the railway.

I want to say how it happened, and I believe this to be an accurate account. I have it in writing here from the late Major Robert Foran, who got it at the Mombasa Club one evening in March 1904 from two survivors of the fateful night, and from a subsequent interview with an English goods-train guard, R. M. Howard, who arrived on the scene only a few hours after Ryall had been taken. An Indian member of the Railway Police, Bishen Singh, who had accompanied Mr Howard, also supplied some valuable details. While Major

Foran has pointed out that the event at Kima is unique, since it 'is the only occasion known when a man-eating lion took a human victim from within a railway coach standing on a siding at a station,' it is certainly not the only recorded instance of a man being eaten by a lion, as we shall see. Nevertheless, Major Foran felt that that which transpired at Kima had a signal peculiarity and that therefore he was bound to report it accurately. In his account, the Major has noted: 'As I happen to possess an authenticated record of the tragic incident when Ryall was taken out of a railway carriage by a man-eater at Kima station, which is most likely not available to anyone else, it seems a duty to pass it on to others if only to counteract the gross misstatements which have been made about the incidents in the past.' Relying then upon Major Foran's word and some information I myself happen to possess, here is how the tragedy must have occurred:

By 1900, after four years of hard work, the line had hardly reached Nairobi, at the time a dismal papyrus swamp; but each day, construction trains would leave the coast and head into the rather sketchily charted nether regions of East Africa, shedding light on the many small jewellike settlements it passed, one of which was situated at Kima, sixty-nine miles along the track southeast of Nairobi.

Now it happens that a man-eating lion, an oddity in nature, had made an appearance in Kima, and the Indian stationmaster, worried not only for the lives of railway workers and passengers but also for his own, for he was no hunter, requested assistance in putting down the killer.

In those days, lions were much more numerous and hence were not infrequent visitors to native villages. In most places, it was not unusual for lions, along with many other species of larger game, to pass to and fro, as they did through the sparse wilderness round Kima, but as I say man-eating lions were rare indeed, as they are still to-day (man-eaters, however, were most remarkable and their presence was sometimes given cartographic significance; and in fact, the station at another place not thirty miles distant from Kima once frequented by man-eaters was called Simba, the Swahili word for 'lion'), and after an Indian pointsman along with several Africans had been eaten, the railway staff stayed in their quarters and would not go out for fear the lion would take them.

One day late in 1899, I think it was on the morning of October 10, a telegram was sent by the station-master at Kima to Mr A. E. Cruickshank, the traffic manager at the new railway headquarters in Nairobi, the town that had been created by the railway only months earlier, complaining of the lion and describing the series of deaths that the beast had wrought. The station-master told Mr Cruickshank that the territory was governed by a reign of terror. Finally, one night as the lion clawed furiously at the corrugated iron roof of the building, the station-master telegraphed to the traffic manager, "Lion fighting with station. Send urgent succour."

In response Mr Cruickshank over a period of weeks dispatched several European railway officers to Kima at different times to eliminate the malignant brute. The first man to come to the station-master's aid was an engine driver who climbed through an opening in the top of an empty water tower near Kima station, and, through a peep hole he had cut in the side, began his vigil, hoping the lion would soon show itself. The lion came as promised, but rather than attack the roof of the station building as it had done before, instead climbed up on top of the water tank and tried to reach the engine driver inside. The beast finally gave up, and the engine driver subsequently fled. Other men were then sent out to Kima, but all of them failed utterly. The man-eater became even bolder and began taking his victims in the middle of the day.

Mr Ryall, the son of George Ryall of the Punjabi Judicial Service, at that time was stationed in Mombasa, but had been informed that official duty would take him to Nairobi. This did not displease him, for his twenty-sixth birthday was approaching on 13 July and he thought he perhaps might be permitted to stay up-country long enough to celebrate the event with friends at Nairobi in pursuit of his special past-time. As an officer in the Punjab constabulary, young Mr Ryall had fostered a keen interest in big-game hunting, a fascination he brought with him to his new appointment to the Uganda Railway Police, and now that his birthday was nearly upon him, he began contemplating its arrival with some pleasure. After all, do we not each have our own personal advent calendar with which we mark time to our own nativity as soon as the day comes into sight? Mr Ryall was in no way different from any of you lads, and he looked forward to joining his friends for an exciting outing. When word of the man-eater at Kima reached him, he was delighted to break his journey there, where he planned to sit up all night in his inspection coach, kill the man-eater, then continue up to Nairobi.

As he was boarding his coach in Mombasa the morning of 5 June, he was approached by a German trader named Huebner, forename unknown to us, and the Italian vice consul at Mombasa, Signor Parenti, initial A. The two men had failed to gain authority to travel on a construction train to railhead, where a porter-safari awaited them to take them on the arduous but perhaps profitable journey overland to Entebbe. Mr Ryall, as kind-hearted a chap as any of you, generously offered to take them in his inspection-coach, but told them he planned on making a vigil at Kima to wipe out the man-eater. The two men accepted his invitation, and off they all set.

When they reached the station at Kima, Mr Ryall arranged

for his inspection-coach to be detached from the train and shunted onto a siding, while the other two men sipped tea and waited patiently. Most probably, they were delighted with this temporary posting, which looks much the same to-day as it did then. The small, colonial station building is clean and bright and smothered in flowers — most enthusiastically by scarlet and purple bougainvillea. A small distance down the track, no more than fifty yards or so and perhaps halfway between the station and the siding where Mr Ryall instructed that his carriage be stopped, is a small park maintained by the railway porters. The station building is the most modern building in sight, as the rest of the village contains architecture of a more indigenous quality, but no fewer flowers. Each small dwelling is surrounded by its own garden, and flower-lined paths lead from garden to garden. The whole scene is delicious. Perhaps poor Mr Ryall should have known what was coming, for he had lived an exemplary Christian life and the station at Kima more than anything else resembled the last stop on the railway to Heaven.

When night fell, the three men climbed into the inspection-coach, which was a composite wagon painted all over in white and with a sliding doorway at each end. In the centre of the carriage was a passageway giving access to the other section of the coach which was used as a kitchen and which was occupied by Mr Ryall's cook, an Indian man, and Mr Ryall's African bearer. Mr Ryall's compartment contained an upper berth on the left-hand side as you entered and a lower one on the right, adjacent to the sliding-panel doorway. At either end of the coach was a small platform.

Mr Ryall and the two travellers discussed their strategy over dinner. They planned that they should remain in the compartment all night and take turns looking for a sign of the killer lion. To lure the lion to the wagon, Mr Ryall thought it

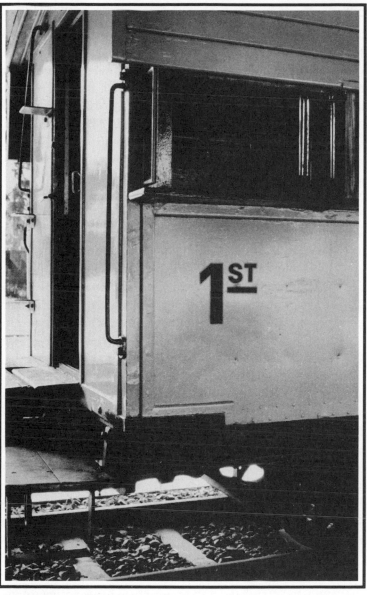

THE INSPECTION COACH, A COMPOSITE WAGON WITH A SLIDING DOOR-WAY AT EACH END

best to leave the door open, the better to whet the beast's curiosity, and to then provide an easy shot when the beast was silhouetted in the doorway. To determine which man would first keep a look-out, they drew lots. In such a way it was decided that Signor Parenti would keep the first vigil until midnight, at which time he would awaken Mr Ryall, who would keep watch until three. Then the German, Herr Huebner, would stand watch until sunrise. Accordingly, Herr Huebner, a tall and very heavy man, kipped in the upper berth, while Mr Ryall took the lower. At ten o'clock, Signor Parenti took up his post near the lower berth and next to the open door. The lamp in the carriage was extinguished, and the Italian, like his German companion, a novice at hunting, waited nervously. His vigilance was rewarded with tedium.

When Mr Ryall's turn came, Signor Parenti wrapped himself in a blanket and first thought to take up a berth, but owing to the cant at which the carriage was parked, feared he might roll out of it; and so instead he stretched out upon the floor with his feet pointed at the door, just as were the other men's. The angle at which the inspection-coach was parked and the effect this may have had upon the sliding doorway has a rather important bearing upon what was to subsequently transpire, and it should not be lost sight of. Rather than disturb Signor Parenti, Mr Ryall, propped up some of his pillows, lowered the window beside his bunk, placed his rifle across his lap, and, reclining, took up his watch. As Signor Parenti was about to sleep, Mr Ryall mentioned that he could see the eyes of a couple of rats 'playing about in the darkness outside' and that 'their eyes were shining like lamps.'

And so, my dear chaps, there we have them. Three men brought together by the challenge of Africa, by the ambition that animated their lives, and by the chance that such a rough-and-ready life provides, in a darkened railway carriage on a siding at a station near the equator waiting for the sun or worse to come to them. By virtue of their circumstance, their desires, and their common cultural background, the three Europeans had a great deal in common, and, as the history of European civil wars has taught us, a great many differences as well; and among the many differences the three men shared was this: Signor Parenti and Herr Huebner were supposed to be sleeping. Mr Ryall actually wasn't.

The eyes of the rats playing about in the darkness grew larger and larger, for they were the eyes of the man-eater who crept silently up onto the platform. The beast snorted softly, then entered the carriage, where he stood upon Signor Parenti's chest in order to reach the face of Mr Ryall in the right-hand lower berth. The sudden lurch of the coach caused the sliding door to come closed and automatically latch shut, while the burden of the lion quite naturally disturbed the sleep of the Italian, who later told Major Foran that he was nearly suffocated by the stench characteristic of man-eaters especially and that he could move but a little, since the brute had him pinned to the floor with its back legs. The German, Herr Huebner, then awoke with the noise and tumbled onto the back of the lion. The combined weight of the confused lion, with Mr Ryall held in its bloody jaws, and the large German was nearly enough to kill the Italian, who all this time was striving mightily to push off the beast that was standing on him. 'His efforts to get free were ineffective,' Major Foran has noted. 'That is perfectly understandable.'

Once he realized his peril, Herr Huebner fairly flew off the back of the lion and fled down the passageway to the door to the kitchen, where Mr Ryall's two servants were reluctant to give him entry. Finally, however, they feared the German would break down the door, so they quickly let him in, bolting the door behind him. Meanwhile, the man-eater must have swung around with Mr Ryall's body held in its jaws in order to retreat by the way of entering the compartment, according to Major Foran's report. He noted also that Mr Howard said that 'on arriving later he found a trickle of blood in a semi-circle, starting from the pillows on the lower berth, continuing over a pair of brown boots in the right-hand top corner of the bunk, and from there to the doorway,' where a larger pool of blood suggested that the lion must have paused while pondering what to do next.

According to Signor Parenti, the lion hesitated briefly at the doorway, then turned, and, with the body of Mr Ryall still clasped in its jaws, managed to squeeze through the window next to Mr Ryall's berth, a window hardly large enough for a man alone to pass with great difficulty! Major Foran has noted that this awkward passage must have taken some time and that Signor Parenti was at that time quite free and in possession of his rifle, but that he didn't shoot at the lion because the horrible affair had unnerved him. Major Foran does not seem to approve of Signor Parenti's hesitancy, noting that 'one would have thought that, if only to protect himself he would have had a shot at the man-eater which was then an absolute "sitter."' Herr Huebner also recalled that Signor Parenti was screaming quite loudly and pleading for entry to the kitchen, which was denied him. Finally, Signor Parenti jumped out of the window opposite Mr Ryall's berth and ran screaming through the night to the station.

'The station-master,' Major Foran has written, 'was scared almost out of his wits when Parenti arrived, shouting out the tragic news and demanding admission.' Eventually, the station-master gave way to Signor Parenti and allowed him to enter. The station-master, himself on the edge of hysteria, telegraphed to ask that immediate help be sent to Kima. Then the station-master, Signor Parenti, and the rest of the station staff all went quickly into a small room in the station building and locked the door and waited for help to come.

The station-master's desperate message was relayed to Mr Howard, who, accompanied by Mr Bishen Singh, arrived at Kima before dawn, where he found everyone in a state of 'helpless panic and confusion' and that no effort at all had been made to recover the body of Mr Ryall. Signor Parenti and the station staff were still locked in the small room in the station, while Herr Huebner was still bolted up in the carriage's kitchen with the cook and the bearer. 'All of them,' according to Major Foran, 'adamantly refused to emerge from their respective refuges.'

Another train, carrying the railway's section engineer, who was a handy man with a rifle, and the postmaster-general of Mombasa, who was not, arrived shortly after Mr Howard, and together some order was restored. A party was organized to find Mr Ryall's body, which was done within a quarter-hour. The lion had left the corpse under a bush, disemboweled, with the intestines scattered about, and with but one thigh and part of the neck eaten through. The remains were shipped to Nairobi, where they were buried in the little cemetery opposite the Nairobi railway yard.

Mr Ryall's grieving mother posted a handsome reward of £100 to the man who could avenge her son's murder, and Sir George Whitehouse, on behalf of the railway's directors, put a £15 per head bounty for every lion killed between Makindu and Nairobi — a distance of nearly 200 miles. Although many lions were slain, and the reward was eventually claimed by a locomotive foreman and a fitter chargeman, no conclusive evidence was ever offered that any of the lions slain had been the lion that had killed Mr Ryall. In 1905, Major Foran, when he was in command of the Mombasa police, was shown a set of photographs by the locomotive foreman, and

IN
LOVING
MEMORY
OF

CHARLES HENRY RYALL A.D.S.
PUNJAB POLICE
SON OF GEORGE RYALL,
OF THE PUNJAB JUDICIAL SERVICE.
BORN JULY 13TH 1874,
DIED JUNE 6TH 1900.

HE WAS ATTACKED WHILST SLEEPING
AND KILLED BY A MAN-EATING LION AT KIMA.

THE REMAINS WERE BURIED IN THE LITTLE CEMETERY OPPOSITE THE
NAIROBI RAILWAY YARD.

he seemed somewhat satisfied that justice had been done, but we may doubt it, since to most of our species, a lion is a lion, a meat-eater always, a man-eater sometimes.

One brave fellow, Rodrigues by name, who had gone to Kima to attempt to claim the reward, swore that the man-eater of Kima was one of the pair of beasts that had terrorized Tsavo a few years earlier. All one can do, he said at the time, was shoot lions until the slaughter stops. Then you can say that you slew the killer beast. But the beast may just have gone away.

To-day, automobiles go faster than the trains in East Africa, so the quickest way to reach Kima is to drive there in a passenger car. As I said, the place is nearly seventy miles southeast of Nairobi. If you go there and you are traveling from the capital, you will pass the Athi River and Salama. Kwamakengi Hill will be off to the west, and soon you will see the sign buried in roadside scrub; but if you pass also the giant mosque at Sultan Hamud, you will have gone too far. At the signpost, make a quick turn off the macadam and proceed down a sandy trail and eventually you will come to Kima settlement. Go directly to the station, and the station-master, a Mr Charles Kogi, identifiable by his crisp, white duck uniform and pleasant demeanour, will direct you to the exact spot where Mr Ryall instructed that his carriage be placed. Perhaps you also will go to that spot and stand there; or perhaps you will stand and discourse with the men who come to the station whenever strangers make an appearance. They will tell you that Kima is at peace, that there have been no lions at Kima in living memory, only goats. One man will be a Masai; he alone will be sorry the lions have gone.

Has Mr Ryall been a good teacher? His lesson was this: Always stay awake on watch, and steer clear of the tall grass in life, you young men, for if your path is not clear you can never see what is in store for you. Like sharks and certain of our own species, lions will kill for the thrill of it, for the blood excitement. If they're moved to do so, they'll kill a man, even if they don't want to eat him. To most lions, people smell quite badly; but a man-eater is a lion with a dietary eccentricity, a lion that will eat just about anything, dear lads. Even the lot of you.

Good night.

INDEX

Abardare Country Club, 166, 188–89
Adamson, George, 182–84
Adamson, Joy, 128n, 182, 184
Aelian, 128n, 217, 220
Aesop, 218
African Lives (Boyles), 151n
African Slave Trade, The (Davidson), 12n, 20n
Africa Speaks (Hoeffler), 219n
Afro-Shirazis, 25, 26
Afro-Shirazi Union (Zanzibar), 25–26
Aga Khan, 9, 37
Agweddo, Cowence, 63
AIDS
    and East Africa, 184
    in Uganda, 201
Amboseli National Park (Kenya), 55
Amboseli plain, 176–77
Amin, Idi, 201, 202
Amnesty International USA, 16n
Anglican cathedral (Zanzibar), 40

Angling. *See* Fishing
Angola, 51
Animals in Art (Rawson), 217n
Animal Kingdom (Cuvier), 216n
Anti-Slavery Society, 16, 16n, 19
    reports on slavery, 17–19
Archer, Tony, 86, 89–90, 128, 137, 153, 221
Aristotle, 217, 225
Ark (animal-observation post), 188
Audubon magazine, 13n

Bagara Arabs, 19
Baker, Sir Samuel, 17n
Balfour Declaration, 108
Battle for the Bundu, The (Miller), 60n
Bearcroft, Michael "Punch," 152
Begin, Menachem, 108
Ben-Gurion, David, 108n
Bennett, James Gordon, 15

Bennett, Norman R., 12n
Black Mother (Davidson), 12n
Blixen, Karen, 5, 148, 157–58, 179
Block, Abraham, 166
Blyth, Audley James, 101–2
Blyth, Ethel Jane, 101–2
Boer War, Patterson in, 99, 103, 104, 106
Bomas of Kenya, 174
"Bombay Africans," 52
Book of the Lion, The (Pease), 219n, 223
Books
  on ancients' knowledge of animals, 217n
  on slavery, 20n
  on Uganda Railway, 21n
  on World War I in East Africa, 60n
  on Zanzibar, 12n, 21n
Born Free (Adamson), 128n, 182
Boyd, William, 60n
Boyes, John, 166
British Empire
  railroads in, 120–21
  and Uganda Railway, 4–5, 23–24, 230
  and Zanzibar, 21–23
Brock, Dr., 93–94, 96, 97, 98, 110, 111
Broughton, Diana (Lady Delamere), 152, 156
Broughton, Sir Jock Delves, 152
Bububu (Zanzibar), 40, 41
Burton, Sir Richard, 12n, 13
Busia (Kenya), 197–201
Butler, A. L., 223
Bwejuu (Zanzibar), 45

Cats, patience of, 97
Capstick, Peter, 83n
Chamberlain, Joseph, 87, 166
Cholmondeley, Hugh (third Lord Delamere), 150, 166, 204–5
Churchill, Winston, 105
Church Missionary Society, 52
Coca-Cola
  in Busia, 199
  and Kenya, 168, 170
  in Kisumu, 211
Cole, Berkeley, 166
Colonialism, 150, 155
Con man, and African tourists, 171–72
Conniff, Richard, 12n
Cooper, Frederick, 12n
Corfield, Timothy, 86, 128, 177–79, 184–85
Coupland, Sir Reginald, 12n
Crewe, Lord, 102
Cricket
  in Nairobi, 153–54
  and Preston, 77
Cruikshank, E. A., 232
Curzon, Lord, 230
Cuvier, Baron Georges, 216

Davidson, Basil, 12n, 15, 20n
Decolonization of Africa, 150, 155
Delamere, Lady Diana, 152, 156
Delamere, Lord (Hugh Cholmondeley), 150, 166, 204–5
de Sélincourt, Aubrey, 217n
Diamonstein, Barbara, 12n
Diet Coke
  and Kenya, 168, 170

in Kisumu, 211
Dinka tribe, and slavery,
  17–19
D'Olier, Elli, 153
D'Olier, Guy, 204
D'Olier, John, 153, 204
Dolphin restaurant (Zanzi-
  bar), 33
Donleavy, J. P., 211
Douglas-Hamilton, Ian, 185
Dyer, Anthony, 86, 88–89,
  91, 128, 222

East Africa
  British expansion in, 21–23
  romantic conception of, 5–6
  See also Kenya; Tanzania;
    Uganda
East Africa and Its Invaders
  (Coupland), 12n
East Africa Railway, 57
East Africa Railways and Har-
  bour, 57
Edmunds, Georgina, 183
End of Slavery in Africa, The
  (Miers and Roberts,
  eds.), 12n, 20n
English Club (Zanzibar), 25,
  33, 40
Equatoria province (Sudan),
  17–19
Esquire magazine, 12n
Ethiopia, killings in, 202

Farquhar (superintendent of
  police), 132, 134
Fashoda (Sudan), 78–79
Felines, patience of, 97
Field Museum of Natural History, Chicago, Patterson's
  lions mounted in, 141

Finch-Hatton, Denys, 158
Fisherman restaurant (Zanzi-
  bar), 35, 39
Fishing, 186–88, 190–91
Foran, Robert, 230–31, 237,
  238, 239
Forests, equatorial, 197
Fort Jesus (Mombasa), 10n,
  52
Fox, James, 70, 152
Frazer, Sir James, 219
Frere, Sir Henry Bartle, 52
Frere Town, 52
From Slaves to Squatters
  (Cooper), 12n

Gai, Martin Magier, 18
Gallipoli, 99, 105, 106
Genesis of Kenya Colony,
  The (Preston), 78n
Goanese Catholic cathedral
  (Roman Catholic), 40
Golden Bough, The (Frazer),
  219
Gordon, Charles George
  "Chinese," 17n
Gordon of Khartoum (Wal-
  ler), 17n
Goss, Ted, 153
Granger, Stewart, 86, 148
Gray, Sir John Milner, 12n
Greenbelt Movement (Kenya),
  163
Guinness, Alec, 83

Haganah, 108
Hairsine, René, 35–37, 38, 39
Hamid-bin-Thwain, Seyyid,
  23
Hardinge (Consul-General at
  Zanzibar), 23

Haslem, Captain (companion
     in Patterson's hunt), 85
Hay, Josslyn (Earl of Erroll),
     152
Hedren, Tippi, 30
Heligoland, 22
Hemingway, Ernest, 102–3,
     179
Hemsing, Jan, 152
Herlehey, Thomas J., 12 n
Herodotus, 217, 225
Herzl, Theodor, 87
Hill, M. F., 21 n
History of the Arab State of
     Zanzibar, A (Bennett),
     12 n
History of Zanzibar (Gray),
     12 n
Hoeffler, Paul, 219
Howard, R. M., 230, 238, 239
Huebner (German trader),
     233, 236, 237, 238, 239
Hunting
   abolition of in Kenya, 181
   organization of, 179
   as poaching control, 181,
     182
   as sport, 220–22
   See also Poaching
Hurt, Robin, 86
Hutu tribe (Rwanda), 150

Ibo tribe (Nigeria), 150
Ice Cream War, An (Boyd),
     60 n
Imperial British East Africa
     Company, 21, 22–23
Imperial Hotel (Kisumu), 206,
     208
India, 4
   slavery in, 19

Indian laborers
   descendants of in Mom-
     basa, 52
   and railways of British Em-
     pire, 120–21
   in Uganda Railway con-
     struction, 71–72, 73,
     75–76, 79, 81, 82,
     114–19, 121–22,
     129–30, 171, 222–23
In the Grip of the Nyika (Pat-
     terson), 101
Irgun, 108 n
Isles of Cloves (Ommaney),
     12 n
Ismail, Khedive, 17 n
Ivory
   and poaching, 184–85
   as Zanzibar export, 13, 13 n
Ivoryton, Conn., 13 n

Jabotinsky, Vladimir, 100,
     106–7, 108–9
Jackson, Stonewall, and Mrs.,
     104
Jockey Club (Kenya), 154–57
Jones, Buffalo, 222
Journeys and Researches in
     South Africa (Living-
     stone), 12 n

Kampala (Uganda), 196
Kariuki, Josiah, 162
Karume, Abeid, 26, 27–28,
     44
Kaunda, Kenneth, 202
Kavirondo, M.S., 206 n
Kennedy, Kerry, 164
Kenya
   government of, 160, 161–
     67

along Lake Victoria, 197
matatus in, 125, 172, 174
Northern Frontier District
    of, 87–88, 101, 153
period films made in, 204
poaching in, 160, 181–82,
    184, 185
railroad stations in, 61, 205
and slavery, 19
Somalis repressed in, 163–
    64
Taru desert in, 61, 79, 147
Timau region of, 86–87
tourists in, 147–48, 170,
    179–81, 185
train ride through, 56–59,
    60–61, 70–71, 119–20,
    141
trout fishing in, 187–88
Uganda Railway through,
    4, 5, 6, 23–24, 195, 230
    (*see also* Uganda Rail-
    way)
white people of, 149–61,
    164–67
See also East Africa; *spe-
    cific cities*
Kenya African National Union
    (KANU), 162–63
Kenya: The First Explorers
    (Pavitt), 12n
Kenya Railways
    daylight service, 60n
    Mombasa to Nairobi, 56–
        59, 60–61, 70–71,
        119,–20, 141
    Nairobi to Kisumu, 195,
        203–204, 205
Kenya-Uganda Railroad, 57
Kenyatta, Jomo
    and corruption, 160

and Kikuyu, 161–62
and Mau Mau, 152
and poaching, 184
and Uhuru Park, 163
and whites, 155–56
Ker and Downey Safaris, 86
Kikuyu tribe (Kenya), 161–62
Kima, 231, 232, 234, 241
    man-eating lions at, 231–
        32, 234–41
Kisumu, 56, 161, 165, 195,
    197, 203, 205–11
Kiswahili (language), 111
Königsberg (German ship), 24
Kogi, Charles, 241
Koppel, Ted, 202
Kora National Reserve, 182–
    83
Krapf, Johann, 13

Lake Naivasha (Kenya), 203–
    204
Lake Victoria, 4, 6, 24, 197,
    205, 219, 230
    Kisumu on, 6, 195, 197.
        See also Kisumu
    ships on, 205, 205–206n
Last Journals (Livingstone),
    12n
Lawrence, T. E., 109
Leakey, Louis, 164
Leakey, Mary, 164
Leakey, Philip, 165
Leakey, Richard, 164–65, 182
Leclerc, Anita, 12n
Lettow-Vorbeck, Paul von,
    24n, 60
Lion Hill Lodge, 205
Lions
    blood lust among, 224–25,
        242

Lions (*continued*)
    cub myths, 217, 225
    difficulties in locating, 220
    eating of, 219
    failure to find, 125, 128
    fat from as medication, 219
    habitat of, 215–18
    as hunters, 90–91, 128n,
        137–38, 223, 224
    hunting of, 220–22
    lassoing of, 222
    leaping ability of, 139
    resting habits of, 223–24
    shooting of, 89
    teeths and mouths of, 224
    and tigers, 215–16
    and tourists, 125
    at Tsavo, 60, 65
    around Uganda Railway
        stations, 219–20
Lions, man-eating, 89–91,
    242
    infrequency of, 231–32
    man as easy prey for, 225–
        26
    vs. man-eating tigers, 218–
        19
    Patterson's hunting of, 85–
        86, 88–89, 91–98, 100,
        110, 114, 122–24,
        128–29, 132–37,
        138–41
    railway construction work-
        ers attacked by, 81–82,
        84–86, 92, 93, 94–95,
        100, 123–24, 128–30,
        140, 222–23
    Ryall taken by, 230–41
    Whitehead attacked by,
        131–32

Livingstone, David, 12, 12n,
    13
Lloyd George, David, 105
Local Food in Zanzibar res-
    taurant, 33
Longonot satellite tracking
    station, 197
Lunatic Express, The (Miller),
    viii
Luo tribe (Kenya), 161
Lyell, Denis, 218

Maathai, Mrs. Wangari, 163
Madagascar, 22
Madonna, 186
Makindu (Kenya), 119
Makupa Creek (Mombasa), 73
Malaba (Kenya), 195
Malaria, in Zanzibar, 45
Malawi, 202
Malindi (Kenya), 54
Man Eaters Motel, 60, 65,
    66–70, 125
Man-eaters of Tsavo, The
    (Patterson), 83, 106
Man-eating lions. *See* Lions,
    man-eating
Marahaleen (Sudanese mili-
    tia), 19
Markham, Beryl, 166
Markham, Sir Charles, 154–
    57
Markham, Gwladys, 156
Marlboro East Africa Safari
    Rally, 170
Martin, Esmond, 12n, 15,
    21n, 25
Masai tribe (Kenya)
    and absence of lions at
        Kima, 241

holy place for, 197
and Zionist delegation, 87
Matatus, 125, 172, 174
Mathews, A. E., 155
Mathews, Sir Lloyd, 23
Mau Escarpment, 196–97, 203
Mauritania, slavery in, 19
Mayers, Ray S., 89
Mboya, Tom, 161
Miers, Suzanne, 12 n, 20 n
Miller, Charles, viii, 60 n
Mohammed (taxi driver), 3, 6, 7–8, 11, 37
Moi, Daniel arap, 69, 161, 162–63, 164, 184
Mombasa, 9, 51–52, 73–75, 82–83
    tourist life in, 55–56
    train ride from, 56–59, 60–61, 70–71, 119–20, 141
    Uganda Railway from, 4, 23–24, 73 (*see also* Uganda Railway)
    and Zanzibar history, 24
Mortensen, Finn K., 37–38, 44–45
Morton, Roger F., 12 n
Mozambique, 19, 22
Mugabe, Robert, 156
Muscat, Sultan of, 13 n
Museveni, Yoweri Kaguta, 201–2
Muthaiga Club (Nairobi), 154

Nairobi
    arrival at, 141
    casino in, 146–48
    and Mombasa tourists, 56
    outlying districts of, 153, 174
    street scenes in, 170–72
    and Uganda Railway, 171
    Uhuru Park controversy in, 162–63
Nairobi National Park, 174–76
Nakuru, 191, 196, 197, 204–5
Nanyuki, 187
Naro Moru, 187, 191
Naro Moru River Lodge, 191
Nasir, Burma, 19
New Africa Hotel (Zanzibar), 33
New School for Social Research (N.Y.C.), 31
New Victoria bar (Kisumu), 208
New York Times, 12 n
Ngong (Kenya), races at, 154–57
Nicholls, C. S., 12 n
Nile River, 5, 230
Njoro (Kenya), 197
Norfolk Hotel, Nairobi, 148, 152, 166–67, 170, 180
Northern Frontier District, 87–88, 101, 153
Nyanza, S.S., 205, 210
Nyanza Club (Kisumu), 208, 209–10
Nyerere, Julius, 26, 26–28, 27 n
Nyeri (Kenya), 187

Obote, Milton, 202
Okello, John, 27
Ommaney, F. D., 12 n
Ouko, Robert, 161

Pappadimitrini, Themistocles,
    93
Parenti, A. (Italian vice-con-
    sul), 233, 236, 237, 238,
    239
Parks and reserves
    Kora National Reserve,
        182–83
    Lion Hill Lodge, 205
    Nairobi National Park,
        174–76
    Shimba Hills Reserve, 55
    Tsavo East National Park,
        69–70, 125
    Tsavo West National Park,
        125
Patterson, John Henry, 82–
    83, 99–100, 103–10
    in Boer War, 99, 103, 104,
        106
    and man-eating lions, 83–
        86, 88–89, 91–98, 100,
        110, 114, 114n, 122–24,
        128–29, 132–37, 138–
        41
    as railway construction
        head, 110–19, 121–22
    and safari scandal, 98,
        100–103
    search for, 98–99
Pavitt, Nigel, 12n, 15
Pearce, F. B., 12n
Pease, Sir Alfred, 138, 219n,
    220, 222, 223–24
Pegasus, H.M.S., 24, 24n
Pemba Island, 4, 26
Percival, Philip, 102–3
*Permanent Way, The: The
    Story of the Kenya and
    Uganda Railway* (Hill),
    21n

Pilkington, Hugh A. W.,
    151–52
Pliny the Elder, 217, 218n,
    225
Plutarch, 218
Poaching, 181–82, 184, 185
    and government corruption,
        160, 181, 182
    and international product
        boycott, 184–85
Pohlmann, Karl, 180
Polybius, 225–26
Preston, Florence, 77, 78
Preston, Ronald O., 77–79,
    81–82, 95, 113, 114n
Preston, Vic, 78n, 114n
Preston, Vic, Jr., 78n
Prison Island, Zanzibar, 9,
    35n, 38, 39–40

Racism, 145–50, 158–59
Railroads
    in British Empire, 120–21
    See also Kenya Railways
Railway, Uganda. *See* Uganda
    Railway
Rawson, Jessica, 217n
Redford, Robert, 158
Rift Valley, 196–97, 203
Ringer, C. G. R., 166
Rizeigat Arabs, 18
Roberts, Richard, 12n, 20n
Rodriguez (Kima lion-killer),
    241
Roosevelt, Theodore, 100,
    103, 166
Rose, Alan, 171, 176, 177–
    78, 185, 187, 188, 190
Ryall, Charles Henry, 228–
    29, 231, 233–41
Ryan, T. C. I., 15

Safaris, 178–81
  newlyweds on, 90
  Patterson scandal on,
    100–103
Said, Sayyid, 12–13
Sam's Hotel (Kisumu), 208
Samuel, Sir Herbert, 109
Sayyid Said, 12–13
Schneider, Paul, 12n
Scholfield, A. F., 217n
Scipio Aemilianus, 225
Seberg, Jean, 41
Selous, Frederick, 139
Seth-Smith, Anthony, 86, 90,
    152, 188
Seton family, 182–83
Shaw, Patrick, 151, 151n
Sheth, Shenti, 179–81
Shimba Hills Reserve, 55
"Short Happy Life of Francis
    Macomber, The" (Hem-
    ingway), 103
"Simba," 232
Singh, Bishen, 230, 239
Singh, Ungan, 85, 91
Slave cave (Mombasa), 52
Slave cave (Zanzibar), 7, 52
Slavery, 20n
  in Africa, 16–19, 25
  and European colonialism,
    150
  in Mombasa, 52
  and Zanzibar, 7, 11, 15–
    16, 19–21, 24, 52
Smee, Thomas, 19–21
Somalis
  in Northern Frontier Dis-
    trict, 87, 153
  oppression of in Kenya,
    163–64
  and transport industry, 199

South Africa, and slavery, 19
Spaulding, Allen, 179
Speke, John Hanning, 13
Spice Inn (Zanzibar), 33
Stanley, Henry Morton, 6, 15
Stewart, James, 30
Streep, Meryl, 5, 157–58
Sudan, slavery in, 16–19
Suez Canal, 5, 22
Sultan of Zanzibar 4, 22, 23,
    25, 27, 27n
Swahili Coast, The (Nicholls),
    12n

Tanganyika, 22
  and Uganda Railway, 5
  and Zanzibar, 11
Tanzania, and Zanzibar,
    27–30
Taru desert, 60, 61, 66, 73,
    78, 79, 147
Tigers, and lions, 215–16,
    218–19
Timau region, 86–87
Tippoo Tib, 15
Tororo (Uganda), 196
Tourists
  and animals, 178, 185,
    188–89
  French-Belgian couple,
    41–47, 145
  and Kenya gambling, 146
  in Kisumu, 205, 206, 208
  and lion-finding, 125
  at Man Eaters Motel,
    67–69, 125
  in Mombasa, 9, 55–56
  in Nairobi, 141, 147–48,
    170–72
  newlyweds on safari, 90
  and poaching, 181, 184

Tourists (*continued*)
  recent Africa influx of, 168,
    170
  and safaris, 179–81
  on train, 57
  in Zanzibar, 30–31
  and Zanzibar transforma-
    tion, 9–11, 33
Tracy, Spencer, 6
Treetops (animal-observation
  post), 188–89
Trout fishing, 187–88
Tsavo, Kenya, 60, 63–66
  and Man Eaters Motel, 60,
    66–70, 125
Tsavo man-eaters. *See* Lions,
  man-eating
Tsavo East National Park,
  69–70, 125
Tsavo River, 65, 66, 79, 84,
  111–13
Tsavo West National Park,
  125
Tschambser, Daniel, 37, 38

Uganda, 196, 201–2
  and Britain, 22, 23
  Kenya incursions from,
    198, 199
  rebellion against British in,
    79
Uganda Railway, 4, 5, 6,
  23–24, 120, 195
  and daylight passenger ser-
    vice, 60n
  and history, 229
  lions at stations of, 219–20
  purpose of, 5, 23–24, 230
  ride on, 56–59, 60–61,
    70–71, 119–20, 141

Uganda Railway construction
  difficulties in, 72–73,
    75–77
  Indian laborers in, 71–72,
    73, 75–76, 79, 81, 82,
    114–19, 121–22, 129–
    30, 171, 222–23
  and man-eating lions, 66,
    81–82, 84–86, 92, 93,
    94–95, 100, 123–24,
    128–30, 140, 222–23,
    230–41
  Patterson's experiences in,
    110–19, 121–22
  Tsavo River crossing, 79,
    84, 111–13

Uhuru Park (Nairobi), 162–63
United Nations Economic and
  Social Council, 16
United Nations Environment
  Programme, 157
United Republic of Tanzania,
  27–28
United Touring Company
  (UTC), 179–80
Usoga, S.S., 206

Van Doren, Mamie, 30
Victoria, S.S., 205
Village Voice, The, 31
Virgin Butterfly, M.V., 41,
  43–44
Voi (Kenya), 59, 66, 69–70

Wakamba tribe (Kenya), 79
Waller, John, 17n
Watson, Rupert, 152
Westland Sundries (Nairobi),
  21n

Whitehead (district officer), 122, 130–32, 133

Whitehouse, Sir George (chief railway engineer), 72–73, 75–77, 78, 79, 130, 239

White Mischief (Fox), 70, 152

Wilderness Guardian, The (Corfield), 177

Wilson Airport (Nairobi), 174

Winfrey, Oprah, 35

With the Judeans in Palestine (Patterson), 108

With the Zionists at Gallipoli (Patterson), 105

World War I, 24, 60
  Patterson in, 99–100, 105–6

Ya Bwawani Hotel (Zanzibar), 33, 38, 44, 45

Yatta plateau (Kenya), 120

Zanzibar, 4, 6, 8–9
  ethnic groups in, 25
  French-Belgian couple in, 41–47
  and Hairsine, 35–37, 39
  heat of, 3, 7
  history of, 11–15, 22–28
  ivory trade in, 13, 13n
  Mortensens in, 37–38, 44–45

restaurants in, 11, 30–35, 38–39

sights and smells of, 7, 22, 39–41, 43

and slavery, 7, 11, 15–16, 19–21, 24, 52

and Tanzania, 28–30

texts on, 12n

transformation of, 9–11, 29–30, 33, 37

Ya Bwawani hotel in, 33, 38, 44–45

Zanzibar and Pemba People's Party, 26

Zanzibar; City, Island and Coast (Burton), 12n

Zanzibar in Contemporary Times (Lyne), 12n

Zanzibar Nationalist Party, 26

Zanzibar: The Island Metropolis (Pearce), 12n

Zanzibar: Tradition and Revolution (Martin), 12n, 21n

Zionism
  and East Africa land offer, 87
  and Patterson, 99–100, 106–10

Zion Mule Corps, 100, 106–108

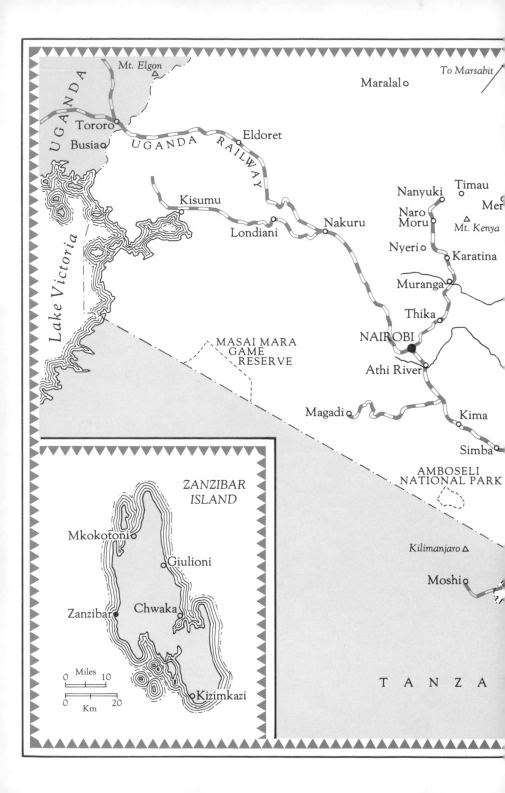